Janice Brown lives with her long-term husband in Central Scotland. She has written several books of teenage fiction. When not writing, her chief delights are travelling, knitting Alpaca scarves, attempting to learn Mandarin and adoring her five grand-children.

Hartsend

A novel

Janice Brown

SANDSTONEPRESS
HIGHLAND | SCOTLAND

First published in Great Britain by
Sandstone Press Ltd
PO Box 5725
One High Street
Dingwall
Ross-shire
IV15 9WJ
Scotland.

www.sandstonepress.com

Hartsend is a work of fiction. Names, characters, places and incidents
are imaginative and any resemblance to actual people, living or dead,
or real places and events is coincidental. Hartsend exists only in the
imagination of its author.

The publisher acknowledges subsidy from Creative Scotland
towards publication of this volume.

ISBN: 978-1-905207-87-9
ISBN e: 978-1-905207-88-6

Cover design by River Design, Edinburgh.
Typeset by Iolaire Typesetting, Newtonmore.
Printed and bound by TOTEM, Poland.

For Rena and Robert

Preface

Rain is falling on Hartsend, darkening the stone needle of the War Memorial and the tattered red wreaths left two months ago by the Boys' Brigade. It's clattering on the roof of the Prince and Princess of Wales Hospice shop in Main Street where Mary Flaherty will come tomorrow in mourning and the hope of finding a black blouse and skirt. It's falling on the Captain's only son in his worn Barbour jacket as he picks up sodden scraps and crisp packets dropped by schoolchildren and windblown all the way up the hill into his garden. It's raining on the Robertson's goldfish pond, where the five surviving fish are barely moving, biding low in the dark water. It's raining on the new estate where, if you place your ear on any interior wall you can hear what the neighbours think of you, and every flush of their toilet. It's filling up the broken end of a Buckfast bottle at the edge of the children's swing park, drumming on the roofs of the travellers' caravans beside the river, falling on the football field and the deer nibbling ferns on the golf course, falling on isolated cottages and small holdings, on fields of wintry stubble and black plastic bales.

The feather

When the rain showed signs of going off, Martine and Josie left the van, closing the door on her. *You're no'comin,* they said, making faces at her through the window, *you're too wee.* In the past she'd made faces back at them, but this time she didn't.

They were going to the golf course again to look for balls to sell. This was the best time of day, when everyone had gone home for tea. They had a torch and a long stick so that they could pick out the balls in the tangled bushes and the burn as the light faded. They didn't want her. She couldn't run fast enough if someone saw them and shouted.

As soon as they were out of sight behind the broken-down wall of bricks, she put on her rubber boots, shoving her arms into her jacket. The dogs paid no attention. With a careful look back to see that her mother, in Nan's van with the baby, wasn't watching, she followed the faint silvery dented tracks over the grass, the green frog faces on the fronts of her boots pushing ahead for her, so she could pretend she was three people, not one.

Away to the left, the cars on the dual carriageway were roaring faintly, their lights just visible, winking through the trees. She felt funny inside. She wasn't supposed to leave the field without telling. Mostly she was careful to be good, but this time she couldn't stop herself. The idea had got bigger and bigger. But it wasn't a naughty idea. All she wanted to do was watch them, and not tell them, not let them know she was watching.

It was hard to keep secrets from them. Anything she tried to hide in the van they found and messed with, but this was going to be a secret inside her head. They wouldn't be able to touch anything inside her head.

She pulled her hood over her head and kept her hands in her pockets to avoid scratches when she passed through the bramble bushes. There was nothing left now but rusty dying leaves and spikes. No warm berries. They'd picked them on sunny afternoons after school, eating them with ice cream from the café. You had to look at them before you put them in your mouth, in case you swallowed a white worm. The worms would grow and grow in your stomach, Martine and Josie said, and eat all the way through to your bottom and come out in your poo. This had happened to one of her cousins. The twins had been in the van at the time and had seen the worms wriggling in the toilet pan.

At the edge of the golf course, a new wire fence kept people out, but she was small enough to go between the lowest strand of barbed wire and the ground, tucking her skirt close against her legs so it didn't get dirty. Not that she was small. She would be five soon. She was going to be beautiful, the beauty out of all the girls, Nan said, brushing her hair slowly each night, plaiting the long strands into one single plait while she ate toast in front of the TV. Nan had been a beauty herself. Don't mind those two, Nan told her, they're just jealous.

The twins were dark like their father. He liked them because they took after his side of the family, Nan said. She was her Mum's girl. Her thoughts faltered. Mum was too tired to do things. She didn't seem to like any of them any more.

Head down, she didn't see it until she walked into it. She jumped back, flailing. It wasn't a ghost though, only a big bit of plastic, caught in the darkening bushes. A big, torn, dirty sheet, not a ghost, not something out to get her. She pulled at it, tried to tear it free but it was too strong for her, too caught and tugged, and the water ran off it, cold up her sleeves.

She rubbed her hands on her skirt, but it wasn't the right kind of cloth for drying hands properly. Should she go back? There was very little noise. The sound of the cars had faded, the birds had finished their early evening chattering. But she was nearly at the burn. She knew where she was. With small careful steps she went on, arms folded. A few moments later there was a glimpse of pink, just visible, not far ahead. She stretched on her toes. The twins, their pink jackets, disappearing into the first of the birch trees . . . She crouched down, in case they might look back.

It was marshy here. She could hear the water, a few yards away, swooshing loud against the long grasses. In the summer it was a good place, but there wouldn't be any tadpoles now, and the tall plants with the purple flowers were brown and slimy, with a funny smell that made her nose itchy.

The ground under her boots had filled up with water. She'd made two pools. Back and forwards she rocked for a moment or two, letting her froggy toes have a drink.

From here to the other side of the plank bridge it would be slippy. Then it was short grass with nothing to hide behind. If Martine and Josie saw her they'd chase her and pull her hair. You couldn't get away from two. One held your arms and the other pulled. *Shh*, she told the frogs on her toes.

There was a long white feather caught in the grass where the plank was wedged into the ground. She reached down. It was all smooth and clean, even at the pointy end.

"Hello. What have you found?"

She put the hand with the feather behind her back as the man came closer.

"It's all right, you can show me. Is it a feather?"

She shook her head, not looking him in the face.

"I won't take it from you. It's yours. You found it, not me."

Slowly she brought the feather round, and held it up, ready to pull away if he tried to snatch it from her.

"That's a beauty," he said. "That's from a black headed gull, I think. They like to live beside the sea, usually. But we're quite a long way from the sea, aren't we?"

His voice was funny. He was carrying a big, black

umbrella, closed up. He stuck the sharp end of it into the grass and began twisting it round and round, slowly, as if it was a stick.

"You wouldn't take eggs though, would you? None of us should take eggs from a nest. You wouldn't do that."

She shook her head.

"Because the mother bird would get upset, wouldn't she?"

He came closer, and squatted down, looking at the feather more closely.

"Can I touch it?" he said, "I promise not to hurt it."

Sharp shoes

Bing Crosby was singing in the hospice shop. Harriet, sixteen, only knew it was Bing Crosby because Mrs Robertson had told her. Mrs Robertson, who might be any age between fifty and seventy, as far as Harriet could tell, said he was much more handsome than that Robbie Williams and a better singer too. Not being much of a Robbie Williams fan, Harriet was quite happy to agree.

She was on her knees at the book and video shelves, arranging the new arrivals. It had been quiet all day, although they'd had the usual lonely hearts, the old biddies that came in all the time, the ones who liked to chat to June, the manager. Mrs Robertson was a volunteer, like her, and like Letty who had Down's but "worked like a wee beaver", according to June.

Mr Mackenzie had been in with a box of Cadbury's Heroes for them.

"He's getting frail," June murmured, when the door closed behind him. "Did you hear what he said? His son invited him out for Christmas dinner, only he told him he'd have to pay for himself? Imagine. And him only losing his wife a few months ago. If I met that boy I'd tell him the time of day all right. He said he wasn't going."

There was a sad little silence for a while, then June said she was going to do some ironing in the back shop. Letty followed. She was at her happiest when close to June. Mrs Robertson turned to Harriet, "Are you all organised for Christmas, dear? I suppose it'll be your father's busiest time."

Harriet nodded politely, still preoccupied with the injustice and sadness of Mr Mackenzie's life. Of life in general. And Letty, whose pale, flat hair was lovingly brushed each morning into a ponytail and tied with a pink ribbon. She was somewhere in her mid twenties; what would happen when her parents grew old?

She took up her pen and finished putting prices on the sticky labels for the new cards. The thoughtless cruelty of human beings continually troubled her. Sometimes Harriet felt she'd been born with thinner emotional skin than other people, with less protection against the things that hurt. She'd stopped eating breakfast in the kitchen because Dad insisted on hearing the news on Radio Four, which was always bad news or arguments and ruined the day before it began. She'd protested for a while. What was the point in knowing about every disaster, if you couldn't do anything?

But what could she have done for Mr Mackenzie?

Mrs Robertson was right. Her Dad was exhausted, and he even had a funeral on Christmas Eve on top of everything else. The tree was up and decorated, the duck was waiting in the fridge, and school was finished for two whole weeks, but with Mum thousands of miles away, there was none of the usual fun in the midst of the chaos. Kerr was home, which was something. She looked at her watch. Three o'clock and getting dark already.

She could hear Letty and June singing along with the CD. June was tanned all year round, thanks to her home sun-bed. She was wearing earrings today in the shape of Christmas trees that twinkled red and green, on and off, which was really naff, but kind of endearing at the same time.

The same could be said of the shop. Harriet's Saturdays here had begun as part of her Social Action from school, but when June asked if she would keep going, alternate Saturdays, mornings and afternoons, she'd said yes. It made her feel virtuous and, besides, gave her a valid reason for being unavailable for the hockey team. June had put her in sole charge of books and videos. ("Harriet here can read a whole book in just a couple of days," she had once informed a customer, adding, "and her brother's at the Oxford University," as if those two facts somehow raised the status of the shop.) Mrs Robertson said she wished she had more time to read. Asked what her favourite book was, Harriet said *The Lord of the Rings*. Mrs Robertson had heard of it, but not read it. But surely she'd seen the film? No. It wasn't about real things, was it? She and Mr Robertson didn't like films unless they were about real things.

"Have you got anything else in black?"

It was their one customer, a stout plain-faced woman with straggling dark hair. Mrs Robertson said she would see if there was anything in the most recent donations in the back shop. "Though it might be needing cleaned, you know," she said.

Harriet watched the woman go to the door. She spoke to a man outside, who reluctantly came back in with her. She began showing him some shirts on the rail. He didn't seem interested. When he turned away, Harriet saw he was just a boy, not much older than herself. His hair was long and dark at the back but dyed blond at the front. A long black raincoat and sharp pointed shoes completed the look.

Disconcerted when he returned her stare, Harriet drew several x's with excessive neatness on the border of the label sheet. That done, she gathered the pile of cellophane-wrapped cards, tapped them into an authoritative stack, and went to the rack beside the door. He had moved to stand beside the till. June, Letty, (still singing) and Mrs Robertson were all in the back shop. His mother, if she was his mother, was examining the inside of a handbag.

He met her eye, gave her a slow smile, leaned over the counter and lifted one of the good brooches from the glass cabinet beneath. He slipped it into his coat pocket. Just did it. Knowing that she saw.

The eulogy

The house is a hundred years old, and much of the furniture in the back room is of the same vintage, having been installed by the deceased's mother and inherited from *her* family. The mourners speak in whispers or are silent, like visitors to a museum. All that is missing is a heavy scarlet rope to keep them from touching the objects. A cream, cordless phone on the sideboard looks out of place, as if a careless curator has left it by mistake.

Facing the stiff rows of chairs (the dining table has evidently been moved elsewhere) is a small gas fire and, above it, a Victorian oak mantel with multiple wreaths of plenty, shelves and small drawers. Somewhere else, given space, it might have been beautiful, but in this small room it is too large. Moreover it is stuffed with train and bus timetables, bills, bundles of recipes cut from magazines, oddments of wool, safety pins and spools of thread, and seems ready to burst out on the room at any moment, scattering its contents over all those reflected in its mirrors.

Not wanting to be first, Walter and Ruby Robertson watched from behind their curtains until they saw some others going in. At the door Ruby found herself hugging Lesley, only child of the deceased. Later she will wonder what came over her. Walter will say that Lesley was probably on Valium and wouldn't remember. They nod to those people they recognise, and slide into the second front row, since they are only neighbours, not relations.

The Robertsons are incomers. They have lived in the street all their married life, but having moved here from the city, they will always be incomers. For almost thirty years they have lived next door to Lesley and her mother, thirty years without a voice raised or an unkind word spoken. Without many words spoken, if the truth be told, although perhaps the hedges are to blame. The high boundary of mixed beech, holly and privet provides sparrows with excellent nesting space but makes casual human conversation rather difficult.

Behind them and ill at ease, never having been to a Protestant funeral before, sits Mrs Mary Flaherty. She felt she had to come, having cleaned and polished for Lesley and her mother for the past three years. She too has moved into the village, but only from a neighbouring village, and more importantly, her grandfather and some of her uncles worked in the local pit before it closed, which makes her almost a local. Beside her sits a pale, sullen young girl in a nurse's uniform and navy anorak, a representative from the Hospice. She speaks to no-one. Doesn't know anyone. She barely knew the deceased. She remembers once cleaning her false teeth, but that's all.

The most important resident of the village has come; widow of the Captain, a smart, sprightly woman, wonderful for her age. Her sandy-haired son and the bereaved daughter, (like him an only child) were friends at primary school. Unable to grow a full beard like his father's, he settled years ago for a moustache, which never suited him and has now turned completely white. He is not near his mother today, he is standing at the back, but it's all right, her thumb will stretch that far.

Precisely at one thirty, the eulogy begins. The minister is a compassionate man. He didn't know the deceased well, having been called to the parish less than a year ago, but he speaks much of Baking Skills, and Visiting the Sick, of Intelligence and Strength Of Mind. He does not speak an unkind word, and at last, to everyone's relief it ends. Stiffly they rise from the hard dining chairs, and move, the women murmuring, the men mostly in silence, to the door and out into the damp December afternoon. They gather round the cars, watching the dirty yellow sky for rain, knowing the interment is still to be got through. And to their eternal credit, not one of them says "Wasn't it just like the old bitch to time her death to ruin Christmas Eve?"

The good daughter

It was very late but Lesley didn't feel ready to go to bed. The temperature had fallen, and the rain had turned to snow, small flakes lightly falling, floating, just visible in the light of the street lamps. If it kept on, the whole village would be a work of art by morning. Everything covered in white: pavements, buildings, the football field, the weeds round the recycling bins. It was all a lie. A white lie. The bad stuff was there underneath.

"This is my house. I am alone in it." She said the words aloud. She had anticipated this moment, touching it lightly now and then over the final months, like someone fingering a birthday gift through tissue paper, afraid to guess what it might be. But now, the funeral over, there wasn't much difference. No relief, no bitterness, no guilt, nothing as identifiable as any of those. Perhaps, she thought, perhaps it was too soon to feel anything.

Did I wish her dead?

She had wanted the waiting for death to end. Not the same thing.

I am glad she's dead?

How strange it was to watch the snow sift down from nowhere, and have no-one calling from the other room, *what are you doing, Lesley?* Just as strange as it had been at tea-time to find the fridge full. Gifts of soup and casseroles and cake had been brought by neighbours. She remembered the smell of the hospital food waiting in the stainless steel trolley in the corridor when visiting was over. A peculiar mix of something fried and something metallic. The nurses said goodnight to her by name, towards the end, grown used to her visits.

What to eat? Or indeed, whether to eat? All her life she'd accepted what was put in front of her when she came home: soup and main course and pudding. She was the shape and size she was because her mother was a good cook. No, she thought, playing with the words, because her mother cooked good food. Goodness as a moral quality was surely something different altogether. *You were a good daughter to her, Lesley.* More than one funeral guest had said it, but how could they possibly know?

If I was a good person, I would feel something definite, something definable. Wouldn't I at least be frightened by this lack of feeling?

She remembered something she'd read once in the *Reader's Digest* about people trapped in snow, how you had to decide which way was up before you began to dig. The way to do this was to spit. You gathered lots of saliva and spat. If the spit ran up your nose, then you were upside down. She had smiled at the idea, but it struck her now that she was that lost individual.

Her descent into the crevasse had been slow, a gradual

daily slide. Hard to tell when it began. At birth? Or on that day when she told her mother she wanted to move out, to share a flat with two of the other girls from the college?

If you leave this house, you will never enter it again.

When she was a child, she played the old game, would you rather freeze or boil to death? Of course the answer was, she didn't want to do either, but in the game she had to choose. The problem with freezing, she saw now, was that you didn't disappear. Had she become an embarrassment to those who were still warm? Her friends had all married or moved away, preoccupied with husbands and children. They still sent Christmas cards, but not so many, and some day, she supposed, even this would stop. Even this shivering hypothermia would stop.

You'll be preserved, she told herself, *like the Ice-man in the Alps, like the bodies on Everest, with the ink stain on your blouse, the shred of cold chicken between your back teeth. You'll stay here in this house until the planet falls into the sun.*

Earthenware

When the evening news came on, Ruby went through to the kitchen and filled the Creda water heater with exactly the amount needed to make two mugs of tea. (The mugs were earthenware. The good bone-china cups were never used, merely washed on Wednesdays and replaced in the cabinet.) When the water bubbled, the machine would emit a piercing sound like a factory hooter.

The room felt cold tonight, and she shivered a little. If only they'd kept the Rayburn, she thought, not for the first time. Lifting a discreet corner of the curtain, she looked across the hedge to Lesley's kitchen window. No light on. She had probably gone to bed.

Maybe the weather would improve, despite the forecast. Still, the cupboards were well stocked, and the freezer was full of neatly labelled packages. Make one, freeze one was a good rule. Taking milk from the fridge, she smiled with satisfaction at the big pot of home-made lentil soup. She had learned early in their marriage that Walter needed something to eat the minute he arrived home, and soup had been the answer, summer or winter. She ate hers in the kitchen, putting the finishing touches to the main course.

As she waited for the water to boil, Ruby felt a little

soreness starting at the back of her throat, and offered a prayer to no-one in particular that this would not be the start of anything serious. It had been bitter on Christmas Eve at the graveside. She'd felt the cold seeping through the seams of her coat. She had said so to Walter at the time, looking with envy at the Captain's widow in her fur. Beaver, she thought it was.

"I'd love a fur coat," she whispered to Walter as they drank their tea at the function room in the Village Hall afterwards.

"When would you wear a fur coat?"

"Things like this. And weddings."

"Who do we know that's getting married?" he said.

"Do you think she'll sell the house?" she asked a moment later.

"What?"

"Lesley next door. Do you think she'll move?

Walter considered the salmon sandwich he had bitten into, as if it might hold the answer.

"Nothing much we can do about it." He lifted one edge of the bread and looked at the filling before carefully extracting a thin slice of cucumber and putting it on his plate.

"I wouldn't like new neighbours, not at our age," she said.

"We might move ourselves. Once I retire."

Ruby stared at her husband of thirty years. He pulled a handkerchief out of his trouser pocket and wiped his nose.

"I've always fancied living near a sea loch. I could fish off a boat."

"But you don't fish, Walter."

"I could learn," he said, putting the rest of the sandwich into his mouth.

The hooter began to sound, and quickly Ruby flicked the switch. Her throat was really quite sore. Perhaps she ought to gargle with salt before bed. She poured some boiling water into a mug so that it would be cool by the time supper was over.

She'd always hated interments. The crematorium was so much nicer, as long as you knew when not to look. She filled the teapot, mopped up a few drips of water on the sink and draining board, added two custard creams to the tray, and took it through to Walter in the sitting room just as the news ended. This ritual, performed every night of their life together, ensured that there was no knowledge of the out-side world in her head that had not been there when she left home.

Mary

Mary Flaherty waited in the Chemist's for her prescription to be filled. Feeling hot and cold by turns, she wondered if she'd caught this cold standing at the graveside. A miserable day that had been, and no mistake. She'd felt peculiar the whole time: all those folk there she didn't know, on the chairs she'd polished herself, and her sitting next to them afterwards eating sandwiches so small they had only two bites in them.

Would she be needed now the old woman was dead? The house was full of clutter, but it wasn't hard to clean, because no-one wanted her to move the clutter. She was fond of the old fashioned ornaments. She liked polishing the brass, and waxing the old furniture, and ironing the old lady's linen pillowcases. In the last few months polycotton sheets had replaced the linen ones, for reasons, Lesley said, of hygiene (meaning that they needed frequent changing) but the linen pillowcases were kept in use. They stayed cool, she learned from Lesley, and were more pleasant against your face. She felt guilty now, remembering how in the last few weeks she'd enjoyed having the house to herself, dusting, hoovering and polishing without the old witch hovering over her. That bath still annoyed her though. She didn't know how they could bear the rusty stain under the cold tap. If it had been up to her, she would have had it out and a nice new white one put in.

Of course Lesley might decide the house was too big and move.

Outside, the coloured Christmas lights were still up, strung between the lamp-posts, Santa and his reindeer swaying in the wind. Had it been a Happy Christmas? Better than some. Her son-in-law had taken Wee Chrissie and the new bicycle out, so there had been an hour of peace. She'd only had to do the one course, roast ham, since no-one liked turkey. Too much food, of course. She saw her shape reflected in the glass and wished again that there had been a dark coat in her size. It was a good coat, and a bargain; she knew what it would have cost new.

The cards of hair ornaments on the wall were all pink or purple, too sparkly, all too young for her now. She had plenty of hair but it was fine and flat. She should have worn it up, but she kept losing the clasps, or else they broke. She sighed. She was silly to think about being attractive now, at her age. That was long gone.

Remembering that she'd given Ryan money the night before, she checked to see what was left in her purse. Ryan was her only boy, the only one still at home. He was eighteen, but still she waited up till she heard him come home. She couldn't help it.

"Who was that?" she would ask when another girl phoned to speak to him.

"Nobody."

His mobile was always set to the answer machine, and if they called the house phone when he was still in bed, or doing something he wanted to keep doing, he refused to come to the phone and she had to take messages for him.

She missed her daughters. They would blether on and tell her all the latest gossip, although maybe not all that they'd been up to themselves. Better not to know, she'd told herself. And they'd had their share of screaming matches, of course, them being teenagers and sharing a bedroom, but at least there had been conversation in the house. This one might as well not have learned to talk.

She worried about him, more than she ever had about the girls. All the junk he ate instead of food, all those chips from Big Sam's, eaten between the bus stop and the house. He'd been such a good eater when he was a wee boy, now he never touched a vegetable. One time when her back was playing her up she'd had a notion for home-made soup, and, both girls being at work, had tried to get him to go down to the Co-op. Her Nan had made proper soup, soup that was good for you, with butter beans and peas, and long strips of boiled beef and big lumps of potato and wee lumps of yellow turnip. Tear up a slice of bread to float in it, and you had a whole family meal for pennies. Her mouth watered at the thought of it.

"And a leek. Make sure it's a good big one."

"What?"

"With lots of white on it. A good sized one."

"I don't know what they look like," he'd said.

Tonight's tea was sausage and egg, the butcher's own square sausage, he would likely eat that. Or if not, there was fish fingers and baked beans.

Bird seed

"Duncan, didn't you say you were going into the village to get some bird seed, dear?"

Duncan's pen halted on the Radio Times. The bird seed was simply a valid reason to go out. Mail order was far cheaper than the village pet shop.

"I was waiting till the rain stopped," he said, not looking round at his mother.

"Well, I would like to get these thank-you letters off, dear, but of course it doesn't have to be today, if you're busy."

"I'll go out before twelve," he said, twelve o'clock being collection time.

She put a small stack of letters down on the desk and tiptoed out of the room.

Duncan stared out at the garden, drawing tiny circles on his cavalry-twilled knee with the capped end of the ballpoint. The previous day's brief snow had been washed away. The climbing hydrangea next to the window was thoroughly sodden, heavy drips gathered along its naked branches. Had it rained so much last December? It had been dry at New Year, certainly, as some of their visitors had walked up the hill rather than coming by car. He wondered if Lesley would come this year, now that she was on her own.

He circled some more radio programmes for the week ahead. He might or might not listen to all of them. He circled the Vivaldi recital. The Scottish Chamber Orchestra was generally acceptable, though in the last year or so he had come to prefer the authenticity of early music specialists. He had, in fact, been in Venice during the night, walking in his dream ahead of his mother and several of the Christmas Eve mourners down narrow streets where all the turns were at right angles, making it impossible to know if they led anywhere at all until the turning point was reached. The responsibility of leading the group was heavy on his shoulders. Why was he in charge? They assumed too much, these people. He did his best to read names and numbers on walls and doors but the words on the ceramic tiles were printed in tiny cramped letters, too small to read. Abruptly they had come upon a stretch of water. The waves were rough and the line of gondolas, deserted, made irregular slapping sounds against the water. When he turned, Lesley was watching him. She was holding out her hands. Did she want help, or was she offering it? As he moved towards her, a man of about his own age appeared, catching him by the sleeve. "I believe I am your long lost brother," the man began, and Duncan knew at once that it was true. With that he'd woken, his first, immediate thought being how on earth he was going to ask his mother about the other child. It took him a few moments to remember that he was the only one.

If he told Mrs Fleming about the dream, she'd most likely enquire how many cups of coffee he'd had the night before. Mrs Fleming was the most recent addition to the staff at the Library. Half his age, with a face covered in freckles, and a small bald baby that her husband brought with him when he came to collect her on late nights, Mrs Fleming was very concerned about his coffee consumption and kept trying to wean him onto something she believed to be healthier. She brought in various fruit teas. He'd tried peppermint to please her. It tasted like hot mouthwash.

"And what are you doing at Christmas, Duncan?" she'd asked.

"Oh, just the usual. Just the two of us. We like a quiet Christmas. We have people in at New Year."

It occurred to him that she might be about to invite him to the party he knew they were having. She had talked about it a lot, a Murder Mystery Evening, with the guests coming in costume. Not something he'd greatly enjoy, he thought, but he pictured himself in his father's old Navy uniform, pre-served untarnished in its dust covering in one of the spare bedrooms. Duncan considered that he had been very kind to Mrs Fleming, changing shifts to suit her, listening with a smile to her chatter about the baby, generally helping her to find her footing. The husband didn't appeal to him parti-cularly, with his leather jacket and untidy hair, but still, he thought now, he might have gone, if invited.

Preparing for the Party

As he stood waiting for the bus, which was more than a few minutes late, Duncan fingered the folded paper in his raincoat pocket. He glanced somewhat sternly at the masculine-looking woman with razor-short hair who was standing beside him in the shelter and whose child was alternately sniffing loudly and coughing without a hand over his mouth. This, Duncan had long since concluded, was a circumstance absolutely to be expected. Although he had a car, it was hardly used. Far more responsible to travel by bus, which was good for the environment, but not quite so good for one's own health. He had solved the problem of keeping his clothes clean by wearing his old navy Barbour, but the thoughtlessness of most individuals, combined with limited ventilation, inevitably resulted in a soup of seasonal viruses which all passengers were compelled to sup, whether they would or no.

It was extremely annoying, but there was nothing one could do. If *he* had a bad cold, and here he stared ineffectively at the woman again, he would travel by car. Had any medical research been done on the effect of bus travel on public health? He made a mental note to run a search when he was back at the library.

His destination was the delicatessen in the next village. Many of the ingredients for his mother's New Year gathering had been mail-ordered as they were every year; the salmon pinwheels and smoked duck mousse from an Aberdeenshire smokehouse had already arrived, along with oatcakes and small biscuits for cheese, while the various cheeses themselves had come from Ayrshire. Tesco would deliver basic items, but still there were some small things that only a delicatessen could provide. For these specialities, one had to go from Hartsend to the neighbouring township, which was more middle class and provided more for middle class needs. It had more or less the same number of shops as Hartsend, but they differed significantly in nature. There was no betting shop and the florist sold only flowers, not fruit and vegetables as well. There was an optician's and an independent shoe shop. There was also a small but very exciting second-hand bookshop, where Duncan had sometimes found poetry first editions at remarkable prices. It troubled his conscience that the owner seemed unaware of the value of his stock, so he always put something in the RSPCA tin on the counter, which seemed to him rather a noble deed since he was not over fond of cats or dogs.

Deep in pleasurable if somewhat anxious anticipation – for the shop might be shut, the owner was erratic as well as unenlightened – Duncan didn't at first realize that his name was being called. The speaker, inside a small black car, tried again.

Stooping, peering in, he recognised the parish minister, disguised in a shabby blue sweater and denim jeans. There was a young girl in the passenger seat.

"I'm only going to Carbennie," Duncan said, adding several thankyous and smiling in case his refusal might seem ungracious.

"That's on my way, jump in," said the minister.

"I'll go in the back, Dad," the girl said, getting out quickly, before Duncan could speak.

His hand thus forced, and constitutionally unable to be rude, he got into the front passenger seat. He felt that his dislike of the man was irrational. In theory, they had a great deal in common. They were possibly the only two in the village who could read both Greek and Latin. More importantly, they were both on the side of decency, both hopeful of improving themselves and the world. But perhaps this was where the problem lay. He himself firmly believed in doing good by stealth. Not letting the left hand know what the right was doing, as it were. To make a living out of this, as ministers of religion did, was, in Duncan's eyes, to make the whole business rather more public and presumptuous than it ought to be. Moreover he had been told that this particular clergyman was happy to quote, in his sermons, from newspapers predominantly left of centre. Today's denim trousers served only to confirm his doubts. The man was, after all, only a few years younger than himself.

"Still on holiday, Duncan?" the minister began as they drove off.

When had they reached first name terms? Feeling something under his feet, he bent down, hoping he hadn't trodden on anything valuable, but it was a brown paper bag, with the words "Burger King" on it. That would account for the rather odd smell then. He left it where it was.

"The college closes for the whole two weeks, but I have some extra days," he replied. He wanted to ask if they might drive a little more slowly, the lane being narrow and the hedges high, but politeness forbade.

"And how's your mother keeping?"

"She's very well, thank you." He gripped the side of the seat as inconspicuously as he could. Was this the right answer? Perhaps if she was "very well" she might be expected to come to church? She had not forgiven the previous minister for remaining on holiday when Captain Crawfurd died, meaning that the man from the next parish, a stripling in his twenties, had had to conduct the service. She still gave money regularly, of course and she had not transferred her lines, but she didn't attend. He himself went faithfully to Communion three times a year, and to Re-membrance Sunday.

The girl in the back seat was just visible in the side mirror. She was exceptionally pretty, and fair-haired like her father, but her face was spoiled by something Duncan could only describe as a disdainful expression. Not an easy child, he decided.

"And your friend, Miss Crosthwaite. I tried to call in the other day, but there was no reply. She hasn't gone away, has she?"

"No, I don't think so."

Duncan felt a pang of guilt. He should have called in himself. Or at least dropped in a card. His mother had sent one, but he should have done something himself.

He hated visiting the sick. It was more than twenty years since his father died, but he still remembered vividly the hospital foyer where they'd sat day by day in that final week, waiting for visiting hour to begin: olive green fake-leather benches, a sludge-coloured carpet, potted artificial plants on either side. In the excessive warmth, he'd felt he was suffocating at the bottom of some murky pond, surrounded by underwater weeds.

He'd been shocked to see how drawn and pale Lesley was at the funeral. Black didn't suit her at all. He'd fully intended to speak to her but she was constantly with someone or other, and when he caught her eye, she seemed not to recognise him. Besides, he was afraid of saying the wrong thing. It was so easy to say the wrong thing in such situations where conversations jumped and jittered around so.

The minister was talking about his son, home from university apparently, and how they couldn't get him up in the mornings. Duncan felt for the sheet of paper in his pocket. There were very specific items on the list. Puréed lemon grass. Pastry shells. Rösti potato mix and raclette cheese. Those very small Belgian chocolates in the shape of Christmas puddings.

Days of servants were of course long, long gone, but Mrs Flaherty would attend the day before the party to help clean and set things out, and on the day after she would come to clear, load the dishwasher with all that was dishwasher proof, and carefully hand rinse the good china. She would be generously reimbursed, and would take leftovers home with her.

Poor Mrs Flaherty. The wild thought had occurred to Duncan more than once in recent years, as some of their guests became too aged or infirm to come, that Mrs Flaherty might be invited to come to the gathering, might sit quietly in a corner with a plate of Tesco's finest lemon cheesecake and enliven the atmosphere by her idiosyncratic use of the English language. (She had once assured him that the "module" under her arm had turned out to be harmless.) Her unintentionally droll commentaries on village life deserved a wider audience, he thought, but he had never mentioned this to his mother.

"Lesley and her mother usually come to us at New Year," he said, becoming aware of a silence. "We have a few people over. Not a late night."

Why did he say this? Was he afraid the minister would think they might be having a rowdy binge-drinking session into the wee small hours?

"That's good. It's such a difficult time to be on your own. I've been worrying about her."

Duncan glanced at the man. What right had *he* to be worrying about Lesley? Lesley wouldn't appreciate such concern. She wasn't particularly religious. Furthermore, she was very capable. She had always been capable.

At school, in the double desk beside him, Lesley had worn

navy ribbons to match her cardigan tied at exactly the same place on each braid, and her white knee socks had remained firmly in place over her stout little calves. Her jotters were covered in smart brown paper. The ordinary village children generally used wallpaper scraps or left-over Christmas wrapping.

"She's a very capable person," he said, more loudly than he meant to. "Before the car park would be fine for me, if you can. At Kelseys," he added.

"The delicatessen? Right. Of course, I don't mean to say she's not capable. But she's not had . . . Ah, well, *de mortuis* etc . . . It would do her good to get more involved in different things now."

Was this directed at him too, at his failure to get "involved" in things? "Thank you for the lift," he said politely.

"My pleasure. Hope your party goes well."

The smile ambushed him.

"Perhaps you and your wife would like to join us," Duncan heard himself say. To his relief he found his offer declined. The minister and his family were already committed elsewhere.

"Big family thing. The men do the cooking so it's a bit of a mess, but you know what they say, if a thing's worth doing, it's worth doing badly."

The car drove off. Unfolding his A5 sheet, Duncan entered the delicatessen.

Fine art

Ryan Flaherty jumped down from the bus, welcoming the cold air after his long journey from the city. Barely half four and it was already dark. He glanced into the café as he passed. There they all were, the usual punters, buying ice cream. Raspberry ripple, chocolate mint, peach, and toffee shortbread. It never ceased to amuse him that people would eat ice-cream on the coldest days. *Don't let the doctor put the wee stick in your mouth till you find out who ate the ice cream.* One of Papa Flaherty's jokes. *How old are you, papa? As old as my tongue and a bit older than my teeth.* He hadn't understood that either, his five year old mind just annoyed at not getting a straight answer. A sense of confusion and the strange sweetish smell of pipe tobacco was about all he remembered of the old man.

That would be some job though, being a doctor, putting things into other people's mouths, sticking things up their bums. Having to look at old people's naked parts. He'd seen his mother's breasts once by accident. She'd been up out of bed, making a cup of tea in the middle of the night, her nightie unbuttoned. He'd just come in. He became one with the coats on the back of the door as she walked through the hall. She'd not noticed him, thank god.

Let me die before I get old . . .

At the Fish and Chip shop he pushed open the heavy glass door and scanned the bright interior. There was a bit of a queue. No familiar faces, except for Sandro busy with the frying, and Michelle behind the counter. She wasn't a friend, but she'd gone with one of his sisters' ex-boyfriends for a while, so he knew things about her, and she knew, so she'd be nice to him. She'd been a couple of years above him at school. 'Jail bait' was his mother's term for Michelle, but now she was older, it hardly applied.

The prices had gone up again. Ten minutes wait for fish, Michelle said. It was worth waiting to get them straight from the fat. What an easy way to make money though, provided you had cash up front. The rich got richer and the poor got nothing. Some of the guys in his class came from his kind of background, but some were unbelievable. The cost of materials was nothing to them, it was like they were buying crisps. Some had even bought the books instead of using the library. It irritated him that he couldn't just despise them. There was one quiet guy who, when he did speak, was so posh you felt like he needed something thrown over him, but his work was brilliant and mad crazy.

He'd not anticipated stuff like this. Ok, he'd assumed that Art School would be hard work, he'd been told that, he was up for that. He knew he had everything to learn. One of the lecturers had even complimented him on that. *That's what I like about you, Mr Flaherty. You know the extent of your ignorance.* It was just that he'd thought life would be better;

the guys around him would all be interested in what he was interested in, unlike school. And it was better, his mind insisted. But not simpler. Better did not equal simpler. So he was envious, but not sure of his envy. Were his thoughts getting deeper, or more shallow?

Sometimes it seemed like you only had to fool enough of the right people enough of the time to be successful. Anyone could end up winning the Turner Prize, given the chance. He himself had a cracker of an idea, which he'd been careful not to mention to anyone. Rows of soiled handfuls of toilet paper, dated by the week, sandwiched between upright slabs of Perspex. Kind of like the Viet Nam war memorial in America, but more visceral. He liked the word *visceral.* He wasn't sure what it meant exactly, but he'd heard someone say it in a review of a Tarantino film, and the one time he'd used it in an essay, he got a massive pencil tick beside it from the tutor. So, right, toilet paper, pure white, no fancy colours. *Production,* he'd call it, with the appropriate year in brackets after the title. He was fairly sure it had never been done. It would be scent free, being encased. *Visually stimulating, thought provoking, symbolic of both the waste of natural resources and the futility of human life* . . . The reviews would be something along those lines except they'd put it better. Originally he'd thought about collecting his nephew Chrissie's disposable nappies, *A resounding call to abandon landfill sites and halt damage to the environment,* but his sister would want to know why he was taking them away and there was the problem of storage. Which of course there would be with the toilet paper too . . .

Michelle, only just contained in her low-cut black sweater, gave him a big smile. She was very tanned. Her skin was orange all the way down her cleavage, thanks to free sessions in the tanning booth. Was this the only village with a tanning booth in its newsagents shop? For the first few days it had seemed out of place, but now it struck him as having a deeper meaning, making some kind of statement about society, he wasn't sure what yet, but it would come to him.

"Lookin' good, Michelle," he said.

She smiled again. Her false nails were immaculate, pale pink with square white tips. She was aware of him these days, he knew it. He was a lot taller than he'd been in school, his growth had come late. He wondered what she'd say if he asked her to pose naked. To help his Life Drawing. He wasn't interested in her, she wouldn't know something was visceral if it hit her between the eyes, but he couldn't help wondering just how far the tan went.

"So what are you up to these days?" she said.

"I got into Art School," he said. "Fine Art."

He was sure she didn't know what he meant. Explaining would have lessened it. Even his sisters thought he was skiving. *That's our taxes keeping you.* His brother-in-law, a plasterer in and out of work, had put it less politely. *You're up your own arse pal.*

Were they right? It was one thing to fool about in the

front of his head about Perspex and used nappies, and to join in the banter and arty chat between classes – he was learning how to do that as cleverly as anyone. But what was he trying to prove? And why? And who to? It could be the whole world was up its own arse.

He'd had a vivid dream once of a stretch of sand, like the one in *The Beach*. Everything was perfect – the sun, the waves slipping over the sand, their stranded bubbles vanishing with a faint "pkkk" sound, the breeze caressing the coconut palms. He was the only one allowed here. Even when he was in the dream he was aware of how clichéd it all was, but it didn't matter, because it really was his island. He took off his trainers and walked for a while. The sand was firm at first, its colour like the tablet his Nan had made when he was small. Then it got softer and his feet slipped about. He stopped walking. He was scared to look ahead, scared to look back . . .

At last the fish was ready. He handed Michelle the money. When he got more change than he should have, he turned away and checked inside the wrapping. Two fish instead of one? She was taking a bit of a risk this time.

He heard her say "The prices are up. You're two pound short." and looked back. Right away he recognised the girl she was talking to.

"I'm really sorry," the girl began. Her voice had no sharp edges, only curves, like pink tulip petals beginning to open. "I haven't got . . ."

"Here," Ryan dropped a five pound note on the counter.

He feels the girl looking at him, stunned by his generous gesture. He holds out a hand, but instead of taking it she comes close. Her hair smells of honeysuckle. She leans against him, murmuring her thanks . . .

"Excuse me."

The sense of unreality persisted. Nobody round here said 'excuse me,' or had flawless skin . . .

"I can't take your money. You can't do that."

"I just did," he told her.

She stared at him. He was made of sand, and it was sliding, as if a hole inside him was widening like some special effect in a movie. And he counted for nothing, because she didn't reply, just turned away, stiffly walking towards the door, her head proud on her neck above the cream scarf.

He followed her out, watched her half run along the street, the way girls always ran, knees stuck together. She got into a car. He kept walking, glanced in. The driver was male, his own age, ok maybe a bit older, with the well-fed, well-groomed, easy on himself middle-class look he now knew so well. He could practically smell the aftershave. Only when the car drove off did he remember his five pound note, lying pointlessly on the counter.

Jenny's chickenpox

"So you didn't get anything? Not even chips? I told you I didn't have any cash, Harriet. If you needed more, I could have got some out of the machine."

"I didn't *know* I would need more. I didn't know the prices had gone up."

"So why didn't you just buy one?"

Because of that horrible creepy boy with the weird hair, she didn't say.

"Are we going to sit here all night?" she demanded.

"Oh sweetest of sisters, your every wish is my command. Where do you want to go?

"New Zealand."

He started the engine. "I take it you just want to go home, then?"

Back in the days when Dad had a real job, there would have been money enough for them all to go and visit. This morning's e-mail had a picture of the latest beach picnic attached: Aunt Rhona and Uncle Malcolm, and the cousins, and Grampa next to Mum, everyone looking very brown and happy.

"Don't you hate this place, Kerr? After Aberdeen? "

They'd had this talk before. He sided with their parents.

This was where their father had been called, he said, so that was that. Blah blah blah. A place was the people in it, he said, not the buildings, and people were much the same the world over. Which was so not true.

"So fitya dee'in tonight? Coming with me?"

The evening had unexpectedly become a blank sheet because of their cousin Jenny's chickenpox. No family gathering. Behind their father's back Kerr had punched the air, with a gleeful, *yes*, and made a couple of phone calls to see which of his friends were around, and where the best party was happening. Her father had decided to take up an invitation from one of his parishioners.

She made a face. "I won't know anyone."

"You know all of them."

"They're your friends Kerr, not mine."

"They all like you."

Right, she thought, as in *I really like children, but I couldn't eat a whole one*. She'd been at gatherings with Kerr's friends before. Never again.

Vitrolite

It was still pitch black outside when Lesley woke. She filled the kettle to make tea and turned on the radio. She had grown up with this kitchen, had hated it for as long as she could recall; the egg-yolk yellow vitrolite tiles on the walls, bordered with black, the everlasting brown linoleum, the pulley overhead. The wood and metal were original, the ropes had been replaced twice in her memory. Everything perfectly serviceable and perfectly hideous. No tile would ever break unless someone swung a saucepan at it. At least she had scored a small victory there. Aluminium had been replaced with stainless steel, thanks to an article in the health pages of the *Herald*, which had convinced Mother that aluminium was dangerous.

She disposed of the leftovers and the surplus food donated by her neighbours, some into the dustbin and some by flushing it down the toilet, in measured amounts, so as not to block the system. Now she had to try to remember which plates and bowls came from whom.

The white stoneware casserole was from the Robertsons next door. She would scour it carefully, and leave it on their doorstep, rather than ring the doorbell. Ruby exhausted her. She sucked up information like a vacuum cleaner sucking up dust. She peeked through her net curtains all the time, and chided the postman if he didn't close the gate after him. She picked up litter from her front garden and threw it back into the street each time she went out. Her husband was always Mr Robertson, never Walter. And the eyebrows! Completely plucked out then painted in blue, they gave her a perpetual look of superiority and astonishment.

The cornflakes had gone stale, but Lesley ate her way through half the bowl before thinking *Why am I doing this? I don't have to eat these. I can eat, or not eat. No-one is going to ask.* The idea rocked her, despite its smallness. She stared at a dribble of milk on the chequered oilcloth.

Careful, she told herself. This might be all freedom amounted to. Until the lawyer dealt with everything, she didn't know whether there was money or not. Too soon yet to throw saucepans at walls, or install a shower, or abandon her job and move from perpetual rain to somewhere warm and beautiful. And where would she go? What would she do, a woman her age, alone? It wouldn't happen. She would go back at work, to the bickering of the other admin staff, and harried teachers' demands, and pupils requesting the toilet key, and the same old post-Christmas conversations. *. . . love them but it's wonderful when they leave honestly I think I've seen that film five times at least if I never eat a mince pie again it'll be too soon you're so lucky Lesley going home to a quiet house and your meal made for you,* *instead of a husband and children mumphing and com-plaining . . .*

No such luck now, if luck it had ever been.

She took her tea though to the front sitting room to begin clearing out the desk. It seemed as good a place as any.

The party

"I'm so glad you decided to come, Lesley. Oh, thank you, you shouldn't have."

What Lesley "shouldn't have" was a box of Arran Aromatics soaps wrapped in flowered paper. She hadn't in fact bought this – it was one of several she'd found in her mother's wardrobe, but there was still a recognisable scent of lavender when she sniffed the box. *Waste not, want not,* she told herself. Duncan, festive in his Crawfurd tartan waistcoat and matching bow tie, was hovering behind his mother, waiting to take her coat and hat.

"And how are you, my dear?" Mrs Crawfurd was wearing cashmere as always. The shade this year was grey, neck and hem edged with a paler silver grey that toned exactly with her pearls.

But all was not as always. This was a new thing, being here alone. And the questioning that began in her head, this was brand new. Was this woman really "glad"? Was she interested in Lesley's wellbeing?

Thank you for asking. Let's sit down for an hour and I will tell you how I am, or rather I will explore how I feel, because I'm not in the least sure. My heart feels as if it wants to burst. Do you think that's possible?

Perhaps Mrs Crawfurd was glad because if people didn't come she would know she had lost her importance as the prize inhabitant of the village. Perhaps her doubts were already growing. So many new people, so many new houses on all sides encroaching on the old village. Perhaps she was already forgotten. The malice of this thought was so sharp and so satisfying that Lesley felt momentarily dizzy.

"I'm quite well, thank you," she said.

Why had she come? She pulled off her boots, (placing them on the newspapers which had been spread on a tray beside the umbrella stand, in advance, as always) and slipped on her good black patent shoes. They were old but immaculate, rather like Duncan's bow tie. He only ever wore it at New Year. Was this why she had come, out of cowardice, out of habit?

Or was being here an act of courage? How much easier it would have been to send a note. *I am still too distressed by Mother's death. I know you will understand.* There was distress, true, but it wasn't her mother's death that was distressing her.

It had been hard and weary work at first, going through her mother's correspondence but without warning it had suddenly become less weary, because, there were, inexplicably, several letters addressed to Miss Lesley Crosthwaite which she had never received or read. A letter from Jennifer, one of her friends at college. A wedding invitation, dated twenty years previously from someone whose name now rang no bell. And a postcard from Canada, from Hector . . .

"Ready? Do come and meet everyone."

The hall through which she followed Mrs Crawfurd was just as she remembered; the nearly black sandalwood chest brought back from the Captain's youthful years in the Eastern Fleet, the gross and politically incorrect cast-iron money banks sitting on it, "Dinah" and "The Jolly Nigger", waiting to raise pennies to their red-lipped mouths, the elaborately framed still life painted by Mrs Crawfurd's Victorian grandmother on glass, the lilies on the glass topped table, pouring out their too-lush scent.

Duncan had disappeared upstairs with the coat. His mother placed a tentative three fingers beneath Lesley's elbow to usher her forward into the conservatory, with its tall plants and white statuary.

"Sherry? Or something soft? Do help yourself. I think you know most people, dear," her hostess added, hastily, for the doorbell was tinkling.

And of course Lesley did know most of them. Her own GP, the almost completely bald Dr MacKinnon, and his nervous wife, whose fair hair had thinned over the years as if in sympathy. The new young doctor whose name she'd heard, but could not now remember. There was no wife beside him, perhaps there wasn't one yet, he looked so young, no more than sixteen. Here was Miss Calvert, the energetic headmistress of the primary school, looking in-complete without her bicycle. Standing apart from these, Duncan's cousins, a couple she recognized but had never spoken to, and the tall bearded man who was something terribly important in the High Court, with his terribly slim wife. The grown-up daughter, not quite so slim, had a man with her this year.

"Glad to see you, Lesley," Dr MacKinnon said.

Since he wasn't a man famed in the village for his bedside manner, his gladness, Lesley thought, was possibly more sincere than Mrs Crawfurd's. He was an intelligent man, and thorough, which was what counted.

She accepted his firm handshake, though even here questions were forming in her mind, because this man had been their family doctor for years and years. *Did you know what she was doing? Did you guess? My heart feels as if it would like to burst.*

"You won't know Dr Gordon," he nodded at the teenager beside him. "Just joined us. English, but it's getting harder to find a man these days, so we took him in."

The young man laughed, but his manner suggested the joke had been told many times. His hair was dark and curly, his skin as smooth and flawless as a baby's. Surely he wasn't old enough to command birth and death and the stretch in between?

"And what do you do?" the young man asked.

"I'm a secretary in the High School."

Instantly Lesley knew that she had been boxed and labelled. Spinster. Overweight. Not very bright. She stared fixedly at the wine glasses on the glaring white linen.

"So you get all these lovely long holidays."

"No," she told him, and turning away, took the nearest

glass. What was she doing? As a rule when this question was asked, she chattered obligingly about how good that would be, and what a pity the office staff didn't get the holidays, but it wasn't so terrible, because the school was quiet without the children etc etc, aligning herself with the other speaker, positioning herself alongside like a friendly little dingy sidling up to a bigger vessel.

"You do know that's champagne," a voice said.

She looked at the glass in her hand, then at Duncan. Dear Duncan. Unchanging as the war memorial. Predictable as winter weather. He was playing with his top waistcoat button. From childhood she had envied those fingers so unlike her little stubby ones. His handwriting had won the class prize year after year. As always, he had written the New Year invitations in immaculate copperplate. Fountain pen, royal blue ink on cream card. And written, no doubt, with his mother at his elbow checking the guest list.

"Not that there's any reason . . ." he began, flushing slightly.

She ought to have helped him, but in her new perverse mood she found herself saying nothing.

"Duncan, dear, can I have a word?" his mother said, ushering forward a new arrival, whom Lesley recognised with slight surprise, for neither Duncan nor his mother were regular church goers. She watched Duncan introduce the minister to his cousin. She didn't want to speak to the minister, didn't want to speak to anyone. She turned away, walking to the window alcove as if to admire the flower arrangement. This was the difference, she saw now. This was what it meant, this being here by herself. She was expected to speak. It was no longer possible to stand beside Mother and smile and make murmuring sounds. How incredibly stupid not to have thought of it before. Her usual stupidity, of course: the failure to think ahead, to remember that she was always seasick until she was on board and it was too late, or to recall that coconut in a cake or a sweet made her gag till the slice or spoonful was irretrievably in her mouth.

There was no-one here she wanted to be with, not her hostess, not the relations, and certainly not robust Miss Calvert, the only other single woman present, who had calf muscles like a man and was always eager to pour forth at length on her latest adventure storming the Alps or the Andes.

"I expect you know everyone here." The young doctor had followed her.

If she said nothing he would surely move away. She sipped at her drink.

How strangely the minister was dressed. Not at all like the man she remembered from the funeral. He wore a checked shirt, with no tie, a brown leather waistcoat, and dark corduroy trousers. He looked like a cowboy. She imagined a horse, tied up to the rhododendrons in the front garden. Duncan had vanished. She assumed he'd taken the minister's coat away.

The young doctor was still beside her, waiting for an

answer. What question had he asked? She took a large mouthful of the champagne, and felt it trickling down inside her chest, bright and cold but somehow warming at the same time.

"Doctor Gordon, have you found somewhere to live yet?"

They both turned. Mrs MacKinnon was blinking at them from under her long, sparse fringe. Her dress was a pale lemon colour, with a pattern of daisies and leaves which looked as if they were wilting, as if the material had been made up the wrong way round.

"Early days, I suppose, but has anything turned up for you?"

"I've been looking at the new builds," he said. "Over at the site of the old brickworks, is that right?"

Mrs MacKinnon frowned. "But they're all so squashed together. You could lean out of one window and hand something to your neighbour. And they're so close to the tinkers' site . . ."

Travellers, Lesley told her silently. She knew two of the children from the school; identical twins, round-faced, with small eyes and long un-brushed hair. They attended inter-mittently but caused no trouble.

"Yes, well at least you know the price," the young doctor said. "I tried for a couple on the far side of the river, but the asking price bears no resemblance to what they go for. It's very different from what I'm used to."

There was a younger child, too young for school, a blond

sweet-faced girl, with huge dark brown eyes who had stared back at her from their ramshackle van outside the Post Office, almost as if trying to read her mind.

Suddenly everyone seemed determined to crowd her into the corner. She tried to move back but there was nowhere to go except into the curtains.

"I believe our Scottish system is better, in fact, but everything's gone crazy these days," Dr MacKinnon rested a large hand on his wife's shoulder. "We were lucky, bought our first house at the beginning of the seventies, six thousand it cost us. Four years later we sold it for eleven. Price of oil went up, you see. I dare say we're sitting on half a million now. "

"Oh, more than that I think," one of the Crawfurd relations commented. "Property in the right place is always going to . . ."

Dr McKinnon interrupted, "Ah, good, smells like the curry's been brought through. Hope you like a good strong curry, Gordon."

But Mrs McKinnon was troubled. "I just think it's all so fast. The village isn't the close-knit community it used to be. There are all sorts of people here now. I came over to the butcher's shop last week to collect our turkey and chipolatas, and the place was full, and when I looked round, I didn't know a single soul. I was the only one served by name, actually. You understand what I mean, don't you, Lesley? There are so many incomers now."

"Well, I hope you don't disapprove of all the incomers,

Mrs McKinnon," the young doctor said. There was a pause, then everyone laughed. Lesley smiled with the rest, wishing she had the courage to point out that Mrs MacKinnon and her husband didn't in fact live in the village any more, but in its much more salubrious neighbour, and that having come originally from an entirely different city on the other side of the country, they were incomers twice over.

A bell rang. There was a chorus of appreciative murmurs from those guests who recognised what this signified, and the tight little press of bodies around Lesley began to loosen. She knew exactly what would be on the table: a large pale salmon with its parsley and lemon slices, tiny pastry shells filled with paté and sunblush tomatoes, honey garlic chicken on bamboo skewers, the famous Malay curry (the Captain's secret recipe), with basmati rice, rösti potatoes in the Delft bowl for those who didn't like rice.

None of which she wanted. There was a metallic taste in her mouth. Had she been grinding her teeth in the night? She looked at her drink. It was a pretty colour, but tasted no better to her than lemonade, an insipid lemonade at that. Why was such a fuss made over it? There was no alcohol in their own house, a legacy of her grandfather's steadfast adherence to the principles of the Rechabites. My house, she corrected herself. My house, where all that has been hidden will be laid bare. Was that the Bible or Shakespeare?

All will be laid bare.

All? She drank some more, and more again.

"Miss Crosthwaite?"

54

The party

It was the minister, gesturing at her, inviting her to come to the table. He really did look like a cowboy without a horse.

Greetings from Calgary, Hector's postcard had said on the front in bright yellow letters, with a mounted policeman holding a long lance with a pennant. On the reverse he'd written, *Hope you're not working too hard. Will write again when I'm settled. Best wishes your friend Hector.*

She had tried to think of some explanation, but in the end there was only one. Mother had ruled out forever the mounted policeman, the impossible shininess of his boots, the assured curve of his legs around the horse, the pure and perfect scarlet of his uniform.

She put down her empty glass, picked up a full one, and went in to the dining room.

The waistcoat and the prawn

"Did you know this was champagne?" Lesley asked the minister.

He nodded. "And a very fine champagne it is."

She moved, and stumbled a little.

"I'm fine, thank you," she said, shrugging off his hand, which for some reason seemed to be attempting to dust her sleeve.

"Why don't you sit here, and let me fill a plate for you."

She sank down into a chair. Above and around her head, people were talking with their mouths full, exclaiming over the food, moving in and out. The minister didn't come back. So much for good manners. Dark suits and bright dresses blurred and the noise level rose, though no-one bothered to talk to her. She might as well have been a cushion. Finding her glass empty, she placed it very carefully on the arm of the chair, then, feeling that might be too precarious, she picked it up again. Very slowly she leaned forward and managed to place it on the floor where, she realized a moment later, it was just as likely to be knocked over. Really, this was all very difficult. They should have put tables near the chairs.

Duncan's mother was coming towards her across the room, a plate in one hand.

Lesley said, "Thank you so much. I'm so sorry. I was having such a problem knowing where to put this beautiful glass. Crystal glass. It's very kind of you. Kind of you." She burped, but only a very small burp, which she managed to turn into a discreet cough.

Duncan's mother didn't answer. She hovered for a moment then for no apparent reason turned away without handing over the plate of food. Puzzled, Lesley watched the immaculate white chignon and its owner disappear into the corridor that led to the kitchen and the pantry. She knew that pantry. At one of Duncan's childhood parties, playing hide and seek, she and another little girl had hidden there in the dark, and when found, had panicked, bringing down the roller towel and its fittings.

"I was so frightened. I thought we had broken it, ruined it for ever," she said.

The important cousin's skinny wife looked down at her, eyebrows raised.

"Nobody told me it wasn't, you see," Lesley explained. "We just ran back to the others. So nobody knew it was me, except that other girl. And now you."

The woman didn't smile back. No sense of humour. Her loss.

"I was never good at hiding. Or seeking, come to that. My mother was. Did you know that? She hid Hector's postcard from me. God knows what else she hid. And not a thing I can do about it now."

The words reverberated, but whether inside or outside

her head she wasn't sure. She sat back. So much noise. Where was it coming from? Where was John Wayne with the promised food? Duncan was in front of her now, and yes, he had brought food, but when she reached up to take it from his hands, the plate unbalanced. Most of the contents flew onto his waistcoat.

She repressed a giggle and tried to get up to rescue a large prawn from his silver buttons. The other way round, she corrected herself. The prawn was dead, there was nothing to be done for the prawn, it was the button she needed to help . . .

"Oh, I'm so sorry, Duncan. Your poor, lovely waistcoat. Cheer up. Here, have a . . ." she stared at the object on her palm, "cherry tomato."

Being helped onto her feet was quite fun, and being half carried into the corridor and into the kitchen was rather like a waltz. It was all different from what she remembered. Lots of white, lots of lovely shiny steel. Where was the pantry? Dr MacKinnon's big, red face blocked her view. His breath was very garlicky. She let him hold her wrist but it was hard to hear what he was saying.

"I believe I would like to go home now," she said.

Terrible things

"Miss Crosthwaite!"

"I am perfectly alright, Dr Gordon," she called, continuing to walk down the driveway away from him.

"Yes, I know, but my car is at the gate and Dr McKinnon doesn't want you walking home by yourself, not at this hour." He was perfectly sober, having stayed with fresh orange juice all evening. She had refused coffee, so McKinnon, satisfied that she was not going to faint, had instructed him to drive the lady home, blaming the combination of champagne and temazepam. Their hostess had become indignant: if she had known Lesley was on medication . . . The elderly bachelor son was worse than useless, flapping about in the background like a demented stork. What a crew.

She stopped abruptly.

"My boots," she said. "I left my boots."

"I'll fetch them for you."

"No. No, leave them."

"Fair enough," he said. "You can recover them another time."

Now, finally, she accepted the offer of his arm, even leaning against him. She was wearing perfume, something old fashioned he recognised but couldn't name, something he thought his mother had worn.

"You'll have to give me directions," he said. "Remember, I'm one of the pesky newcomers."

"You must think . . ."

"I must think what?"

But she didn't finish her sentence.

He got her into the car with no further difficulty. He'd dismissed her initially: one more menopausal spinster. Then he'd seen her face change at the use of the word "tinker": he wondered if there was more to her. She'd seemed profoundly unhappy, despite the fixed smile. Only when they slowed to a stop outside her gate, and he looked up at the dark house did he remember being told that she had lost her mother recently.

In his best bedside voice he said, "This is a very hard time for you. I think everyone understands that."

"I don't care if they understand or not."

"Good for you."

She twisted round to face him. "Why did you come here?"

Her face was jaundiced in the yellow light from the street lamps.

"I was asked to see you safely home."

"No, here. This village."

It was the first time anyone had asked him. "I needed the job," he told her. "I've been a locum for a long time. It was a case of . . ."

"This is a terrible place. Terrible things happen here. Terrible things have happened to me."

He waited for more, but nothing came. He got out and went round to open her door.

She peered at him. "How can you be a doctor?" she said. "You're so young."

"Thirty two. Not so very young." He held out a hand, but she made no move.

"I never thought I would be fifty. I have no idea how it happened. One day I was seventeen and now look at me. I might as well be dead."

"Come now, don't talk like that. Let's get you safely home."

She let him help her out.

"You'll feel better in the morning, once you've had a good . . ."

"Oh, go to Hell," she said loudly, slamming the car door. She pushed open her gate and closed it behind her with unnecessary force.

He watched her progress up the path. It occurred to him that there might be stacks of prescription medications in the house after the mother's long illness. It would be irresponsible not to check. He dialled Dr MacKinnon's mobile number.

e-numbers

"There's a little custard left," Ruby called through the hatch into the dining room.

"No thank you, dear. That was just fine."

Why was there always just a little custard left? Because Ruby still cooked enough of everything for Walter Junior, who had left home three years before. He was always offered the little custard, or the little stew or whatever, and always said no, in the hope that someday, some happy day, Ruby might accept that Walter Junior was not coming back, not even for special days like this. They didn't make much of New Year down south, he'd told Ruby, trying to help.

"Tea? And a biscuit?"

"Just tea, dear. That would be lovely."

"I'll bring you a Digestive in case."

He studied the fish tank for several minutes, looking at each of the residents to make sure they were swimming correctly, that their eyes were clear, that each fin was erect. He loved his fish. Their effortless meandering from frond to frond with no contact or conflict seemed to him a way of life little short of perfection. No-one was allowed to touch the tank or do anything to it and its occupants. He had had a bad scare some years back, when Ruby decided to clean the outdoor pond. Happily tonight all seemed to be well with each little Platy and Angel Fish. He dabbed his lips with the napkin, and made his way through to the sitting room. Tonight's pudding had been tinned pears in fruit juice. He wasn't over fond of pears, particularly in juice. Sometimes they had a sharpness that annoyed the tongue, but he wasn't allowed the ones in syrup any more

Healthy eating was Ruby's latest thing. The weekly shop was taking a lot longer, now that she had to read for e-numbers and saturated fat. He missed a few of the old favourites. A little of what you fancy, they used to say, even though there was less to fancy back then. You had your carrots, onions and peas, your potatoes mashed or chipped. The young ones had laughed at him one day at work, when he said he remembered where and when he'd first tasted sweetcorn. Ruby was on at him to grow their own vegetables come Spring. The back garden was big enough, but he wasn't persuaded. Her enthusiasms tended to diminish if ignored for long enough.

He switched on the TV, turned the sound right down, and rested his head back on the settee, closing his eyes. His uncle, also named Walter, had been a great gardener. There was a greenhouse in the garden in Peebles, not a particularly large one, but inside it Uncle Walter had a vine that produced luscious black grapes year after year, apparently unharmed and untainted by the smoke from Uncle Walter's pipe.

"Piddle," Uncle Walter had announced solemnly, one early summer afternoon, when they were standing together, looking up at the small green fruits, the man puffing on his pipe, the small boy passively inhaling. "That's the secret, laddie. Plenty of piddle. Great for the parsley too."

He remembered still the feeling, half terror, half joy that thrilled through his eight year old body. Was he going to be asked to contribute? Would he be able to pee on demand? But the invitation didn't come. He knew now that Uncle Walter would have used a jug or a bowl when he went to the bathroom, the greenhouse being in full view of the neighbours, but for years the image of his uncle spraying cheerfully in the greenhouse and over the parsley bed cheered him when school or life in general became dull or difficult.

What would Ruby make of that one, he wondered. Where's your e-numbers now?

"Here you are, dear," she set his cup and plate down and returned to the dishes in the kitchen. It was always tea now. She wouldn't let him drink coffee in the evening. "We're not as young as we were," she said. He knew he was meant to say something flattering about her when she said this kind of thing. Sometimes he did and sometimes he didn't. What life really boiled down to, he mused, biting into his organic Digestive, was knowing when to play dumb. *Kid on you're daft and you'll get a hurl on the barra.* Playing dumb took a certain amount of finesse, all the same. He bought a large Dairy Milk every morning when he stopped for his paper, but he never brought any of it home, not even a couple of pieces for a sly nibble. Ruby would have smelt it when she turned out the trouser pockets for the wash. He stared at the silent screen. For the first time it occurred to him that retirement might involve difficulties he had not so far considered.

"Walter," she sat down beside him with her latest copy of Puzzle Monthly and her rubber-tipped pencil. "I've been wondering."

"Have you?"

Behind the glasses, her eyes were large and earnest. "I've been wondering if we should ask Lesley next door to come in for tea now and then. She'll be lonely. I don't like to think of her on her own."

He said nothing.

Much later, when the TV had been switched off, and Ruby had already gone upstairs, he was checking that the front door was locked when he heard a bang. Car door, he told himself, not loud enough for fireworks. These had been going off through most of the evening. No doubt there would be more at midnight.

"Did you hear that?" Ruby called from upstairs.

"Hear what?"

"There's a car at our gate."

"I don't think so, not at this hour." And if there was, it wouldn't be Walter Junior, that was for sure. When he went into the bedroom, she was standing with her nose through the curtains.

"Oh my," she said. Closing them carefully, she darted to the side for a better view.

He sat on the bed, pushed each slipper off with the other foot, and began unbuttoning his trousers.

"Oh. Oh my goodness."

"Why are we whispering?"

"Lesley's sitting on the path."

"Hers or ours?"

With a sigh he rebuttoned himself and joined her. Sure enough, there was Lesley, sitting on her own path beside the doorstep, facing the street.

"Do something, Walter."

He scratched the back of his head. It was all very well to say do something, when you didn't have to do the doing. He was still trying to think of an answer, when a male figure opened Lesley's gate and began walking up the path. The man helped her to her feet, and then, Walter surmised, there was an exchange of words. He gently detached Ruby from the window, letting the curtain fall, deaf to her whispered protests.

"It's none of our business," he said.

Ruby smoothed Nivea over her face and lay on her back for a while to let the cream penetrate before her skin touched the pillowslip. She had put ear-plugs in, to counter-act the bangs which would continue into the wee small hours, and she lay as still as possible, so as not to disturb Walter. Her mind meanwhile was anything but still.

Love

The ruined factory with its gaping window frames and rusty pipes smelled exactly like the abandoned buildings of his childhood where he had stripped with closed eyes. When he moved the brick and shone his torch into the space, the roll of fruit sweets was gone. From his coat pocket he took its replacement, a chocolate egg this time, plastic wrap over the bright coloured foil to protect it from dirt and damp. He put it into the hole, repositioning the brick, imagining her delight when she found it.

He switched off the torch and started back to the track. He had never hurt a child, and he never would. Everything was under control. He couldn't harm a child. All he wanted to do was show them love.

He was drawn to unloved, lonely children, those who were troubled as he had been troubled. Often the loveliest children were the most troubled. What a lovely child, what pretty hair, people said, out loud, wanting the child to hear, but their saying it changed nothing. It did not make the child feel lovely, did not make the child feel loved.

When he was older he had taken his bike for long rides, choosing villages where he wasn't known. Winter was better than summer, with darkness coming early. From a back garden he watched till a child was put to bed. He would wait in the darkness, then flash a torch into the bedroom window so that the child would get up and look out.

No-one had been hurt. He wouldn't hurt a child. No-one saw him, and he was careful never to return to the same place.

Child's play

Being an only child, Lesley had learned to play on her own. When she was a toddler, her father made a sandpit for her in the back garden against the stone wall at the end next to the coal shed. She spent a lot of time there in summer and on dry winter days, building little mounds that were houses, and gardens with stones for walls. Doorways were made by inserting a thumb and moving it from side to side. Gardens came alive with fallen rose petals. Water from the rain butt and daisies and buttercups from the drying green were also allowed. She knew that fairies weren't real, just as Santa wasn't real, so she had no foolish thoughts about little people coming to live in the mounds overnight.

Had Mother ever come out to watch or give suggestions? Or praise? It seemed to her that she had played alone, completely contented, hands muddy, the scent of the summer roses all around her. She knew now what she hadn't then. It was as simple as sunlight. What she had loved was the freedom to make something without help, the freedom to choose, and perhaps the fact that no-one ever told her to make it better.

She would be fifty on her next birthday. Far too old to have children. Some of the staff her age were bringing in photographs of their grandchildren. They all looked exactly the same. If Hector was still alive he would be fifty three. It must be almost thirty years since she had tried to invite him home for tea. She hadn't made a fuss when Mother said no, since he was only a friend, not a boyfriend. She'd assumed, at twenty, that there would be, if not plenty of young men, at least some to choose from. But all the time, there was Mother, keeping her safe, letting her make her mud-pie houses, watching from the window.

Ryan's night

Ryan's night began well. He met with everyone down Dimity Lane, happy in his new limited edition trainers, a joint present from his sisters, and happier still when a pint of beer was passed to him by someone he didn't know. The street was heaving with people, the queues for the bars were mad. No neds anywhere; the street was closed except for ticket holders, but one of the class had got tickets, his Dad had contacts, so that was good, and everyone was allowed to drink outside, which was brilliant, because the rain was off and now and then you could see stars overhead when the clouds cleared, and there was a great mix of people, and just a few policemen watching with impassive faces. Along with a couple of his pals, he cracked himself up playing "spot the media type" for at least half an hour. The guy would have square thick glasses, the woman with him would be in trendy clothes that were too young for her. It was a doddle, it was like they had a lifestyle catalogue of their own they had all bought from.

He wished he'd a scarf, some dull colour like grey in cashmere would have been perfect, or maybe white silk, he'd seen a photo of Sting wearing white silk, but otherwise he felt he was looking just about right. There were loads of students, some of them from wealthy backgrounds, going by their voices, but hey, it was the West End, so everyone had made a lot of effort to look as if they hadn't made an effort. Really all he'd done was take a short cut. Fine Art students like himself were always more scruffy than the rest anyway. You could spot the Design types a mile off. The t-shirts had to have cool graphics, the necklace would be some surfer type thing.

The girls were amazing. He got talking to one, almost as tall as himself, who said her name was Scarlett, which he doubted, but so what, she was seriously amazing, the whole front of her hair cut in a fringe, slanting sideways across her eyes to the level of her ear, but after a few minutes, it was obvious she'd done a few cheeky lines already, and he moved on. He couldn't stand the nonsense.

After a while, they all moved on via the Underground to the city centre for the fireworks display. Not so good. The crowd was more aggressive, a lot of fast drinking going on, a lot of joints being smoked, and other stuff, which was fine if you were the one doing them, but he'd promised his school art teacher, the one decent guy on the staff, that he wouldn't and so far he hadn't. That was one guy who knew what it was all about.

He kept a smile on his face, avoided eye contact, stuck close to those he knew. To his relief, soon after all the bangs were finished, someone said it was time to go if they wanted to get to the party while there was still transport. He was tired now, the earlier glow was wearing off, leaving him almost sober, and almost inclined to go home, but hey, it was New Year.

Good Decision. The party – he didn't know whose house it was – was well stocked, at the start anyway, and not too many people, though it was definitely a weird mix. Some were old for this sort of thing, and some of the girls, even made up and in the low lighting looked way too young to him. He hung out in the kitchen when it got busier, avoiding the casualties, and the daft hyper girls with their breasts falling out of their tops talking nonsense in the middle of the living room. The music was better than it had been all night. The bass was deep and satisfying. The guy on the decks had good taste. Going to the toilet, however, was a fucking pain, having to defend his manhood in the queue of girls. Then suddenly it was time to go home. He'd been stressing about it for a while. He'd totally drunk himself sober.

For the first couple of miles he had company, an older guy and his girlfriend, but after that he was on his own. It had occurred to him earlier that he might phone his married sister, but he'd been sick once in their car. A loving father would have been handy.

There were no photographs of his father in the house at all. Both of his sisters remembered him, but neither they nor his mother ever mentioned him or why he'd gone, months after Ryan's birth. It was pathetic, not knowing what your own father had looked like. Not his hair colour, or his eyes, not whether you looked anything like him, nothing.

He turned into a doorway for a moment, to let a couple of

mental-looking guys go past. The wind seemed colder now. Everyone on the street felt like a potential hazard. Kids in groups hailed him; he called back. Cars passed, there were lit windows, and now and then bursts of music. He wasn't exactly alone. No, he was always alone, that was the truth of it. This is how I am, he thought sadly, this is my life. This is my grim journey, fighting the wind, in the dark. He felt almost heroic for a few yards, until reality thudded back. Being alone was nothing to be proud of. It was a simple fact.

On the far side of the road, inside a bus shelter, an older couple were fighting one another, mostly shouting but with raised fists. The woman had weight on her side, and a bag with a useful silver chain. On his side another small group of neds was coming closer.

Everything as usual

When Duncan came down a little after nine, Mrs Flaherty's coat was already hanging on the rack beside the back door. His mother was still asleep, and would not descend for some time, but Mrs Flaherty had let herself in very quietly with her own backdoor key.

He looked into the front porch, irritated by the absence of post. He found himself disliking this disruption of normality more each year. Once he was back at work, there would be plenty to do: e-mails and letters that hadn't been replied to, photocopying needing done urgently by disorganised lecturers, and all those troublesome requests with not enough information that were put to one side by less diligent members of Library staff to be dealt with "when there's more time."

Not that the week would be empty. He would have to drive Mother into town. He had two book tokens and a gift voucher for Boots the Chemist, but with browsing time strictly limited and the streets and shops even more crowded than usual, he would probably end up choosing things he didn't need or want. Once he'd bought a book he already owned, caught out by a change in jacket design. He made a mental note to buy deodorant as he had almost run out.

He'd once believed that deodorant was unmanly, but had recently begun using it after hearing the female staff discuss the man who looked after the photocopier.

"Good morning, Mrs Flaherty," he called, giving plenty of warning as he approached the kitchen. She was a woman who responded badly to the unexpected. Not a nervous woman, exactly, but one who was happier with order. She seemed to experience profound delight when scrubbing surfaces, and although he approved of this perfectionism, it concerned him that she went through so much bleach and anti-bacterial cleanser. "Think of the oceans, Mrs Flaherty," he had said, trying to introduce her to the idea of eco-friendliness, but the oceans were nothing to her compared to the satisfaction of a gleaming sink.

She straightened up from loading the dishwasher. "Oh, thank you for the picture frame, Mr Crawfurd." Her red face beamed. "It was very kind of you and Mrs Crawfurd. I've put my grandson in it."

He imagined that sturdily built infant with his head stuck in the frame after the manner of the traditional child in the park railings, but merely nodded as he moved towards the coffee machine, repressing as one so frequently had to with Mrs Flaherty the urge to say something which would only confuse her.

"And did your night go well, Mr Crawfurd?"

"Yes, thank you, everything went as usual."

This was a lie. He switched on the machine and reached into the cupboard for a fresh packet of beans.

"And yourself?" he asked. The sealant strip seemed to resist him deliberately, breaking half way round.

"Oh, just a quiet night. That wild boy of mine was out with his pals, of course. Only came in when I was getting up . . ."

In the past he had made the mistake of showing interest in this Ryan, and particularly in his success in getting into Art School. Mrs Flaherty now assumed that he wanted frequent bulletins. Fortunately she seemed happy with short comments on his part, and the occasional prompt kept her going for a while.

". . . and to tell the truth, Mr Crawfurd, I'm glad when it's all over. It's getting worse every year. It all starts too early . . ."

He nodded again, assuming a listening expression while the foam formed on his cappuccino. Then he reproached himself. She was right. In fact, despite being Mrs Flaherty she was often right. It was simply unfortunate that the flat nasal tone made her statements ludicrous when they were perfectly reasonable, and that her lack of mental subtlety made irony a country forever unexplored.

He dipped his tongue into the thick, warm foam. He ought to be more kind. She was hard working, honest, self-effacing and possibly the least vain woman he had ever met. A crueller man might say she had little to be vain about. If only she would wear clothes that fitted her. He glanced at the troublesome upper arms, bulging from the short sleeves of her pink nylon overalls. Was he unkind? He didn't mean to be.

At the door he paused. "You'll make yourself a parcel, as usual, Mrs Flaherty, won't you?"

"If you're sure . . ."

"Oh, of course. No sense in waste. Mother left out the containers for you."

He took his cup through to the study, closing the door so he wouldn't hear the clearing of the previous night's debris. Not that she was noisy. The dishwasher would be stacked and set but not switched on, nor would she approach the vacuum cleaner until Mother was up.

There was a patch of blue sky beyond the church spire on the opposite side of the village. The day might yet improve. He stood by the window, sipping his drink, relishing the contrast of the milk against the heat of the coffee beneath, the slight bitterness of the cocoa against sweetness of the chocolate dusting. In the branches of the rowan tree, a patch of reddish brown caught his eye. *Erithacus rubecula*. He was fond of his robin, glad to see it reappear each winter. He recited Hardy's first lines aloud.

> *"When up aloft*
> *I fly and fly,*
> *I see in pools*
> *The shining sky"*

A sad poem, but unlike Hardy's, his robin was in no danger of starving. There weren't any birds at the feeder, but the level of seed had gone down since yesterday, so presumably they had come and gone. All in the garden was as it should be.

His own feathers were still ruffled. If anything he felt more aggrieved.

"Why is that man here?" his mother had asked, *sotto voce*, thrusting the Reverend's red jacket into his arms. At first he'd only half heard, troubled by the sight of Lesley drinking champagne. And not sipping either, but taking great swallows of it.

"I invited him. Mother, have you noticed that . . ."

"I assumed *that*, Duncan, since as far as I know we have not placed an advertisement in the Post Office window. I'm asking you why?"

"I . . ."

"I cannot believe you would do this, Duncan. Without even having the grace to mention it to me?"

He worried for the pearls, so tight was her stranglehold on them.

"Well, what's done is done. We'll just have to keep a close eye on things. But for heaven's sake, don't let him get near Eunice Calvert. She can't abide the man. I am very upset, Duncan."

He took the coat to the downstairs cloak room and hung it beside those of the other guests. How could he have known the man would come? The invitation had been lightly given and immediately declined. It wasn't his fault if the fellow didn't have the good manners to let them know he'd changed his mind.

He turned from the window and switched on Radio Three, but after a moment switched it off. It was a string quartet, something he could not abide. There seemed to be an unending supply of them at this time of year. Scraping the last of the foam with the teaspoon, he stared at the bookshelves. His eye lighted on a dear friend, Jonsson's *Birds of Europe*. He eased the volume off the shelf and sat down.

A consultation

Miss Crosthwaite was tense, Dr Gordon thought, and perhaps a little thinner since their last meeting. How much of that night did she remember? He had tried to calm her down, assuring her of his sympathy. It must be terrible to care for someone for so long, to lose someone you loved so much.

"I'm not entirely sure I loved my mother at all," she'd told him, enunciating the words with great care.

Her face looked so tragic he had to fight the desire to laugh.

"I see. Well, at the risk of being slick and trite, I would suggest that . . ."

". . . that I forgive her? I can't. She ruined my life."

The words slipped round his cynicism.

"Then don't let her bloody well ruin the rest of it," he said.

To his astonishment she had leaned forward, lifted his hand and kissed it.

He began now as he always did. "So how are things?"

"I'm getting there, thank you."

He had never been sure what that meant. It reminded him

of another tired lie, the one about Time being a Healer. So much depended on how much Time you were talking about. A year, a lifetime?

"And what can I do for you today?" he asked.

No make-up of any kind brightened her complexion. The beige raincoat with its overlarge collar and tie belt did nothing for her.

"I'm not sure I'm ready to go back to work. I'm getting a lot of headaches."

Headaches. Every doctor's favourite symptom. Start with the usual culprits and work down the list forever.

"Fair enough. Can you think of anything that might be causing them?"

Without moving his head he glanced at his watch. He still had a couple of phone calls to make. Mrs Turner, thirty eight weeks pregnant, needed extra iron, her haemoglobin being far too low, and the Respiratory Physician who'd called about an abnormal x-ray would be on his own way home if he didn't ring back before six thirty. He took a deep breath and relaxed back into the chair, signalling his readiness to listen to anything, no matter how esoteric or banal.

"I don't know where to start," she said. She was sitting very straight, her feet tucked under the chair, well away from his size nines.

"That's all right. Start in the middle somewhere and we'll muddle along together."

*

Dear God, how often had he used this line? It wasn't his being a doctor – whether they knew his occupation or not people unburdened themselves to him constantly, as if a luminous message, "Tell me your life story", came and went across his forehead like a film title pulsing around a cinema frontage.

"I found some letters addressed to me in my mother's bureau. I don't know what to do about them."

Neither do I, he said inside his head, *though as always, I am flattered when my patients assume I am the source of all wisdom.*

"Yes?"

"Very . . . important letters. She was keeping them from me."

"I see."

Where was this going? Her life, he recalled, had apparently been ruined by the mother. He hadn't known the woman. She'd been McKinnon's patient.

"I see," he said again. "And you feel you ought to . . . to do something?"

She was shaking. He leaned over, taking hold of her left hand. It was clammy and cold.

"Deep breaths," he said, feeling for her pulse. "Deep breaths. That's it."

"I'm all right."

"I know. But just take a minute."

He pushed the box of paper handkerchiefs closer to her, in case tears came. After a while, he let the wrist go, and sat back. The heart was strong and had steadied reasonably quickly. He made his voice quiet but firm. He had a good voice. Reassuring. Patients had often told him so.

"There's no hurry. We can talk if you want to, and stop whenever you feel like stopping. You know I'm here to listen, and help if I can. Let's just take a look at your blood pressure, anyway."

It was perfectly normal, and he told her so. He expected her to look relieved, but there was nothing. "These letters," he said. "Were they . . . unpleasant . . . anonymous?"

Or perhaps imaginary? There was no reference to any psychiatric problems in her scanty notes, but she was at an age when odd things often began to occur. When it became obvious that she was not going to say more, he reached for his pen. He would speak to McKinnon before he did anything much.

"I don't feel you need any medication at the moment. I think you're tired out, that's all. If the headaches continue, use paracetamol, not more than the stated dose of course."

He looked over her notes again, and suggested she make an appointment with the practice nurse, to have her blood and urine checked.

"Are you feeding yourself properly?

She nodded.

"And sleeping?'

Another nod.

He decided not to ask whether she was still menstruating, but made a note on her page to do so at the next visit.

"Let's make it two more weeks off, shall we? Come and see me before then. Especially if the headaches get worse. And don't feel guilty. That's the last thing we need. I want you to be kind to yourself."

Her unhappiness lingered in the room after she left it. Why had she begun if she didn't want to talk? If she didn't trust him, why hadn't she asked for one of the others? He stared at what was visible of the world through the vertical window blinds. Once upon a time he had imagined that helping others would be a way of helping himself.

Would they ever get round to redecorating this room for him? The previous occupant had clearly fallen for the theory that pink walls helped patients to relax. The curtains, beige on brown, were particularly hideous, possibly left over from the seventies. His table was a mess. He checked his watch against the round chrome and white desk clock, Viagra, in blue, stamped arrogantly across its face. A pill for every bloody ill.

And what might he have offered poor Miss Crosthwaite, to whom "terrible things" had happened. Counselling? HRT? The simple answer was, nothing. Not until she was ready to be helped. All these middle-aged women conforming in silence, feeling guilty at the least suggestion that they might have any right to happiness. What century were they living in, for God's sake? Would she even make a return appointment? He gathered up the urine samples to take down to Reception for the morning van.

"Everything all right, Miss Kennedy?" He paused at the

secretary's door. He ought to go in for the usual few minutes chat, but he was tired of being nice.

"I left a message for Mrs Turner to phone us tomorrow. Did you remember to phone Radiology?" she said.

"Damn. It'll have to wait till the morning. Can I give you a lift?"

"Oh no, Doctor. Robert's coming for me."

Every week on her late night he offered her a lift and she refused. It wasn't correct for Doctors to drive secretaries home in this part of the world.

It still surprised him how early darkness came this far north. He keyed the car. The lights flashed obediently. He flung his case onto the back seat.

I want you to be kind to yourself.

His words stayed with her. It would have helped more if he'd given some examples of what being kind might mean. She had no idea where to begin. Should she spend money? For there was plenty of money. Despite her mother's hints over the years about this charity and that, everything had been left to her. "Completely straight-forward," according to her mother's lawyer. He had been very kind.

The nurses too had been kind to her in the last days, taking care of her, telling her to go down to the WRVS tearoom, saying they didn't expect anything sudden. They would call her if anything changed.

She was noting how her mother's breasts had shrunk away to nothing, actually watching the rise and fall of the nightgown, when things did change. All movement ceased. She called for the nurse. The nurse came, checked her patient and took off the wedding ring, giving it to Lesley in a brown envelope. In the taxi coming home a strange anxiety gripped her. She couldn't remember whether Mother had breathed in and not out, or breathed out, and not in again. It seemed terribly important that she should remember.

The day of the funeral was a blur in her mind, although she remembered being surprised that the room was full, having assumed that Mother had outlived all her friends. One detail only of the interment remained with her. A bird paused on the green mat beside the coffin. It flew onto the lid, then flew away, and there was a communal sound, not quite a sigh, from those around her.

We're so sorry. When certain people said this she wanted to ask why? Why did they feel sorry? They hadn't shown their faces in the last long weeks when her mother's mind had deteriorated. Was that what they were apologizing for?

You were so good to her. This too was said by more than a few.

Had she been good? She had done no more than she had to. Knowing what she knew now, would she have behaved differently?

When the doorbell rang, she went to the front room, adjusting the curtain to see who it was. With some reluctance she went to the door. The outside air was icy, with a north wind.

"Mrs Flaherty?" she said.

"Not to disturb you, Lesley, but I was passing and . . ."

"Come in out of the wind, Mrs Flaherty."

"Oh no, I'm fine. I was just wondering if you . . ."

"But all the heat's going out. Come in for a moment."

She led the way into the back room, switching on the light, for the morning was dull. Mrs Flaherty took off her black woollen cap and shook out her hair.

I want you to be kind to yourself.

"I was just wondering if you would still be wanting me," she said at last. She seemed very uncomfortable, fidgeting with the large toggle buttons on her coat.

With a start Lesley realised what was meant. She was about to say no, having more or less determined even before the funeral that a cleaning lady was no longer a necessity, but with Mrs Flaherty in front of her she hesitated. It occurred to her that Mrs Flaherty needed the money. She'd had three weeks without. Need had brought her here despite the embarrassment entailed.

"Oh, yes. That would be fine," she said.

"Just the same hours?"

"I'll have to get you a key," she said, thinking aloud. "A back-door key. Would that be all right?"

Mrs Flaherty nodded.

"Well, that's settled then."

What was she waiting for? Was she owed money?

"Am I owing you, Mrs Flaherty?"

"Oh no, not at all." Her face reddened.

The Christmas present. Lesley couldn't remember what it was, but there was a present laid aside. Bought in September, wrapped, and labelled. She drew aside the curtain that hid the walk-in recess, and after some searching found the brightly wrapped object. Dutch Speciality Chocolate Chip Cookies, she recalled, feeling the shape of the tin through the paper.

"I'm so sorry, Mrs Flaherty. What with everything. This was for you. I won't say Happy Christmas, of course. Oh,

Mrs Flaherty, please, it's just a token . . ." she added, taken aback by the tears that suddenly were welling up.

"I'm sorry, Lesley. I shouldn't be . . ."

"No, it's all right. Sit down for a moment."

The woman avoided the nearest armchair, Mother's chair, and chose instead one of the hard chairs next to the table. As she sat down her grey trousers rose up by a couple of inches, revealing mottled skin above white ankle socks.

"You don't knit, do you, Mrs Flaherty?" Lesley said hurriedly. "All these knitting patterns. It seems a pity to throw them out. Maybe you know someone who would like them?"

More tears. Lesley wondered tentatively about leaning over to pat an arm. This must stop soon, surely? Should she offer a glass of water?

Mrs Flaherty wiped the tears from below both eyes, using her fingers.

"I don't know what to do," she said.

"About what?"

Mrs Flaherty's pale eyes were on her, bewildered, fearful.

"You can tell me, if it helps, Mrs Flaherty. I am not one to gossip."

There was a longish interval. Nothing violated the heavy silence except the slow tick of the onyx mantel clock, and the muted sound of a plane overhead.

"He phoned this morning. I knew it was him. I should've put the phone down."

I want you to be kind to yourself.

"Who phoned?"

"Johnny. Mr Flaherty that was. Nearly sixteen years it's been. What am I going to do?"

The doorbell shrilled. As if one they sat, motionless, waiting. It rang again. Mrs Flaherty began to rise, but Lesley stayed her with a lifted hand.

"No," she said. "They'll go away."

Shopping

"Mother, let me take them for you," Duncan offered, pulling the car gently to a stop. "I think the rain's coming on."

"I'm not an invalid yet, Duncan. You've parked rather close to the hedge, dear," his mother added, inspecting the ground below the opened door. It was hard to tell what might lie beneath the brown mush of dead leaves and twigs. "You'd better go up to the end and turn round before I come back."

Lesley had not been picking up her phone. Mrs Crawfurd did not believe in leaving messages on answering machines. She did not intend to go inside the house, merely to hand in the boots. It would be sufficient to mention the words "city", "motorway", "traffic" and "parking" to excuse the brevity of the visit.

The pebbled path to Lesley's stout oak door was indeed long, and uneven, but the parcel of boots was not heavy, and it suited Mrs Crawfurd to return them herself, because she was not altogether certain that Duncan would come immediately back to the car. He had been in something of a mood since Christmas. Holidays, she felt, did not agree with him. When idle, he was inclined to mope, and to cast about for inappropriate affairs in which to busy himself. She was sorry for Lesley's loss too, of course, but people had to have privacy and take their own time to re-establish themselves. It had been unwise, if well-intentioned on his part, to invite Lesley, so soon after the funeral, especially when, as Dr MacKinnon explained confidentially after the distressing scene, she had been neglecting her own health during her mother's last weeks.

Both of the heavy outer doors were shut. Mrs Crawfurd pressed the doorbell firmly. No response. She peered into the sitting room. Seeing no-one, she went to the side gate. Unfortunately, this was locked.

"Are you looking for Lesley?"

She turned. The speaker, coming up the path in the neighbouring garden, was an odd-looking woman with blue-pencilled eyebrows, and a scarf that resembled a piece of orange fishing-net. The plastic bags in her hands suggested she had been shopping at the village Co-operative store.

"I beg your pardon?"

"If you're looking for Lesley, I think she's at home."

"And you are . . .?"

"Mrs Robertson. Her neighbour."

Mrs Crawfurd pressed the doorbell again, and looked up at the gathering clouds.

"I think she might have a visitor."

Mrs Crawfurd turned.

"A man came to the door when I was . . . She seems to

have quite a lot of gentlemen calling. At all hours." A little nervous laugh. "Not that she shouldn't. It's quite right that friends should rally round. She's on her own now, you see. She lost her mother recently, and as I said to Walter, those of us who . . ."

This was becoming ridiculous. But there was the problem of the boots.

"Perhaps you would give her these, when you see her next," Mrs Crawfurd extended the brown paper parcel. Not the most satisfactory of solutions, but what else could be done?

"Who will I say . . .?" The voice followed her down the path.

She lifted a gloved hand without looking back, a hand that contrived to be dismissive but courteous at the same time.

"How is she?" Duncan asked, switching on the wipers as large spots of rain began to hit the windscreen.

"She wasn't at home. I left them with her neighbour. I must say, the garden looks very neglected and sad. Perhaps her new gentleman friend will do something about it."

She watched him out of the corner of her eye for several seconds, but there was no sign that he had heard. He had the same annoying habit as his late father of not hearing unless a sentence was prefaced with his name.

Every year the pattern was the same. They would go to Boots, then Mother would visit Marks and Spencer to choose some item of clothing, while he went to the nearby bookshop. She would come for him, then they would cross the street and have lunch.

The restaurant had changed hands more than once, but the furniture remained the same. The chairs and tables were a faded pink, Lloyd Loom originals. The square tables with their protective glass tops had cross struts below that made stretching one's legs impossible.

Members of the library staff had recommended other places, which Duncan would have been happy to try, but this was the one his mother insisted was his favourite. She liked a window seat on the upper floor, and was prepared to wait for one so that they could look down on the shoppers in the street below.

He placed the plastic bag with his purchase carefully on the carpet at his feet. *The Poetry of Birds*. He had read the reviews some weeks earlier. According to the *Telegraph* the poems were "set in acres of space which makes the reading experience pleasurable." The reviewer had also praised the "striking red endpapers." He had read the contents page already, and the thought of the evening ahead when he could recline and settle into it was wonderful. He was still undecided as to whether he should limit himself to one poem per evening.

What would he like today?

Quickly he looked at the menu. Last year he had tried the Turkey Toastie with Cranberry Sauce. It had proved to be dry. He ordered the Tasty Macaroni Cheese. He'd liked it since his boarding school days. Did Lesley eat macaroni cheese? Did she know how to make it? He hoped she was looking after herself properly.

A rivulet of cold water fell on his neck. He turned to protest. But the woman holding the umbrella was elderly. He contained his annoyance, took out his handkerchief and patted himself dry.

Mother was absorbed by the scurrying bodies below. Now she turned to take a spoonful of broth and a small piece of unbuttered roll.

"I ought to have got you a new cardigan in Marks. You're terribly hard on elbows, Duncan. I've given up looking for darning wool. Marjory says nobody darns any more. If I could find leather patches . . ."

Lesley would probably have darning wool. Her mother had never thrown anything out. The drawers of that dreadful mantelpiece were probably stiff with darning wool. He looked over at the nearby tables. Had one of the husbands taken his shoes off? There was an unmistakeable odour of feet.

". . . such a mercy they deliver groceries now. Of course it pays them, because one buys more, naturally. I do feel much happier when the freezer's full at this time of the year. One doesn't mind paying a little more for quality food. And the lemon sole alone is worth the trip . . ."

He hated fish. He loathed the small bones that stuck between one's front teeth and had to be flossed carefully out. He longed for a total moratorium on fishing to be introduced by the governments of the world. How did she know there was a gentleman friend? If she was waiting for him to ask, she was going to be disappointed.

"Are we all right for time, dear?"

He nodded. One hour and fourteen minutes left on the meter. Lesley didn't drive. She would come into the city by bus, if she needed something. Of course, she could walk to work, the High School being less than half an hour away. He often caught sight of her when he was coming or going on the bus. There hadn't been a car at her front door today. Of course, a gentleman friend might not have a car . . .

"Would you like to see the sweet menu?"

He looked up at the waitress, recognising her from previous years. She wasn't young, though her hair was completely black. It was pulled back so severely from her face, he felt it must hurt. Mother asked for white coffee but he shook his head. It would taste terrible whatever way they made it. He watched the woman pass between the tables towards the kitchen. Did she like her job? Were people generous with tips? Was she happy?

Moving on

He checked his hairline in the bathroom mirror. Nothing untoward seemed to be happening. It looked as if he hadn't inherited his father's genes in that particular area after all.

He and his father had never spent enough time together to talk about such trivia. Money, yes. There was always time to talk about money. And if he could have talked politics or pretended an interest in Test Match scores, they might have been closer. Instead he had slipped, or been dropped, whatever the correct word was, into the role of mother's little companion. He had at first accepted her loneliness and frustration as a normal state, with no idea that things should or could have been different. Only when he grew old enough to play at other boys' houses, did he meet mothers who smiled a lot and even played games in the garden. At around the same time he began to dislike bed time conversations where she lamented her husband's shortcomings, hugs that were too close and lasted too long so that he came away smelling of her scent, and praise lavished too publicly on his intelligence and successes at school.

Long before he became an adult, he recognised that all

was not as it should be. He made allowances, adjusted his attitude to her and, generally speaking, moved on. He'd used the very words in conversation with someone at school who asked if he still enjoyed bike rides. "Oh, I've moved on," he'd said.

Bringing back the shoes

"Hello. Can I help you?" Not recognising the bald boy in the dripping anorak, Harriet smiled generously, as she always did with strangers on the manse doorstep.

"Can I help you?" she said again, more slowly. His mouth had opened and closed. He might be hard of hearing, or an asylum seeker with poor English.

"Yes, that's my Dad," she said, looking at the slightly damp card he held out, her voice softer, for people who accepted one of her Dad's cards were generally people with troubles.

"I'll just get him for you."

"No," he said. "I've brought these." He took a pair of men's trainers out of a Primark bag.

She hated doing this to people. But you couldn't buy things that were most likely stolen. He didn't look exactly like a down and out, though. His eyes weren't bloodshot, and he didn't smell.

"I brought them back, ok? He lent them to me."

"Wait a minute," she said, as he began to back away. "I'll get him. He's not busy."

"Dad, there's a hairless boy in the porch with a pair of Nike trainers," she announced, going into the sitting room, "which he says you lent him."

"Hairless?" her father said.

Kerr raised himself on both elbows.

"Well, his head is. But since when did you have trainers?"

"Now there's a thing," Kerr said. "I thought they were gone for good." He got up from the couch and went out.

"What did you say?" her father asked, not turning from the TV.

"A boy at the door. Kerr's gone to speak to him." She stared at the letters on the Scrabble board before her. She had a q, but no u to go with it. Then suddenly she saw it, a stray r, just begging to be used at the end of "fever." She put letters on the board, and began to add up her score.

"Your turn," she announced.

Her father glanced over, "Nope. There's a u in that as well."

"No, there isn't."

He had turned back to the screen.

"It's a kind of tunnel, Dad. I've used it before."

With a humph of annoyance Harriet stood up, knowing that unless she brought down the Shorter Oxford and showed him the actual word on a page, he wouldn't accept it. And even so, he'd probably object that it was a foreign one.

At the foot of the stairs she paused. That voice. Where had she heard it? With a frisson she remembered. She looked round the kitchen door.

"Ah, there you are," Kerr said. "This is Ryan. He borrowed my shoes the other night. Ryan, this is my sister, Harriet, who's going to make us some coffee."

"Am I?" she said.

The boy said, "I'd better get on."

Kerr made a face at her. "I can boil a kettle. Wait till the rain goes off a bit."

"You're busy."

"Watching *The Great Escape*. Again. Tea or coffee? Or a coke?"

Trust Kerr, champion of waifs and strays, embracing all comers with the friendliness of a lolloping Labrador puppy. She opened the oven door, looked at the potatoes and shut it hard, hoping Kerr might get the message. The Ryan person's answer was lost in the thud of the room door as she closed it behind her.

"Don't mind Harriet," the brother said, pouring Coca Cola into two glasses. "She's in a bad mood because nobody would drive her into town this afternoon."

Ryan didn't think that was the reason. She hadn't recognised him at the door, welcoming him with a smile that turned his knees into silly putty and wiped everything out of his head. By the time she came into the room again she'd remembered exactly who he was. She had the same look on her face as she'd had that very first time, just waiting to see what bad thing he'd do. Sod you, he'd thought, taking the brooch to see what she'd do next. When he'd put down the money for the fish, trying to be nice, that had somehow turned into a crime as well.

He'd brought the shoes back. Time now to make some excuse and get out. He cleared his throat. The brother, Kerr, was rummaging in the freezer. Straight hair, not so fair as hers, the face broader, the chin receding slightly. His navy woollen jumper was unravelling at the shoulder seam.

"Lemons," Kerr explained, pulling out a small plastic bag. "You slice 'em up and freeze them. Works with limes too. Dad," he called, "d'you want something to drink?"

A voice shouted no.

The iced lemon fizzed in the dark liquid. He'd never been in a house where people kept slices of lime or lemon in the freezer. What else was in there? Caviar? Steaks and oysters? Something good was cooking in the oven.

"So you made it home ok."

"Yeah."

"Did you report it? The shoes."

"To the police? No point," Ryan shook his head. "They're no' interested."

"I suppose. It could've been worse. At least you weren't hurt."

The guy was right. They'd taken his phone, his cash, his shoes and socks, and written very rude words in black permanent marker on his bum, but yes, it could've been much worse. So, hah hah, good natured theft and humorous assault. Happy New Year.

"Thanks for stopping. I should've said that first."

"You thanked me at the time. How many of them were there?"

Somewhere in the house a phone rang and was picked up.

He couldn't remember. "A crowd. Full of the gear."

103

"Nightmare. Not a lot you could have done. So, are you working? Or at college?"

Ryan explained. He sipped at the coke, watching the shut door, only half listening when the other spoke. They talked about music. He was surprised and cheered to find that they both liked the same bands, because Kerr didn't sound or look like the type who would. Then the door opened, but it wasn't her.

"Dad, this is Ryan."

"Hello, glad to meet you," the man in the priest's collar grasped his hand. "We'll have to talk again, I'm sorry. Sudden emergency. Don't finish the chicken, Kerr. I'm not fussed about the veg."

"Potatoes?"

"Just a couple."

Grabbing a red jacket from the coat-rack behind the door, he was gone.

Ryan found his voice. "Is he a priest?"

"What? Oh right. Because of the collar. No, it's just a clerical collar. He says it's more comfortable, plus you can wear it with an ordinary shirt. And we're doing our own ironing while Mum's away, so that's a big thing. Are you Catholic?"

"Depends. No' really."

"Are you vegetarian?"

Had he heard right?

"I'm starving. But if you were vegetarian, I wouldn't eat it in front of you, so we'd have to wait till you left. But there's plenty. Harriet kind of overdoes it when it's her turn."

Kerr stretched out backwards, and opened the oven door. The smell that poured forth made Ryan's mouth water. But the girl would be furious if he stayed.

"Well, I'm no' a vegetarian," he said slowly.

"Good. Knives and forks in the top drawer."

The kitchen was totally middle class: white units, plants on the window ledge, blue and white curtains with tie backs, blue mugs matching them on a white mug stand. He hung his coat on the back of the door where the father's jacket had been, and began taking out cutlery.

Upstairs in her father's study Harriet took volume M to Z from the bookcase. Flicking over the pages, she found the confirmation she needed. 'Qanat. A gently sloping underground water tunnel.'

She waited and waited where she was, ears straining to hear the sounds of their visitor leaving. She needed to eat. The rich smell of Chicken Forestière and roast potatoes had spread through the entire house. The parsnips were probably overdone by now, but she wasn't going down till she was sure he was gone.

Why had Kerr given him shoes? Where had they met? A thud from below told her the front door had been opened and shut. Well, thank goodness for that. Her head was beginning to hurt. She shrugged off a miniscule feeling of guilt. She hadn't actually said anything nasty. And she'd been nice at the door. More than he deserved, really.

Chocolate

Walter was taken aback to find Lesley on his front door step offering him an empty Pyrex dish.

"Ruby's having a bath," he said.

"I just wanted to hand this back. It was very kind of you, thank you."

She looked cold, despite being wrapped up sensibly.

"Please tell Mrs Robertson it was very good."

"Oh, she does a good beef stew," he said. It occurred to him that perhaps he ought to ask Lesley in, this being the season of goodwill. *In or out of the bath, Ruby won't like it* warned a voice in his head. Neither Lesley nor her late mother had ever crossed the door. Moreover he was aware that Ruby's attitude to their neighbour had undergone a subtle shift at New Year. He could hear the faint sound of the radio upstairs in the bathroom.

None of our business, he told himself again.

"Come in for a minute," he said.

"No, I mustn't keep you back."

"Oh, you're not keeping anyone back. Just for five minutes."

He put the dish on the hall table, then led her into the front room, where he switched off the television. The silence seemed louder than the newsreader's voice had been. He sat down in the opposite armchair, only then noticing a red stain on the cuff of his fawn pullover. Bolognese sauce from teatime. "Would you . . ." he stopped. He wasn't sure whether to offer her alcohol or not, and it was such a long time since he'd made his own tea or coffee that he doubted his competence.

"Nothing for me, please," Lesley said. She had unwrapped her scarf, folding it into a neat square, but her coat remained buttoned, and she sat forward on the edge of the chair, as if ready for flight.

"A chocolate then?" There was a large tin of Cadbury's Roses on the coffee table. One of the reps had brought it into the office. He wrestled the lid off and slid it over to her. "Take more than one. Take some for later. Ruby's only letting me have one a day. They'll last till Easter." He chose an orange cream for himself, and slipped a toffee into his pocket.

Her quick smile was like a young girl's, not a middle-aged woman's. He wondered what age she actually was. She looked younger, close up. The old mother had been eighty two, according to the funeral eulogy, but Lesley was the only child, so she might have been a late surprise.

She was looking at their wedding photograph. Thirty years next year, he thought.

"I like what you've done with the fireplace, Mr Robertson."

"Walter, please. Yes, I'm happy enough with it. Took me longer than I thought it would though."

"You did it yourself?"

The admiration in her voice was nice to hear. "Oh, there's nothing much to it," he stretched his arms and folded them, turning the stained cuff over. "When you're in one trade, you have a fair grasp of the rest." He unwrapped his chocolate, making two bites of it. In his boyhood days he had played with chocolate creams, tonguing the soft centres out until the shells were left. "But you've got the originals, Lesley. This is all reproduction," he gestured at the Art Nouveau tiles and pale pink marble. "Whoever had this place before us should've been prosecuted. You shouldn't modernise these houses, you have to go with the plaster and all that. And you've got those beautiful stained glass windows."

"Mother didn't care for change. But they're very draughty."

"I'd keep them myself. You could put in secondary glazing. Or fit the stained glass into double glazing panels. Cut out all the draughts. I know a good glazing firm."

"It sounds rather expensive," she said.

He saw he'd overstepped himself. He cleared his throat. "I'm sorry, I shouldn't be telling you your own business . . ."

"No, I'm sure you're right. The bills would be smaller, I suppose. It's just that there's so much . . ."

"Yes. Takes a lot of getting used to. Just you take your own time, pet, and don't let other people try to run your life. It's early days."

He'd seen tradesmen take advantage of single women. Silly prices and shoddy work, and charm. Not in his firm, he made sure of that, but he'd seen it happen. He wondered if she'd be all right with no-one else in the house. His mother had kept his father's police hat and raincoat on the pegs in the hall for years, so that no caller would think she lived alone. He and his brother Archie had cleared the garage and sold the car. She wouldn't let them clear out cupboards, wouldn't let them do more than paint the anaglypta downstairs.

Lesley got up from her chair, "I'd better get back," she said.

He followed her into the hall and she opened the door herself, before he could do it for her.

He switched on the outdoor light. Within seconds she was halfway down the long path.

Just as he closed the door, he heard Ruby coming cautiously down the stairs. She was in her dressing gown, the pink plastic bath cap still on her head.

"Who was that?"

"Lesley next door. She brought your dish back."

"How long was she in?"

"Long enough to give me the dish back."

"Did you give her the boots?"

"What boots?"

"The boots that woman left for her. "

"I forgot. I'll run after her," he said.

"No, it's all right," she said. "I'll take them round myself tomorrow. What were you talking about?"

"Fireplaces," he told her.

The place to be

Walking home with a strong wind at his back, his head freezing cold, and too many thoughts jigging inside it, Ryan tried to make sense of his evening. Light from the street lamps shimmered in the puddles. Every house with its curtains open looked like a treasure cave. A woman walking a big black dog smiled at him when they passed, and he smiled back, though he'd never seen her before. Man, had he eaten some weird things. Parsnips, sweet and mushy. Long thin green beans, French beans they were called, OK but not great. Roast potatoes he'd had a lot of times, but not like theirs. There were small round objects in the sauce, which turned out to be mushrooms, and squarish bits that he recognised as bacon.

The girl had avoided looking at him, which left him free to look at her. The set of her ears entranced him. Where in his skull he'd found that word he didn't know, but it was perfect. She had her hair caught back in grips, so that the ears showed, and every time she turned her head, like when she talked to Kerr, he traced the curves. The way they leaned away from her head at the top made him think of elves. She wasn't wearing earrings, and the lobes weren't pierced. He supplied a pair – gold because of her hair, with pale blue stones to match the sweater. After a minute he took the stones away. Plain gold was better.

He'd taken some of all he was offered, eating slowly in case he gagged. Kerr did most of the talking, but after a while, politeness seemed to get the better of her, and she asked about the trainers. Then she wanted to know the whole story, and she actually looked quite upset. Kerr didn't say anything about the fact that he'd been too pissed to protect himself.

"We don't get presents worth stealing any more," she said.

"That scarf thing of yours wasn't cheap," Kerr protested. "What you have to understand, Ryan, is that this child," he gestured towards her with his fork, "is very greedy. She misses the good old days when she and her buddies went round every shop in Aberdeen every Saturday. She has the biggest wardrobe in the house. She could start her own clothes shop."

Ryan's sisters were the same, but wise for once, he accepted more gravy without saying anything. With them it was shoes. Mostly shoes that didn't even fit. He remembered them throwing gravel at his bedroom window to get him to open the back door in their late night dancing days. They'd hobbled in, heels and toes raw and bleeding. He didn't think they went to the same shops as Harriet though.

He had to wait for several cars to pass before he could cross Main Street, but there weren't that many people on foot at this end of the village, away from the shops. An older couple with another dog, this one straining on its chain as if it wasn't walking fast enough. One cyclist. Not anyone he knew.

He crossed the footbridge. The river was noisy, high from all the rain. He pulled the hood of his jacket tighter, wishing he'd had the sense to wear a hat. On his right the houses had sandbags stacked beside their low walls and hedges; there had been flooding a few years back, he couldn't remember exactly when. They hadn't been in any danger themselves, being higher up the hill. Big private houses were being built much higher up, on a new road, well away from the river, on land that would have been too difficult or too expensive to build on in the past. "The Place that's Going to be the Place to Be," according to the hoardings.

Different planets. With each stride he felt himself resenting what he was going towards. Their house was as clean as the one he'd just left – his mother cleaned as if that was what kept the planet turning, but that was all you could say. Nothing matched. Every window ledge had some stupid, cheap ornament on it. Two furry kittens in a basket adorned the bathroom cistern. He'd tried and failed to find some kind of symbolic significance in that. On the kitchen wall hung a calendar with red print and green exotic birds, a freebie from the local Chinese takeaway. Why she kept it, he didn't know, since there was nothing written in any of the spaces. In the living room on top of the fireplace sat his all-time favourite, a glass vase decorated with a hand-painted teddy bear in a tartan scarf, and the words *A Present from*

Ullapool in gold script. Ullapool had probably been glad to see the back of it.

He vaulted over the front gate. The catch was stiff, and there was a metal bit that could catch the delicate skin between your thumb and first finger if you didn't do it right. Just one more shitty detail in his life. Up till now he'd managed to convince himself that money and class and all that crap didn't matter because his day was coming, the day when everyone would see that he, Ryan Flaherty, was right up there. Inside he was a genius, inside he was different from everything and everybody round about him. God, it was easy to despise the bourgeoisie when you hadn't tasted their parsnips.

"Is that you, Ryan?"

"No, Mum," he muttered, "it's Pierce Brosnan come to take you dancing."

Loud canned laughter burst from the TV in the living room as if the studio

audience got the joke.

"Your tea's in the oven, son."

"Ah'm no' hungry," he called back.

He kicked off his shoes, hung his coat over the post at the foot of the stairs and was halfway to the upper landing when the phone began to ring. Usually it was for her – one of his sisters complaining or passing on some piece of trivia. But it might be for him. He'd told them his name. Kerr had written down the address and phone number.

"Dinna answer it!"

His mother came rushing from the living room. Her face was flushed.

"What?"

"Pit that doon!"

He did as he was told.

She turned away, bumping into the doorframe before finding her way back into the room.

"What's happened? Wha's deid noo?" He shouted after her.

He stood where he was for a few moments. She'd been up at the chapel again, he guessed. Every time she went she came back with news of some fatal illness or sudden death. That and a fresh sense of shame because her son never showed his face at Mass.

She was staring at the screen and didn't turn her head.

"Talk to me." He moved between her and the set. "What's the matter? Am ah in trouble again?"

She pressed her hands against her eyes. "You're in the road. Awa an' have your dinner. It's waited for you long enough."

Behind him the studio audience ooh'd and aah'd.

"D'you want a cup of tea or somethin'?"

She shook her head, her hands still up against her face.

In the oven he found a foil-covered plate of boiled potatoes, with three slices of fried bacon and some baked beans. He wrapped most of it in the foil, binned it, and put the dirty plate next to the sink. He could have washed it, but she'd only wash it again.

Up in his own bedroom he closed the door and locked it. His most recent sketch lay on the desk. He lifted it by the two top corners, but after a few seconds laid it down. Why take your anger out on a decent drawing, an innocent sketch of wind-blown branches?

There was a pencil lying on the carpet beside the bed. This he picked up, and holding it in both hands, forced it until it shattered, startling him, so that one of the broken ends stabbed the soft cushion of flesh below his right thumb. He watched the bright blood well up, then smeared it over his jeans. If she asked, he'd say it was a nose bleed.

He switched the light back off and went to the window. The radiator was hot against his legs, the window glass chilled his upper body. He couldn't see Harriet's house for trees, but he knew where it was now, knew she was inside it, putting plates back in the white cupboards, watching TV with her brother, or reading some fancy book, just generally being a nice girl. He kicked off his shoes, lay down on the bed and pulled the quilt over himself.

This room had been his for three years, since Kelly moved in with her boyfriend. He'd painted the walls dark red, put up some posters, and binned the pink curtains.

"Ah'm no' buyin' new ones," his mother told him. "There was nothing wrong wi' those. An' they were lined."

"Ah'm no needin' curtains anyway."

"You'll feel it come winter."

She was right. The heat didn't extend more than two feet into the room. Some day he would have his own place, with more than one room to himself. Two or three rooms. One just to paint in, loads of space with a wall of glass and nothing outside but the ocean. There would be one room to sleep in, with a double bed, so he could turn over without fear of falling out, and a ceiling painted dark blue, with small lights in it like stars. There'd be a jacuzzi bath at the far end, behind a wall of glass bricks, and a fitted fridge and bar in an alcove, really tasteful and discreet, and a few bits of antique sculpture under subtle spotlights, and the wall that faced the sea would have sliding glass panels so that on hot nights the whole thing could be opened up. And maybe above this, he'd have another room for music, with perfect acoustics, and the best Bang and Olufsen system money could buy.

She walks out of the ocean like that actress in the old Bond film. He pretends not to see her walking up the beach towards where he sits on the veranda shaded by palms, he keeps his head down, keeps going with the sketching. All day it's been hot. Now it's late afternoon. Maybe there's going to be thunder and a quick rain. Her shadow falls across him. She says hello. He grunts, as if he's too busy to notice her. He's so famous for his art now, he doesn't like visitors.

Maybe they met somewhere else the day before, she was buying mangoes and the bag burst and he helped her pick them up, and she offered him one as a reward, and that was it, and once he left, she asked the stall holder who he was, and now she's tracked him down. Leaving tiny grains of

*sand from her soles, she goes around the room. It's on two
levels, with a high ceiling. She loves everything she sees: the
paintings, all originals (but not his own, these he'll show her
later), the subtle colours, the sound system, every piece of
furniture. He keeps quiet about the fact that these are
exclusive pieces he's designed himself. He's won awards
for design, big international prizes.*

*She wants to see what he's working on, but he says, no,
it's not ready. Now she says she's hot and thirsty, so he puts
down his pencil, makes her something with ice, some drink
she's never heard of. She tastes it and says it's wonderful. He
acknowledges this with a modest nod of the head. She's
wearing a one piece swimsuit in the same creamy colour as
the dress she'd had on the day before. A butterfly darts in
through the open wall, and settles on her shoulder, attracted
by her perfume. He reassures her, tells her what kind of
butterfly it is, because he knows that sort of thing. He asks if
she'd like him to put on some music. He can smell her hair
when she kneels down beside him to look at all his CD's.
She undoes her sandals, or maybe she doesn't have sandals
on, since she was swimming. Or maybe they're in her
canvas bag with her towel and sun-cream. She lies back
in one of the recliners, running her fingers along the
butterscotch Italian leather . . .*

The ring of the phone woke him. The heating was off and
the air in the room was freezing. He looked at the bedside
clock. Half one. The phone rang until it rang out. Seconds

later the whole thing repeated itself. He lay for a while waiting. Silence.

Wide awake, he went down to the kitchen and heated some milk. There were strange-looking pastry things in the fridge, and small cooked potatoes with bits of green stuff on them, but luckily there was still some bread in the box. He made himself a sandwich with red jam. His hand hurt a bit, so he ran cold water over it for a time. Sandwich in one hand, milk in the other, he stared at the phone in the hall. He put the mug down on the ledge and dialled 1471. It wasn't a number he recognised. He pressed three.

"Hullo."

A male voice.

"Hullo? Who's that?" it repeated.

He put the phone down without answering.

Going like a fair

When Duncan returned to work the Library was depressingly quiet, with only a few students around, and none of them needing assistance. More importantly, little Mrs Fleming who brightened his mornings and chatted with him while she ate her packed lunch was missing, afflicted by a viral infection, which was a great pity, as he had rehearsed a conversation in which he would ask about her Murder Mystery evening, and she would learn about the new bird book, which he had brought with him. Mrs Fleming was quite interested in birds, and quite interested in poetry, so he felt she would be very interested in a book where the two were combined.

So far he had been surprised and pleased by how accurate the poems were in their choice of detail. Hardy's robin poem was the only one he had encountered before, (There was another poem in the collection, "The Darkling Thrush," but he was keeping his rule, and hadn't reached it yet.) and though he liked the first three verses, he disliked the last one, not merely because Hardy allowed his robin to die of starvation, but because in Duncan's experience, birds fluffed up when sick and did not resemble balls when dead. Besides, although he had never been able to discuss this with a poetry expert, he was unsure about the bird knowing how it felt to be dead. Since he was very fond of Hardy's poems, it was easier to leave the last verse unread.

However, this new book was proving more than satisfactory. He *had* allowed himself to glance at the afterword, written by one of the editors, and it seemed to him to be as poetic and accurate as the chosen poems. He was, in fact, beginning to feel rather excited, like someone discovering a new continent, like the chap in the Keats poem who stood on a mount in Lebanon, or wherever it was. Perhaps Mrs Fleming would be back soon.

His bus journey home was uneventful until they came within two miles of the village, where the nearside lane was cordoned off and a queue had formed. Eventually they reached two police cars with lights flashing. A uniformed officer signalled to the driver to open his doors, spoke to him and went away.

The bus driver swivelled round and shouted, "Right, everybody. We've got a wee problem up ahead. Big Sam's chippie's on fire at the moment." He talked on over the buzz of voices. "So we're no' goin' through the village. We're goin' off by the old farm road and back on at the other side at Bogend. So if any of youse want to walk the last bit, you'd better get off now."

Duncan stepped down out of the warmth of the bus, grasped his umbrella firmly, and pulled his scarf a little higher. The smell of smoke was apparent even this far away. With his long stride, he was soon ahead of the others. He had never been inside Big Sam's establishment and was unable to feel a great sense of loss. Besides, he was forever lifting greasy cartons and paper from where they had been stuffed into the back hedge. It seemed that a portion of fish and chips could be consumed in the time it took the average teenager to walk from the shop to that part of their hedge bordering the shortcut through the golf course. He had never visited the Tandoori Takeaway, or Ming's Oriental Restaurant either but sometimes they too made their presence felt. On a summer evening with the French doors open, the breeze would now and then blow from the north, wafting the smells of fried pork, papadums and curry all the way from the centre of the village.

None of these establishments had existed when their house was built. None of the roads was tarred. The doctor of the day had owned the first motor car; the District Nurse used a bicycle. In summer the children went shoeless. Year round, each Friday, they watched the big plough horses being shod where Mr Ming's restaurant now stood. When the school bell rang, they hurtled across the old bridge. Being late mattered in those days. The blacksmith's shop had still been there in his own childhood, though the horses had gone.

People were milling about on the traffic-free High Street, everyone cheerful and excited as if some festival had been announced. The side street itself was cordoned off, and blocked half way along by two large fire engines. There was plenty of smoke, but no flames that he could see. An ambulance and a couple of police cars were parked beyond the fire engines. Someone had put up a step ladder on the pavement, and there was a man with a camera on it, while others were holding mobile phones high to take photographs. Going like a fair, Duncan thought: bustle and jostling and shrieking children and yelping dogs twisting on leads to get at one another. The village sergeant and constable were trying to soothe a group of irate-looking bystanders. He recognised one of the local councillors, who on seeing him, waved, as if to say, Come over here, Mr Crawfurd, I'll tell you all you need to know. Duncan nodded in a non-committal manner, slowly turned himself around, and began to walk away. The man had a habit of pausing for breath in the middle of sentences, so that you could never interrupt without talking over him, besides which, having lived in Hartsend all his days he took it for granted that the village was the centre of the world. His conversation moved inevitably into detailed news about people he assumed Duncan knew and cared about, or worse, news about people *those* people knew, who might be dead, missing, or living in Patagonia for all Duncan knew or cared.

He felt a gentle tap on his arm.

"Lesley? Shouldn't you be at work?" What a silly thing to say. It sounded like criticism. "My bus was diverted. I've had to get off at Peathill," he added quickly.

Should he ask how she was? His mind tossed up suggestion after suggestion and the slight wind was enough to blow them away.

"Did you get your boots?" he said finally. They were walking side by side, and he had to bend a little to hear her over the noise around them. He had forgotten how short she was.

"My boots?"

"Mother gave them to your neighbour the other day."

"Really? "

He remembered the gentleman friend.

"I think you . . . had a visitor."

"I'm sorry. Was that you? I didn't realise . . ." An ambulance siren submerged the rest of her words. ". . . Mary Flaherty. It was very difficult."

"Yes," he said, wanting to be helpful.

"I've just been to see her, but I don't think I did much good."

"Oh dear, that's a pity."

"Has she spoken to you?"

"Well," he said. "I'm not sure I ought . . ."

They had to separate to go round two young women with prams. What had Mrs Flaherty to do with the boots, he wondered. And what was difficult? Was the family in trouble? He understood the son-in-law had not yet found employment. He hoped Mrs Flaherty hadn't been pestering Lesley to help the man in some way . . .

"Isn't that her son?"

"What?"

"Her son," she pointed to a dark-coated figure leaning against the window of the Hospice Shop. "She said he'd shaved all his hair off. Peculiar thing to do in the middle of winter, don't you think?"

A girl in a beige-coloured duffel coat came out of the shop. She said something to the boy, and they turned in the direction of the New Bridge.

"I know that girl. That's the minister's child," Duncan exclaimed.

"Hardly a child, Duncan."

Lesley had stopped. He stood beside her. They watched for a moment. Should he express approval or disapproval? Or change the subject? Could he tell her about his new book? It was glowing quietly in his briefcase. "Darien," he said out loud. That's where the mount was, not Lebanon. He'd known whole chunks of Keats by heart once.

"Pardon?"

"Oh. Nothing," he said. Yet at once he wondered if she would like to see the book. She might understand his delight.

But she was saying goodbye then and see you again soon, and pushing open the door of the shop beside them, and gone. Taken aback, he stood outside the shop for a while, his explanation ungiven, until, noticing from the window display that it was the ladies' hairdresser, he grasped what had happened, collected himself and walked on.

He crossed by the old metal footbridge, letting the ferrule of his umbrella trail with a series of rapid clicks along the wire mesh. Then he realised what he was doing. Fortunately it wasn't scratched. A clear thought rose above his mind's restless surface. Lesley was always discreet, but her tone of voice had given the game away. The Flahertys were Catholic. The son had formed an attachment with the Protestant daughter of the local minister.

He could understand Mrs Flaherty's distress, although frankly it was ridiculous in this day and age. Nor was it right of her to trouble Lesley, not at this time. Lesley had no-one to protect her.

"You've led such a sheltered life, Duncan," Mrs Fleming had said more than once, smiling, as if a sheltered life was something bad, as if sheltering her baby was not Mrs Fleming's own first priority. As if sheltering his family was not the first priority of a husband, even Mrs Fleming's husband, a man with beads on a leather string round his neck who held his baby under his arm like a parcel.

I want to shelter Lesley.

The idea grew and grew until everything else was gone from his mind. The terrible completeness of it stunned him.

It brought no delight. Instead he felt as if he were walking towards a huge blockage, a wall, something that would stop him in his tracks like the immense steel buffers at the end of a station platform he'd seen once as a small child.

The wind had shifted, what little wind there was. It blew now from the north, bearing the acrid smoke from the ruined shop further along the valley, lifting it in a long plume, dark against the pearl-coloured sky.

Treasure

She was a very beautiful child. Her face had been dirty that first day and he had ached to wipe it clean for her, but he knew instinctively that this would have been a mistake. Her eyes were wonderful – generous, innocent but aware at the same time. He knew children's eyes were big compared to the size of the face, so that they would be more appealing, a louder cry for the parent's care, as it were, but he had seen a lot of very plain, mean-eyed children in his time. It was easy to tell she was a gentle soul from the way she held the feather, from the fact that she'd picked it up in the first place and hidden it protectively from him. She was so solemn, agreeing with him that eggs should never be stolen. He looked round the room, wondering what small treasure he might carry in his pocket the next time he went for a walk. What might he give her? What would she like?

Clamped

Harriet recognised Ryan through the shop window, just as she was putting her coat on. She made some excuse to June and went through to the back, hoping he'd be gone when she came out.

He wasn't.

"Comin' to see the fire?" he asked.

"I'm going to the Post Office."

"There's nothin' much to see now, anyway, unless you like dirty water. I took some photos earlier." He patted a bulge in his coat pocket. "They might come in useful."

"Good for you," she said.

"There's no' been excitement like this since McIntyre's cows got out the dairy."

"Before my time," she said.

The whole of the village was on the streets, it seemed: several shop owners in their doorways, young children sleeping or getting impatient in pushchairs while their mothers talked, and drivers whose cars were stuck in the parking inlet arguing with Brenda, the lady traffic warden, who had one hand clamped on her ear while she tried to talk into her phone. Clamped. That's quite funny, Harriet thought. Not funny enough to share. Not with him.

Across from them in the Millennium Garden the Pensioners Refuge looked deserted. All the old men seemed to have come over to the edge of the grass to see what was going on. One of them had a mug in his hand. Another had lit a cigarette and was coughing badly.

She was being unfair. He wasn't that awful. At least he didn't smoke. He looked better with his hair gone than he had before. It was just that he made her uncomfortable. She couldn't help speaking the way she did. She sounded so posh, but they weren't posh. They hadn't been posh, even in Aberdeen when they had money . . .

"I'd better get on," she said.

"Wait."

"I'm sorry?"

"There's a thing you could do for me. Help me with."

He pulled out something from an inside pocket. The brooch.

"Come in the shop with me."

"I'm sorry?" she said again.

"Come in with me, and I'll put it back." He began picking bits of fluff off the scrolled silver leaves.

"You can't. . . . You shouldn't have taken it in the first place."

"I only did it 'cause you were expectin' me to."

"What?"

"Come on, admit it," he looked from the brooch to her. "You were watching me out of the corner of your eye, like a fucking raptor in the jungle."

The word was like a slap. She turned, her face burning. That word still had the power to sicken, no matter how often she heard it. Overhearing was bad enough. To have it so close, to have it said to her . . .

He had caught up, was walking next to her again. She kept her head down. He said nothing more, but he didn't go away either.

When eventually they reached the Post Office, he said, "I'll wait here."

"Please don't bother. I might be quite a while."

There was no queue. The letters were weighed. She pocketed the change and the receipt. He was leaning against the window, rocking slightly, as if some tune was playing in his head.

"I'm perishin'. You want to go to the café?" he said, the minute she reappeared.

"No, I have to get home. Goodbye."

"I'm not good enough, is that it?"

"What?"

"What, what, what? I'm offerin' to buy you a diet Coke, no' cocaine."

"I have to go home."

"Sure you do. OK. How's Kerr?"

"He's fine. He's off bouldering with some friends."

"Bouldering? What the fancy fuck's that?"

"Don't!"

"Don't what?"

"Use that word."

He stared at her, eyebrows raised.

"You're no' real," he said.

The road was clear. She darted over, walked quickly, ready to run if need be.

His voice pursued her, "I said, you're no' fucking real!"

Margaret doesn't work here anymore

Lesley lay back with her head in the basin, agreed that the water was fine for her, and let the junior begin the shampooing. She recognised the girl, one of the more pleasant children whose uniform and appearance had always been neat. The mother had been a willing helper at parties and days out. Sick notes were spelled correctly, written on proper paper, not on a page from a jotter.

"I don't like the head massage, Candy," she said, as the water began to flow. She had to speak quite loudly against the background music.

"Oh, do you remember me, Miss Crosthwaite?" The girl sounded pleased.

They talked a little about school, and what Candy's friends were now doing. Her fingers were very gentle, in fact it was so soothing that Lesley felt after a minute or two that she might fall asleep.

The stylist brought her back to full wakefulness. She was new and wore a small diamond stud above her right nostril. Her hair looked as if it hadn't been combed and there was a disconcerting purple streak in front of one eye.

"Who cut your hair last?" she asked, lifting it up at the back.

"Margaret." Lesley felt like a traitor. "But I haven't been in a long time." She had originally asked for Margaret, only to be told that she had retired.

"Right. Well it's not in very good condition. You're not using conditioner, are you? So how much are we taking off? We'll need to take all these split ends away."

Candy appeared with a cup of tea and placed it on the small shelf in front of the mirror. "No sugar, Miss Crosthwaite, was that right?" she said. "Would you like a magazine?"

To her embarrassment, Lesley couldn't immediately tell the stylist which side her parting was usually on. The girl handed her a comb to help her remember.

Between snips there were attempts at conversation. Was she going anywhere special that night? Had she enjoyed Christmas? Was she working? Lesley held the magazine up resolutely, trying to ignore the woman, though conscious at the same time that it might be dangerous to antagonise her. She thought of Margaret who had looked after her for years, and had known exactly what to do without being told.

"Have you considered using some colour?" the girl said, twisting a section of front hair and catching it in a clip.

"No," Lesley said quickly, keeping her eyes on an advert for face creams. Seven different products by one manufacturer, at prices she considered ridiculous. Why did anyone need seven different things to make their skin presentable?

"Well, I would if I were you. A whole head of grey hair

can be very attractive in an older lady like yourself, but lots of grey hairs amongst the brown isn't really so nice."

"Hello, Lesley, how are you today?"

A young woman she didn't know from Eve was smiling at her in the mirror, dressed in a trim white uniform like a nurse.

"This is Claire, our new beauty therapist," the stylist told her.

Lesley accepted the leaflet out of politeness.

". . . and we have a special deal today for £10. Just a file and polish. It hardly takes a minute. Would you like me to do it while Marie's drying your hair?"

Candy brought her coat. Lesley had hoped for this, and slipped some pound coins into the girl's hand. She had no intention of putting money into a fund that would be shared by everyone. She paid the bill, which was more than she expected, by credit card. While they waited for it to clear, the receptionist said how nice her new nails were. Two women waiting to make appointments agreed they were really lovely. Lesley looked down at her terracotta finger tips and wanted to scream.

Respect

After a dinner of tomato soup followed by lemon sole, "lightly dusted with a seasoned dressing" according to the label, Mrs Crawfurd went upstairs. Duncan stacked the dishwasher, made himself a decaffeinated latte and sat down to watch the news on the small kitchen TV. Generally this was enough to send him into a light doze. He wondered if Mrs Fleming would be back soon. Perhaps he would suggest they send a card. From Mrs Fleming his thoughts drifted without hindrance to Lesley. In truth, worrying about Mrs Fleming's health was more of a delaying tactic for preventing himself from thinking about Lesley.

How had this happened? One moment Lesley was an old friend whose company he enjoyed, and whose views he respected. The next she was something else entirely. He stepped back from defining the "something". At last the idea of a gallant knight in armour came helpfully to mind. But how exactly was he going to shine?

You could have insisted on seeing her home at New Year.
He'd been willing but Dr MacKinnon had overruled.
You could have insisted on taking back the boots.
True.

*Have you ever asked her how she is? Have you offered
her anything?*

She knew he was concerned. She knew where he lived.
And she was a private person.

When someone knocked loudly at the back door, he
wondered wildly whether it might be her. He didn't feel
like answering, but Mother never went to the door at this
hour, despite the fact that the security light illuminated
everything with a blaze worthy of a concentration camp.

Close to, the Flaherty boy was taller than Duncan remembered, able to look him straight in the eye, which he
now did, with a look entirely devoid of . . . of what,
exactly? Deference was hardly the right word. Respect?
He was wearing a knitted hat pulled low, almost down to
his eyebrows. His eyes were so intensely blue it crossed
Duncan's mind he might be wearing coloured contact
lenses. The young did such things.

"Mum's no' well. But if she's better by Friday, she says
she'll come then. If you want her."

"Mrs Flaherty."

The boy nodded.

"Wait here a moment." Duncan indicated the general
area of the porch. He closed the door into the kitchen
proper, dismissing the impulse to slide the sneck over as
uncharitable.

There was nothing on the calendar, so he assumed that
the Friday morning would be suitable as usual. Friday was a
big day. Sheet washing and ironing. Mrs Flaherty was of

course restricted to the downstairs of the house. Mother managed her own bed linen but he stripped his bed and carried everything down to the utility room.

When he came back to the porch, the boy was pressing the scented geranium leaves and sniffing his fingers.

"Friday would be suitable," Duncan said. "Please give Mrs Flaherty our best wishes for a quick recovery."

The boy stuck his hands in his coat pockets and sauntered off. Not kicking at the gravel, thankfully. Duncan watched him all the way to the side gate and out into the street. He looked at the geranium leaves. An odd gesture for a barbarian, he thought.

Better. He tried the word aloud, the way the boy had said it, with the hideous glottal stop. It was hard to imagine him as an artistic soul. Lacking any academic qualifications, he was nevertheless, according to Mrs Flaherty, so talented that he'd been accepted into the School of Art on the strength of his portfolio alone.

The last inch of the latté was cold. Duncan picked up the Herald, begun that morning at breakfast, and tried to summon some interest in the Blogs. He wondered whether the boy could even write in proper sentences.

He glanced at the mantel clock. Lesley would be asleep. She would be having a late meal. She would be . . . any number of things, and possibly more than one at once, but whatever these might be, he knew for a certainty that, following her custom of the last several days, she would not pick up the phone.

Leave a message. Ask her to phone back.

Mrs Fleming was right. She was shaking her head at him, the bald baby on her lap, both laughing at him from the chair opposite.

Why do you want to phone her, Duncan?

I'm worried about her.

That's good. Nothing wrong with that.

And Mrs Flaherty, of course. I'm not indifferent to her problems.

Then what's stopping you? For all you know, Lesley could be sitting there in that big empty house, looking out at the unkempt garden and the bare branches of her willow trees, wishing somebody would phone her. Besides, you can ask if she got the boots. Your mother would appreciate you asking.

There was that. And he might mention the gentleman friend.

The bald baby frowned and Mrs Fleming shook her head.

He was stunned when Lesley's live voice answered.

"Yes, ah . . . Duncan here," he said.

"Hello, Duncan. Is something wrong?"

"No. Well, not exactly. I was thinking . . . Mrs Flaherty."

"Yes?"

"Her son . . . came by just now. Apparently she's . . . ill."

"What happened?"

"Well, I don't think anything happened exactly. He said she's not well. I thought it was perhaps a cold. Bad time of year for colds." He picked up his pencil and began doodling in the newspaper margin. "Just that you mentioned her earlier. Decent person, Mrs Flaherty. Wouldn't like to think she was neglecting herself. Needing the doctor in and not calling him, that sort of thing."

"Well, she has two daughters," Lesley said, "They both live locally. I expect they're looking in on her."

"Right. Anyway. Just in case you hadn't heard. Sorry to bother you at this hour."

"No, it's all right. I'm glad you phoned. You know he's called Ryan, don't you? Not Darien."

"Of course. Well. You know where I am. Anytime."

"Thank you, Duncan. I appreciate that very much."

"Right."

He put the phone down and sat back in the chair. There was no sound from upstairs. Of course Mrs Flaherty had daughters. They'd be doing all that was necessary. Damn, he thought, he'd forgotten to mention the boots. She was glad he'd phoned. He allowed himself a smile. He was glad too. No harm had been done. She'd appreciated his offer of help. He turned to see if Mrs Fleming and the baby approved, but they had gone.

Clichés

Lesley rose early, meaning to begin sorting clothes from her mother's drawers. Some would go to Oxfam, and some into the recycle bins behind the Co-operative store. She took a roll of black bin liners into the front bedroom and emptied the contents of the bottom drawer onto the bed.

Two neatly folded pink bed jackets wrapped in tissue paper. Scarves in their original cellophane packets, never worn, Fair Isle gloves ditto. Two knitted tea pot cosies with felt flowers on the sides, red with green, and green with red. A box of gents' tartan handkerchiefs. The next drawer up was full of tights and socks. Long winter socks, grey and darned at the heels in a lighter shade, folded in pairs.

She had a vague memory of these from her childhood, on her mother's feet, worn inside rubber boots when she brought in coal from the bunker or scraped snow from the steps. Everyone had identical rubber boots then. And every winter brought snow. It occurred to her for the first time that these socks might originally have been her late father's.

It was barely seven o'clock. Outside the sky was dark blue, just beginning to grow paler where the sun would eventually rise above the hills.

At the back gate she turned to look at the house. She'd left some lights on to fool the burglars. Anyone passing might assume that a cheerful breakfast was going on behind the partly drawn curtains. Next door, the Robertson's house was in darkness. She stared at the windows upstairs, but there was no sign of Mrs Robertson, no twitch of a curtain.

For the first several minutes she felt good. She had acted on impulse, made an instant decision, and done just what she felt like doing, with no one to stop her. Cars were moving on the motorway, but there were few people about. A handful waiting in the bus shelter. A few walking their dogs. But by the time she reached the War Memorial, she was beginning to feel conspicuous, walking with no purpose, and no direction. Blessed are the early morning dog walkers, for they do not look ridiculous. Not that she was fond of dogs. A cat would be easier, but she actively disliked cats: their unreasonable behaviour, their torturing of small mammals and birds, their indolence. Besides, the spinster with the cat was such a cliché.

She passed the wooden hut where once upon a time she had been a cheerful Brownie. All those happy hours ironing a yellow scarf, polishing a leather belt and purse. And the games, the singing, the making of scrapbooks under the benevolent smile of Brown Owl, whose black hair was so shiny, whose pink-tipped fingers had curved elegantly like some oriental dancer's. How full of good intentions she had been; a small, round Gnome in plaits with brown ribbons, fully determined, as their particular rhyme put it, to help mother in the home. And how wonderfully helpful she had continued to be, through High School, and college, on and on and on . . .

Enough. She made a right turn into a well-lit street that would take her back in the direction of home. Duncan clearly thought she should still be doing helpful things. She was surprised by his concern for Mrs Flaherty. To be completely honest, she was a little surprised that Mrs Flaherty had confided in him. Although of course Duncan was the kind of person in whom one might confidently confide. Straight as a ramrod, always the perfect gentleman. Just as well Mrs Flaherty wasn't the sort of woman to take advantage of him. Dear Duncan. She had known him all her life, but she hardly knew him at all. She had exchanged more words with him in the last two weeks than in the last ten years.

The Dust Heaps

"Thank you so much for coming, Harriet," Mrs Robertson said, "June had such a sore throat on Monday I just knew she wouldn't be well enough to come this morning, and Letty's still at her Auntie's . . ."

Harriet smiled back. She hadn't wanted to come, but it was better than having to start revising for prelims.

". . . going to send a manager over, but I just thought, with it still being the holidays, we could open up if you could be here for a couple of hours . . ."

Mrs Robertson's eyes, enormous behind her glasses, were deeply disturbing. They reminded Harriet of a picture of the Cheshire Cat in *Alice In Wonderland*. Her hair was just as worrying. She had a girlish deep fringe, and her back hair was combed in a straight line from crown to nape where it turned under abruptly, as if she'd set it on tight curlers.

"What would you like me to do first, Mrs Robertson?"

"Would you like to refresh the window, dear? I feel I must vacuum this awful carpet before I do anything else. And of course we should take the decorations down."

The beige carpet, 100 percent nylon and resistant to the removal of stains, was the bane of Mrs Robertson's life, but no-one else was allowed to do battle with it. Refreshing the window was less prestigious, but still a mark of approval. Letty, eager to please but "not quite all there", was never allowed to "refresh" the window, which involved taking everything off the three glass shelves, wiping them and choosing some new arrangement of delicate objects. These generally included various china vases with floral designs, ashtrays, jam dishes, condiment sets and crystal milk and sugars. On the top shelf, at eye height for anyone passing by, stood three very large coffee pots. They were in perfect condition, but bore no famous maker's mark on their bottoms. As June said, they were too large to be useful. No-one made coffee in china pots for eight people any more. She had tried putting flowers in them, but they remained obstinately pot-like, and unsold.

Nevertheless like everything else in the shop, they had to be kept clean. "We're not a second-hand shop," June regularly reminded them. "We are a Charity Shop."

It was an important distinction. And to support it, there were always brand new goods for sale, such as handbags in imitation leather, and fridge magnets in the shape of bright coloured abstract cats or dogs; new bracelets for £4.99 each; "magic" gloves, where one size fitted all; Scottie dog key rings made in China.

In the back room, Harriet dug out the box for the Christmas decorations. The three sided mesh cage against the back wall was piled high with bulging black plastic bags, waiting to be emptied out onto the table. This task made everyone nervous. No-one liked opening bags if there was no label to say who had donated them. "Do we look like the kind of shop that would take stained goods?" was the regular pained cry on discovering an offending object.

"Mmm. The Dust Heaps. Very Dickensian," her father had commented, when she'd described her first day.

"Meaning?"

"People sometimes throw out valuable things by mistake."

"Not very often," Harriet said. All the antique programmes on TV had made people much more aware, according to June. Now and again something would be found, like a Delft vase, or a piece of gold jewellery, or brooches that turned out to have real stones, but all such things went to auction. The brooch Ryan Flaherty had stolen was pretty, but not real silver. Which didn't mean it wasn't theft.

She began to clear the shelves, disentangling the gold tinsel and fairy lights from the vases. Behind her the vacuum cleaner roared. June made cups of tea first, but Mrs Robertson had to clean. How old was she? Her trousers, always navy or dark grey, came just short of her ankles. She wore pale flesh-coloured nylons. Her shoes, (Harriet had described them to her mother as "old lady shoes") had low heels, navy when she wore navy trousers, black for the grey ones.

Christmas was long gone. The prelims would begin a few days after school began. Tonight she'd make a timetable.

Making a timetable was a good start. She carried the cardboard box into the backroom and half filled the red bucket with hot water.

The electronic door alarm did its loud "Peep poop" noise as a customer came in. It was the man they'd given a lift to, the thin tall man with the sad eyes. "Poor Duncan," her father called him. He had two large plastic bags in his hands, which he put down carefully on the counter before removing his cap. Mrs Robertson switched off the vacuum cleaner and went over.

"Just some oddments," he said in a gruff voice. "And some gloves. Leather. Hardly used."

Harriet picket up the bucket and cleaning rags and went through.

Mrs Robertson trilled, "Oh, thank you so much. We're always in need of new items after Christmas."

"Why 'Poor'?" she'd asked her father.

"Not financially poor. He lives with his mother in that huge house near the woods, the one with the turrets. I called in not long after we came. He made me a cup of very decent coffee, and we sat out on the terrace. Very pleasant it was, watching woodpeckers on the feeders. He's terribly keen on birds. Then his mother appeared and he shrank into his chair," her father mimicked the action, drawing his shoulders together. "It made me think of those plastic things you and Kerr used to put in the oven."

She remembered the smell of the plastic as it cooked, and Mum's insistence on keeping the kitchen door wide open.

Kerr hadn't been all that interested after the first session, but she'd made endless rings and charms to be worn on string necklaces, and badges to be given away to selected friends and relations.

"That's three pounds, please," Mrs Robertson said.

Evidently he'd bought something. Harriet didn't catch his reply.

"Oh, thank you. And please do say thank you to your wife for the last bundle. She has such good taste. Those Liberty blouses just flew out of the shop."

"My wife?"

Harriet looked round at Mrs Robertson.

"She always looks so elegant, I think. We do appreciate all her donations. If only more people would be so thought-ful."

Harriet waited for him to correct Mrs Robertson. Instead he touched his cap and went out. Mrs Robertson kept the smile on her face until the door drifted slowly shut behind him, then began examining the contents of the bags. *You stupid, stupid greedy woman*, Harriet said silently, turning back to her shelves. *I hope you find something you totally can't live without.*

No-one on the staff was allowed to buy items until they'd been on display for two full weeks. June had told her about an Italian silk scarf Mrs Robertson wanted so badly she kept putting it under other items. When the two weeks were up June pretended she'd sold it, but she relented afterwards.

Poor Duncan had left his book on the counter. It was an old hardback, the lettering on its blue spine too faded to read. While Mrs Robertson was fighting dirty marks on the carpet beneath the DVD shelf, Harriet slipped it into her own bag.

Age

On the way home Duncan was overtaken by Miss Calvert, pedalling hard against the gradient. She lifted one mittened hand from the handlebars as she passed. He touched his cap in acknowledgement.

Miss Calvert wore bright berets in winter, set at an angle, an imitation, he assumed, of the continentals she so revered. Today's was scarlet, with a matching scarf tucked into her jacket. She couldn't be much more than forty yet he thought of her as being much older than himself.

Not an attractive woman. For one thing, she never truly listened to anyone but herself. A word of conversation instantly triggered in her a memory of somewhere she had been, a view of the Jungfrau, or a "first-rate" hotel. If it was term-time, she would be pronouncing on staff shortages or some new folly of the local Education Department. All entirely predictable.

How predictable am I? he wondered. The pattern of his days hardly varied: Imperial Leather soap in the shower, Weetabix sprinkled with bran for breakfast (porridge in winter), no coffee after six pm, decaffeinated being anathema, the regular radio programmes he listened to, the TV programmes he despised and avoided . . . His life might easily seem dull to someone else, someone ignorant of the welter of thoughts that coursed around inside his head. He'd decided to work part time because it gave him afternoons to follow his own interests, not because he was old, or unable to cope.

That girl kneeling at the window, the minister's daughter, she had heard everything. She'd taken it all in.

He passed the Pensioners' Refuge, a white-painted wooden hut, next to the remaining beech tree in what had been re-christened the Millennium Garden. Storms in past years had brought down the other two. Their sad stumps remained, incised now with slogans and profanities by the village youth.

Mr McKenzie, who for many years had taken care of their garden, was standing in the doorway. He touched his forehead and Duncan saluted back. The man was old now, and stooped, but Duncan remembered watching one hot summer in profound envy as he and his two teenage sons, naked to the waist, the boys pale-skinned and the father deeply tanned, had chopped down an overgrown rowan and constructed a tier of raised beds out of old cobbled stones, so that his mother could grow herbs near the kitchen door.

Forty years ago, at least. The old man's passage through the village was slow these days, and getting slower; a few steps, then a long wait for the breath to come back, then a few steps more. It was perhaps made bearable, he supposed, by the fact that the old man was well known, that so many stopped to exchange a word. And yet with every year, there would be fewer of his vintage left, clay workers who had turned to other things when the factory closed.

Mr Mackenzie was wearing a traditional tweed cap very similar to his own. The label would be different, of course. He glanced back, noting the old man's training shoes, worn grey trousers, and black fleece jacket. It was likely that Mr Mackenzie did not own more than one cap. Or perhaps two. He himself had five: this all-purpose checked one, a waxed Barbour to be worn with his raincoat, a soft leather one for his brown tweed jacket, and two for summer, one in cream and one in light blue. He was fond of caps. They kept one's head appropriately warm or cool, and had brims broad enough to shade the eyes. He had always felt that a cap made a man look dressed whatever the situation. A cap enabled one to behave like a gentleman. Or did it merely enable one to look like an old age pensioner?

The simplest explanation, he told himself, was that the woman in the shop had mistaken him for someone else. She'd always struck him as being a little odd. She always spoke with particular care, as if she might too easily mispronounce words.

The girl had noticed everything. She would think it was amusing. She would tell her whole family the joke, and then she would tell the tale to her friend, Ryan Flaherty, and he would laugh too. He would tell his mother and she . . .

No. Mrs Flaherty wouldn't laugh. She would stop the boy short. *That's a terrible thing to say*, she'd tell him. *Mr Crawfurd's such a nice gentleman,* she'd say. *Imagine thinking him the same age as his mother.*

The sugar bowl is broken

"Mr Crawfurd, there's someone at the door."

Mrs Flaherty's shout roused Duncan from his reverie. He went unhurriedly down the stairs, cup in hand, trying to make out who it was through the glass. From the distant sounds of drawers opening and closing, Mrs Flaherty had evidently gone back to the kitchen.

The Reverend's daughter. Why was she here? Was she was collecting for some good cause?

"I brought your book. You left it behind this morning."

"Oh, thank you." He took the small volume from her. "Yes, you were in the shop." How loud and rough his voice sounded. He cleared his throat and tried again, "Very kind of you."

She was shivering. He glanced beyond her for a car. She wasn't wearing a coat, just a cardigan. Boots yes, and a knitted scarf, but no hat, no gloves.

"You're not on foot, are you?"

"I just came from the shop. I usually just do Saturdays, but Mrs Robertson was short staffed."

"Mrs Robertson."

"The one with the blue eyebrows."

"They are rather blue, yes." He was unable to repress a slight smile.

"I didn't mean to be rude," she said.

"No. Of course not."

"Will I make another pot, Mr Crawfurd?" A voice from the far end of the hall.

His mother was out. But Mrs Flaherty was in. Where was the harm?

"May I offer you a cup of tea?"

When she said yes, he had to think rapidly. The kitchen would be best. Mrs Flaherty would be ironing in the utility room and could chaperone from there.

He seated the girl in the wicker chair beside the window.

"So, do you enjoy working in the Hospice Shop?" he began.

When she didn't answer he went on, "It's a very worthy cause. At least, I hear people say so, I don't know how much of the . . ."

To his surprise, she broke off and stood up. "Mr Crawfurd. I wanted to come and tell you . . . because I saw . . . I wanted you to know that . . ." She took a deep breath as if to steady herself. "To apologise . . . Mrs Robertson . . . everyone knows the clothes are from your mother. She's a very . . . She's just weird. I'm really sorry."

Before he could answer she was heading back towards the hall. He just managed to get to the front door before her.

"Thank you so much for bringing the book," he said

hurriedly. She looked as if she wanted to vanish into thin air. "It's quite a find," he went on, "I'm quite ashamed that I only paid three pounds for it. No dust jacket, unfortunately."

Her face was reddening.

He heard himself wittering on, "That's the term used for the paper cover. It's always more valuable with the original cover. Well-known author on birds, James E Whiting. Perhaps you'll let me know if you come across any more . . ."

He closed the door behind her. *Idiot, idiot* he muttered under his breath. She would know perfectly well what a dust jacket was. It then occurred to him that Mrs Flaherty would still be constructing a cup of tea for his visitor and would have to be stopped. As he pushed the kitchen door, he suddenly remembered that the girl whom he had been momentarily entertaining might be said to have a connection to the said personage.

"Good Lord!" he exclaimed.

Mrs Flaherty jumped. The gold-rimmed tray tipped off the work top, cascading cups and saucers, milk jug, sugar bowl, biscuits, spoons, the whole caboodle onto the floor.

Words essaying comfort, and the rescue of pieces followed. It was not as bad as it might have been, but bad enough. The teapot had not yet been filled with scalding liquid, but the sugar bowl had suffered and was neatly split in two. He became alarmed when tears threatened, taking hold of her plump shoulders and directing her into the conservatory. He made her sit down, placing in her hand a clean handkerchief, ironed by herself on a past occasion.

His first instinct was to cover the mess with a tea towel, rather in the manner of covering a body on a battlefield. This, he quickly realised, would solve nothing. His mother was due home at any moment from her committee meeting. Mrs Flaherty could not be asked to help. He alone had to clear things up. The undamaged items he put back into their places in the cupboards, then was at a loss as to what to do with the spoiled sugar cubes. Finally he gathered them into a plastic bag, along with the broken pieces of the bowl. At the bin he hesitated. If they went into the kitchen bin, Mother would find them . Even in the wheelie bin outside they might not be safe.

He went upstairs to his own room. He took his summer sandals out of their box, placed them boxless back into the shoe cupboard, put the plastic bag inside the box and pushed the box under his bed. He got to his feet. Now to dispose of Mrs Flaherty.

She was exactly where he had put her.

"I have tidied the kitchen myself, and there is no reason for you to feel upset," he said.

"I'm that sorry, Mr Crawfurd," she began, "The good china . . ."

"The fault was entirely mine, Mrs Flaherty, and I want to hear no more about it."

"Mrs Crawfurd's goin' to . . ."

"No, she won't. And if she does, I will deal with it. You're not yourself, Mrs Flaherty. Perhaps you should have taken a few more days off. Miss Crosthwaite and I are both concerned about you and your worries."

He liked this linking of himself with Lesley. Besides, it was true, they were both concerned for her well-being. Each in their own way. He felt quite exhilarated.

"About me? She telt you about him?" Mrs Flaherty's mouth fell open.

"No, no," he said hastily, sensing danger in the shape of a long conversation, "not in any detail. None whatsoever. No, hold on to it meantime," he added as the handkerchief was proffered.

"It's very nearly your stopping hour," he hurried on, lifting his wrist to make it plain that he was looking at the watch. Often it was helpful to give Mrs Flaherty visual aids when saying something important, "and after the shock I gave you . . . I believe we could call it a day, don't you. If you want to do a little more next time . . ."

In his study, he opened the Whiting, but could not concentrate. What a strange afternoon he'd had. Poor Mrs Flaherty. Odd that she and not the minister should be the one worrying about her child's relationship. There was the difference in religion of course, but it seemed to him that he had himself misjudged the girl. A little moody perhaps, but well-intentioned and thoughtful.

He stood to look at himself in the oval mirror above the fireplace. He hardly thought himself middle aged. His hair was as thick as it had ever been. Each month the village barber commented on it approvingly. And his teeth were his own. The back ones, – he studied them now, his mouth wide – were well-filled but the front ones were still straight and serviceable. "Metal fatigue," his dentist had assured him. "That's all you have to fear now, Duncan. And the gums of course. Keep up the flossing. Are you seeing the hygienist regularly?"

He was, though he didn't enjoy it. The hygienist was a small, fierce woman, armed with various sharp metal instruments. *Raise your hand if it hurts.* He didn't dare. Were his reading glasses possibly a little old-fashioned? The optician had mentioned new frames when he'd last had an examination but this seemed to him simply another way of increasing the bill. Leaning forward, he examined his nose. It was unremarkable, inherited, like his vigorous hair, from his mother's side of the family. With an index finger he stroked each side of his moustache. The hairs were mixed, more white than brown really. He laid two fingers above his upper lip and wondered.

Gorgeous

The street lights came on as Harriet neared the bottom of the hill. She pulled her hood up, glad of the dusk, wondering if her face was still as red as it felt. Everything had seemed very clear cut when she set out. She'd looked up the telephone directory for the address, worked out where it was, and full of righteous indignation had marched to Mr Crawfurd's door. But before she could decide where to leave the book, on the shelf between the pot plants, or on the tiled porch floor, a woman in a blue checked housecoat had seen her through the bay window, nodded and pointed with her finger towards the door.

But the woman hadn't come to the door. It was Poor Duncan himself, with bits of his hair standing up at the back and his moustache drooping, a mug in his hand, and his shirt tail escaping out of his trousers beneath the maroon sweater. She should have said no to the tea, but it seemed rude. And then she'd felt so uncomfortable, she'd blurted out all that stuff about Mrs Robertson instead of explaining sensible, so badly did she want him to know that it was only Mrs Robertson and no-one else was so stupid. Meaning herself. He'd looked shocked, as if he'd forgotten all about it.

There was something at her heels. A dog, a thin, grey-brown mongrel with spindly legs and a long thin face, sniffing at her. She stopped.

"Go away," she said.

Its wet pink tongue hung loose from its mouth. It made to jump up with its paws at the front of her cardigan. She stepped back. It jumped again.

"He's just being pally!"

Some boys were coming up the hill. "He'll no' hurt you, Missus," one called.

It was trying now to wrap itself round her boot.

"Aye, he's just a wee bit randy. Kinda like yourself, Stevie."

"Call him off, please."

"Ooh, call him off please," one of them said, mocking her accent. Instead of doing anything to the dog, they gathered round. They were younger than her, but there were four of them. One pulled down her cardigan hood. "What's your name?" he said.

"Hey, Stevie."

They looked round. "Hey, Ryan," the one in the leather jacket said. "How's things?"

"You lot got nothin' better to do?"

They exchanged glances, and slowly began to walk away. One snapped his fingers and called roughly to the dog.

"You all right?" Ryan asked, his eyes on the departing boys.

She stared at the muddy streaks on her skirt. It would

need dry-cleaning. She should have taken Mum's advice and gone for black or navy.

"Come on," he told her, "I'll walk you to the main road."

"I'm not good with dogs," she told him.

"I got that. So, how many points have I earned so far?"

She looked up at him.

"For no' swearin'," he explained. "No' even at those eejits."

"Why did you say I wasn't real?"

He shrugged his shoulders.

"No, seriously. Just because I don't swear, it doesn't mean I'm an idiot."

"I never said you were an idiot. I don't think you're an idiot. You're.." He took a detour round the lamp post then fell into step beside her again. ". . . gorgeous."

"What?"

He didn't say anything, just looked at the river, a slight smile on his face. The arrogance! Though it was nice to know someone thought you were gorgeous. Of course, as she had often been reminded, being nice inside was more important. Was it really a compliment when it came from someone you weren't certain you liked all that much, who thought he could get away with anything just because he was hot.

"Cross by the road bridge," he suggested. "You'll be ok. There's plenty folk around. It's no' five o'clock yet. What's the matter?"

"Nothing."

"They're no' comin' back, if that's what you're worryin' about. What're you doing up this bit anyway?"

"I had to deliver a parcel," she said.

"To old man Crawfurd? I saw you come out his gate," he explained. "He's a weirdo. We used to play in the woods behind his house, and he'd come out and watch us with these massive binoculars. What was the parcel?"

She didn't want to talk about it.

"Thanks again," she said. "I'll be all right now."

She had gone a short distance when he called after her.

"Hey. You want to do somethin' sometime?"

She shook her head. "I'm studying. Exams."

"Well, if you get bored, give me a phone."

As if, she thought.

Sugar

As usual, Mrs McKinnon did not park her cheery red Clio directly outside the Crawfurd house. The road there was rather steep, necessitating a hill start which was not her favourite manoeuvre. Instead she stopped where the road flattened out a little further on which allowed Mrs Crawfurd to make her way back down to her own gate with the assistance of the handrail on the sandstone wall, a handrail which, as visitors to the house were always told, was of historical interest, having escaped Lord Beaverbrook's hunt for iron during the Second World War when railings in the poorer part of the village had been cut away.

They had just begun their discussion about the afternoon's high and low points when the doctor's wife glanced in the mirror and said, "Edith, is that someone coming out of your front gate?"

Mrs Crawfurd looked in the side mirror.

"Possibly. I don't know who it is."

It was a woman, quite a young woman, judging by the skirt which ended above the knees, and the black tights and boots. The hair, what one could see of it escaping from the hood of her cardigan, was blond. Unfortunately the woman didn't cross the road before she was out of sight, so there was no opportunity to see the face, but young or old, the tights and the short skirt propelled her immediately into the category of "hussy."

"Were you expecting someone?"

"I imagine it was another piece of mail gone astray," Mrs Crawfurd said calmly, "They've named one of the streets in the new estate Hawthorn Bank . . ."

"And you're Thorn Bank. I see. It must be very irritating for you. Of course, you can just readdress it, you know. That's what I do. Most people don't realise they can do that, of course. As long as you don't open it. Oh, I know what I was going to say," she became animated, "Tell me, did you think Helen was a little subdued today, or was it just my imagination?"

They exchanged views on this and other subjects for quite a time, then finally Mrs McKinnon took her diary from her handbag. "So, our next turn for doing teas isn't till the 14th. Are you sure you want to bake, Edith?"

"I have sponges and shortbread in the freezer," Mrs Crawfurd assured her. "Thank you again for the lift, Marjorie. Do drive carefully."

There was no flier on the porch floor, nor any letter or parcel on the hall table. Presumably the caller had. . . . But what *had* the caller done? No easy solution presented itself. Nor was there any sound in the house, which was surprising. There was a distinct smell of lavender polish, but surely the vacuum cleaner should be on. Mrs Flaherty did things in the same order each time; she always came in to the sound of the vacuum cleaner.

"Duncan!"

He appeared at the top of the stairs.

"Did Mrs Flaherty come?"

"Yes. Umm. I sent her home. Didn't think she was quite herself. I believe she's done most of it, though."

"I do hope so."

"I said she wasn't to worry. She could do a little extra next week."

Mrs Crawfurd half turned, then called back "Duncan, dear?"

His head reappeared.

"Did I miss anything? Any phone-calls?"

She could not bring herself to be more specific.

"No, nothing." he said. "How was your meeting?"

She didn't answer. The Discussion Group seemed neither here nor there.

She made her way through the house. Everything seemed normal in the sitting room: floor swept, the Doulton ladies dusted, fallen petals removed from the arrangement of apricot-coloured roses on the pedestal table. She preferred scented blooms but the colour was heart-warming in winter. Across the hallway, the cloakroom floor was still damp but everything was otherwise satisfactory. In the kitchen, the sink shone and the ironing pile was neatly stacked on the table. The board and the iron itself were back in the utility room, and the newly washed clothes lay folded in the wicker basket on top of the tumble drier, as always. Mrs Flaherty, though the most trustworthy of cleaning ladies, (and Edith had met some untrustworthy ones in earlier times; there was the disappearance of the fur lined gloves in Devonport for example) had never quite grasped the significance of "low" and "high" on the drier control panel, and she preferred to do this little task herself. Could the blonde have been some relative of Mrs Flaherty's?

She was walking back through the kitchen when something crunched beneath her shoe. Sugar? A sugar cube? But no-one took sugar. Not herself, not Duncan. And Mrs Flaherty would never drink anything other than hot water when she came.

The blue and white box of cubes was in its usual place in the cupboard, the tab folded into the slot. She dampened a piece of kitchen towel and gathered up the pieces of sugar to drop into the bin. But the bin had not been emptied. Presumably Mrs Flaherty had become unwell before she had time to attend to it.

Who then had been using sugar? Had Duncan been entertaining someone? Mrs Crawfurd, still in her coat and gloves, carried her curiosity upstairs. Duncan's bedroom door was firmly shut. She raised her hand to knock. Then lowered it. She would not pursue the matter. There was a small mystery here somewhere, but she would not enquire. All would eventually become known.

Jumble

Saturday morning began brightly, but clouds gathered gradually over the hills to the north. Duncan was not at peace. He watched his mother make her way round the various tables in the Church Hall, talking to this acquaintance and that. Before breakfast she had asked him to empty the kitchen bin, usually Mrs Flaherty's task. It was of course an entirely innocent request. There was no evidence in the bin. She might have noticed that the sugar bowl was missing. But if so, why had it not been mentioned?

Another small thing. Mother came to the Boys' Brigade Jumble sale every year, but it was unlike her to want him to bring her, since she had several friends who still drove. She also had made rather a point of his staying. He might see something he needed, she said, and besides, she felt she might get tired and want to come home. Winter, especially a wet winter such as this, seemed to drain her more than in the past.

Tea and coffee were being served in the downstairs basement hall, but she declared herself not quite ready, so he went down alone. It was a windowless room, with pale pink walls, decorated by pictures drawn by the Sunday School children and photographs of African orphans for whom they collected pennies. Duncan bought tea and a cheese scone, and stood beside a radiator with his back to the wall rather than sit at a table where he would have to make conversation. Lesley was sitting at the other side of the room. But she was with Miss Calvert. Still, there was a spare seat. Before he could decide, another woman sat down. Mrs McKinnon, underneath a very large black fur hat.

"Mind if I share your radiator, Duncan?"

He moved over a little. Dr McKinnon propped something against the wall at his feet, a heavy squarish object in a plastic bag.

"Did I tell you Marjorie has taken up Art? Arranging flowers isn't enough for her, she has to paint the bloody things. Costing me a fortune, all those squirrel brushes. And now we're collecting frames. I haven't a clue where she's going to put the finished articles. The girls won't take any more. If she offers you one, Duncan, say you'd like two and put them in the attic."

"Wouldn't she notice? Their absence, I mean? When she visits."

"I shouldn't think so."

"She would ask Mother."

"True. That stuff drinkable?" he indicated Duncan's mug of tea.

"Slightly stewed, I'm afraid."

"Always the same at these things. Ideal if you're in need of a diuretic. No, she doesn't miss much, your mother. She saw your visitor leaving the other day. I'll bet you didn't count on that."

"My visitor?"

"Blond lady with black leather boots."

"That was the Reverend Smith's daughter."

"Ah."

"I took a bundle to the Hospice Shop for Mother, then I bought a book and left it on the counter. She very kindly brought it round."

"I knew there would be some dull explanation. Marjorie watches too much television. I won't enlighten her just yet. The minister's daughter, eh. Well, the mother's genes won out there. They'd better get started building the moat and drawbridge round that one."

"Too late for that."

"Really?"

"She seems to have attracted Mrs Flaherty's son."

"Mary Flaherty's boy? Is he that age? I suppose he must be. Last time I saw him, I was suturing his head in my kitchen after he fell out of one of my trees."

"He's a very strange-looking individual."

"Probably what attracted her. The stranger the better. Katy and Lillian brought all sorts of peculiar boys home at that age. I kept well out of it, let Marjorie do the sleepless nights and tantrums."

"Where did you meet Mrs McKinnon?" Duncan asked.

"What? Oh, mutual friend introduced us at a birthday party. She had a car and I didn't, and she took me back to my digs. Why d'you ask?"

"I just wondered."

"Duncan, why don't you go on one of those cruises?" Dr McKinnon said, after a moment or two.

"I'm sorry?"

"Don't say you can't afford it. One of those National Trust cruises would suit you nicely. Scandinavia. Or the Antarctic. Lots of penguins. Even an albatross or two. Packed to the gunnels with single women and widows, those ships."

"I don't think Mother would . . ."

"No, she wouldn't. Go by yourself, Duncan. You might even buy yourself some new clothes. I believe I've seen that jacket on you for at least ten years. Oh, happy day, we seem to be done."

Mrs McKinnon had risen from her chair, and was waving to them.

"Remember what I told you about the paintings, won't you?" the Doctor said.

Disgruntled, Duncan watched him join the women. It was the word "dull" that had triggered it, the man's assumption that anything connected with him would be "dull," would have a "dull" explanation. It had stung more than a little. He dropped his chin, trying to see himself. What was wrong with his jacket?

"Well, whoever made these is not half the baker your mother was," Eunice Calvert announced, inspecting the inside of her scone. "I can't see more than three sultanas in total, and I suspect they were made with very cheap margarine."

Lesley felt the eyes of both women regarding her sadly.

"You must find the house very quiet, dear," Mrs McKinnon ventured as she pulled on her gloves.

Lesley smiled and nodded. Mrs McKinnon was such a gentle, well-meaning soul. She must, once upon a time, have been a very caring nurse.

"The thing is, you have to remember what she would have wanted." Eunice wiped her lips with a paper napkin, a Sunday School Christmas leftover, Teddy Bears decorated in holly leaves and red berries. "You have to give thanks for all the happy memories, Lesley, and go forward into the rest of your life."

"But it's early days yet, Eunice," Mrs McKinnon pleaded.

"Of course it is. I'm not suggesting it isn't. But the fact remains that we all have to consider how we . . ."

"How are we all, ladies?" Dr McKinnon beamed down at them. "Have you made some exciting find? Not more wool, Eunice." He poked at the plastic bag hung on the back of her chair.

"My Primary Sevens enjoy learning to knit, even the boys. Hardly any of their mothers know how. "

"I have drawers full. I should give you some," Lesley said.

"Oh, you'll use it up yourself," Eunice said.

"Actually I hate knitting."

She had silenced them. Eunice was baffled. Mrs McKinnon looked stricken.

"Perhaps painting would . . ." the latter began.

"Behave yourself, Marjory," Dr McKinnon said. "Lesley

needs less clutter, not more. If this continues," he hefted his parcel higher, "we'll have to move to a larger house."

When they were out of hearing Miss Calvert said, "He's such a very big man, don't you think? Most men shrink as they get older but he seems to get bigger somehow."

Lesley felt irritated. What did the woman want? A world populated by men under five feet four?

"Now, as I was saying . . ."

Lesley interrupted, "Forgive me, Eunice. I really must have a word with one or two people. Please don't wait for me. I have my umbrella."

She carried her cup and saucer over to the kitchen hatch. There was no-one serving, so she put them beside some others, and turned round, right into Duncan's Barbour jacket.

They both apologised, then Duncan said, "Did you find something on the stalls?"

"Just a book."

"Something interesting?"

She slid the small volume out of its bag. A Ladybird book. *The Story of Joseph.*

"A bit ridiculous at my age," she said. "I had this as a child, but it got warped after I dropped it in the bath." She thought he might smile at this but he didn't.

"You know, some Ladybird books are very valuable," he said, as they moved to let two small girls dance past. "The early editions, especially in good condition. And it's important to have the dust wrapper."

How earnest he always was. He was an early edition himself, complete with dust wrapper, pages unmarked.

"I think there's a whole box of these in our roof space," she said.

"Really?" He grew more earnest. "You should search the web sometime and check them. Not that you haven't got plenty of other . . ."

"You've shaved your moustache."

He cleared his throat. "Ah. Yes. Is it all right?"

"It looks fine. What made you decide . . ."

"I did it last night." He coughed again. "Actually, you're the only person who's noticed, apart from Mother. That is, she looked at the space where it had been," he tapped his upper lip, "but she didn't comment. I suspect she doesn't approve. I must confess, the wind felt a little cold this morning," he smiled shyly at his own joke. "Probably the wrong time of year to do it."

"Well, in summer you'd be left with a strip of white skin, and the rest of your face tanned."

"Right. Hadn't thought of that one. I thought more people might notice," he added.

But no-one looks at you, she thought, feeling a little shiver of sadness. Faithful Duncan, always ready to be of use and never appreciated.

"Well, if you want my opinion, I think you look much better without it."

"Really?"

"Yes."

It was true. Without the moustache, his face was . . . softer?

"No going back then. Right. I should perhaps check whether she's ready to depart."

Lesley walked with him towards the stairs. Just before they reached the door into the main hall she said, "Duncan."

"Yes?"

"What you were saying, about the Ladybird books. I don't have a computer. Could I look on yours sometime?"

"Of course. Whenever you like."

The done deed

Walter opened the back of the van and looked with satisfaction at his new fish tanks. He laid hold of the nearest one,
bending his knees to avoid straining the back, a life-long
habit he had always tried to pass on to his apprentices, then
hesitated. Mouth pursed, he closed the van doors and
turned the key.

When he went through the gate into the back garden, he
saw Lesley on the other side of the hedge, taking sheets
down from the washing line.

"Not a bad drying day," he called. She waved back. How
awfully like her mother she looked, with that scarf tied
round her head. The sheets would be more frozen than dry.
A tumble drier was what she needed. Ruby never hung
clothes out between December and the end of February,
except for tea towels and the like.

He had a quick look at the goldfish then continued up the
long path towards the back door.

"Mr Robertson."

He turned. She had left the clothes line and was just
visible across the hedge.

"I've been thinking about double glazing. You mentioned
you knew someone reliable . . ."

He said he would find the man's card and slip it through her letter box, entering his own kitchen with a smile on his face, glad that she was doing something to benefit herself, and glad too that he had been the one to give the good advice in the first place.

"That was a long day, dear," Ruby said, not looking up. She was chopping carrots. He could smell onions frying. What she meant was, what have you been doing all day.

"Oh, I just had a wee wander around the town while I was in."

He had gone into the city with the gift voucher Walter Junior had sent for Christmas. It had taken him five minutes in the store to be certain there was nothing he particularly liked. The next hours had been happily occupied in collecting the fish tanks, discussing his ideas with the proprietor of the Tropical Section, and reading his newly purchased magazine in the cafe nearby.

"Did you have some lunch?"

"I had a cup of tea." And a slice of something called Mississippi Mud Pie.

"And did you get a new jumper?"

"There was nothing I fancied. That smells good, dear"

"Lentil and carrot soup," she said, "and there's beef olives."

" Lovely. Home made? Not the ones from the butcher's?"

"Of course not," she said. "How could there be nothing

you liked, Walter? I saw lovely cardigans before Christmas. That old green one's not fit to be worn in public. "

Tropical Freshwater. He unrolled the magazine and fingered the glossy cover.

"I don't know how they keep finding new things to say every month," Ruby said. "Would you like me to make some croutons?"

He wondered what Lesley was having for tea. She seemed to be getting thinner and thinner.

"Are we having Lesley in sometime?" he said.

Ruby stopped chopping, knife in mid-air. "What for?"

"You said you thought we should have her over for tea, now that she's on her own."

"She doesn't seem to be on her own very much, if you ask me."

Walter hung up his jacket, and, glancing back to see that he was not observed, went through to young Walter's bedroom.

He sat down on the bedside chair. In his mind's eye he cleared the room, except for the desk and the bookshelves. They could stay. The breeding tanks would sit against the side wall away from direct sunlight and the outside wall of the house. He had settled on Guppies after much deep thought. A few top quality fish would suit him. They were hardy little fish, but high stocking levels would mean more frequent water changes, and he could not risk leaving this to Ruby. The filtration was crucial.

First of course he had to overcome Ruby's resistance. The

best thing might be to confront her with a "done deed" as the Americans put it. He'd order a skip and get a couple of the lads to empty the room. She'd make a fuss, there might even be a tear or two, but it wouldn't last long and she'd be on to something else soon enough.

Guppies

"I've jumped the gun a bit," Walter explained.

"How big are they exactly?" Lesley asked.

"Not very big, "he told her. "The big one holds about forty five litres."

"But they would be empty."

"Oh yes, of course. I was going to put them under the roof of the garage, but it's not good for them to be in such a cold place, you see. Even with the wee heater on. And it wouldn't be for long. I just need to find the right moment. I'm sorry. I shouldn't have asked you."

"No, it's all right," she said. Though it wasn't really. "Would the front sitting room do? I haven't got central heating, but the storage heaters keep it reasonably warm, and it gets any sun that's going."

She hung up the phone and turned to her visitor. He was looking properly ministerial today, in a dark suit and clerical collar.

"My next door neighbour," she explained coming back to her chair. "He's bought himself new tanks for breeding guppies and he needs to store them somewhere for a few days until he breaks the news to his wife."

"I haven't heard that one before. Very odd,"

"Oh, this village has more than its share of odd people. Hardly anyone's normal."

He smiled, "Apart from you and me."

He seemed not to realize she was being serious. Mother had blamed the many eccentricities and peculiarities on inbreeding; cousins intermarrying year by year in small hamlets where, without effort or ambition, sons followed fathers into a trade, farming or the brickmaking works. There was just enough employment, Mother said. Less would have driven them out, more would have brought new people in.

Mother always said. The words took shape in her head. No, she told herself. Mother had no voice now. Her opinions, right or wrong, didn't count. *Don't let her bloody well ruin the rest of your life.*

The minister couldn't read her mind, but he was watching her, letting her choose what to say, where to go. Waiting for her to unburden her secrets? Well, he was in for a disappointment. That wasn't why she'd phoned him. It had been her intention merely to outline Mrs Flaherty's problem and ask for an answer. But the daughter had answered the phone. He was on his mobile. He asked, via the daughter if he might call round on his way elsewhere. He had not taken off his coat, signalling that he did not intend to stay long. She in return had not offered to make tea.

"I wanted to speak to you about someone I know," she began briskly, "not a church member, but someone I feel obliged to, if that makes sense. She's having quite serious problems. She doesn't want to ask anyone for help. I think she needs to, but I don't know who to speak to, or how to go about it."

In case he still imagined she was talking about herself, she added, "This person has a family, grown up children, so she isn't on her own, but she says she can't tell them what's happening. She's very protective of them."

Tooprotective. There was a difference in taking care of your children and becoming a doormat for all and sundry. Especially when the children earned more than Mary herself did.

"And you feel you can't break this confidence and tell them. What's happening exactly?"

'Very little' was the true answer. Mrs Flaherty was a circuitous story teller, and Lesley had had to listen hard to work out what exactly she was afraid of. It was more a case of what might happen.

"She was separated from her husband a long time ago. Separated rather than divorced. He abused her rather badly, and was rough with the children, so she threw him out, with the help of her parents, who were still alive at that point. She moved here with the children. Now he seems to have reappeared, and wants back into the family."

"And she doesn't want him back?"

"She's terrified of him."

"And the police won't be interested, since he hasn't done anything. Or has he?"

"So far all he's done is make phone calls. He's told her he's a changed man."

"It can happen. Presumably he wasn't abusive when they first met."

"I don't really know. She said he was the best-looking boy in the village, and everyone knew he got violent when he drank, except her. All her friends knew. And afterwards she said to them, 'why did none of you tell me?'"

"Why didn't they?"

"They told her they thought marriage might change him."

"Ah. The love of a good woman," he said, with a deep sigh. "Well, love just doesn't cut it all of the time. I take it her parents are dead?"

"The mother is. The father's in a care home somewhere."

"And there's no male figure who can intervene in any way? No brother or uncle . . ."

"I don't think so. I suggested her priest and she was horrified. She would be very upset if she knew I was talking to you."

The minister folded his arms behind his head and stared at the ceiling, as if admiring the plaster work. She was fond of it herself. And the fireplace was handsome, as Mr Robertson had said. But the rest of all these too-large, unrelentingly solid family heirlooms that left so little space in which to move: the bookcase full of books unread for decades, the pink-flowering cacti that only flowered for a fortnight and looked so depressed for the other fifty weeks of the year . . .

"Did you know," the minister said suddenly, "that guppies were named after a clergyman in Trinidad?"

It took her a moment to remember that she was the one who had mentioned them.

"The Reverend Robert John Lechmore Guppy. What a leisurely life he must have had, the dear man." He looked up at the clock, and got to his feet. "I'm sorry. I'm afraid I'm full of useless information. We play a lot of Scrabble. You don't need an answer from me right now, do you? For your friend? Give me a day or two."

She closed the door behind him with a feeling of relief. He hadn't once tried to turn the conversation round to her situation. "You're looking better," he'd said when she opened the door. She glimpsed herself in the hall mirror. Perhaps he'd meant it. The woman with the diamond in her nose had actually cut her hair very nicely. She might ask for her again. But not the manicure. She'd bought nail polish removal pads on the way home, unable to think straight until her fingers looked like her own again.

Intarsia

Duncan felt that fate was blessing him when his mother mentioned that it was her turn to host the Knitting Circle. It was still called the Knitting Circle, though few of the ladies knitted any more. The exchange of news was reason enough to keep attending. Supper was never lavish. The hostess was expected to provide tea and biscuits and there was a rota for the bringing of a plain iced sponge. Over the years Duncan had overheard mysterious words like *intarsia* and *self striping* and *double front cross*, but his mother never attempted anything complex now. She was content to make crochet squares that someone else sewed into blankets destined for Peru. Those ladies with grandchildren made small pastel-coloured items. It was a monthly ritual that seemed to gain just enough new members to compensate for the loss of others.

If Mother had been going out to the group, there would still have been problems. She might change her mind, there might be snow, her knee or her neuralgia might play up. Hosting the Circle, however, was a matter of honour and duty. She would be preoccupied with her own visitors, and although winter vomiting was doing its rounds and might keep some away, it was most unlikely that everyone would cancel.

What pleased him most was that there was no need to lie. He'd failed to mention that Lesley was coming, but he hadn't lied. And now, soon, when it was too late for Mother to change anything, when her first fellow knitters were beginning to arrive, Lesley would turn the corner, and her brave little boots would ascend the hill towards him. As soon as he saw her, he would go and announce diffidently that she was about to arrive.

There was a fluttery sensation inside his chest. That very morning, Mrs Fleming had asked if he was doing anything interesting at the weekend.

"A friend's coming over for coffee tonight," he'd said, wondering how much he might say, if she asked what for, or who.

She had not asked.

From his position on the upstairs landing, he could see everyone before they reached the house. It was an easy matter to reach the door just as Lesley pressed the bell.

"Did I say something wrong?" They were in his study.

"Wrong?"

"Your mother looked . . ."

"Flustered?" he suggested.

"I was going to say surprised. "

The correct word for Mother's expression was "astonished", so astonished that she had gone back into the lounge, completely forgetting to help Lesley off with her coat. It was her good one, he saw, with the velvet band round the edges of the collar, not the brown one she wore every day.

"Here, let me take . . ." He hesitated. If he went back to the hall with her coat, he might be caught and questioned. "Let me put it here." "Here" was a row of small hooks on the back of the door where he kept his caps. He put one cap on top of another to clear a hook.

No woman, except for his mother, and Mrs Flaherty who was permitted to vacuum the carpet and dust around objects without moving them, had ever been in his study. What would Lesley think of it, with its shelves of magazines and books, paintings inherited from his grandfather and great grandfather, the line of boxed Dinky cars that stretched along the top of the fireplace. Suddenly everything looked commonplace to him, even the Melville original.

Lesley had seated herself in the leather recliner.

"If you push that button, you can lie back," he told her. "That is, if you were wanting to make it recline. Not that you look tired. I mean, you're looking well. Very trim. Not that you were needing to lose weight . . ."

"Yes, I was. And I still do. Mother went on cooking for three after father died and I ate for two."

He was burbling on like an idiot. And *trim*? *Trim*? Where had that rusted relic of a word sprung from? He'd never used it in his life. It was a word for a vintage car, or a gent's haircut . . .

"I made a list of the books." She took a sheet of paper from her handbag.

He switched on the computer, the word "trim" still spinning in his brain. His screen saver was a photograph of his favourite bird, a robin. Oddly, there were two in the garden this week, both males, and furthermore they seemed to be ignoring one another, which was strange. Robins were so territorial . . .

"Here we are," he said.

He placed the list on the desk and Lesley stood behind him. The most valuable was *The Story of the Motor Car*, for sale at £15. None of the others, including *Sleeping Beauty* and *The Ugly Duckling*, was worth more than five pounds.

"I'm sorry," Duncan said, swivelling round. "I shouldn't have raised your hopes."

"No, that was fun," she said, moving back to her chair. "I don't mind if they're not worth anything. Some of those were Mother's and some were Sunday School Attendance prizes. I don't think I'd like to sell them anyway. I used to read them over and over, probably because the illustrations were so good. *Joseph* was always my favourite."

"The one you bought at the Jumble Sale."

He did a quick search. "How much did it cost you?"

"Ten pence."

"A bargain. There's one here for 99p."

"He looked so sad, I think that was it. I was furious when his brothers put him into the pit and sold him."

"I don't think I won any prizes. I must have missed too many Sundays."

"You won the writing prize in Primary Seven."

"So I did," he said, remembering. A Parker pen. It was probably still in a drawer somewhere. Mottled green, with a silver clip. He hadn't been allowed to use it at the time.

"You know, Duncan, I always wondered why you didn't learn the piano. You have such long fingers. Wasn't there a piano in the back sitting room?"

"It made too much noise," he said, trying not to look at his hands. "And it was a very old piano. I suppose if I'd shown any proficiency, they would have let me continue."

"But you love music, Duncan."

"I expect the world has been spared another dreadful amateur," he put on a smile. "Would you like some now?"

She nodded. "You choose something."

Beethoven. Brendel. Not the *Appassionata*. He settled on The Late Piano Sonatas, Opus 110.

Why *had* he stopped? It couldn't have been his decision. Of course he had been deported to boarding school around the same time. But some of the boys had music lessons. Why hadn't he?

"Actually," he said, "I do feel strongly about it. I wish I hadn't stopped. Which is rather a waste of emotional energy."

"Take lessons," she said.

"What?"

"Take lessons. Lots of people do. I would, if I wanted to."

As the first notes of No. 31 trickled gently into the room, he pictured his "long fingers" on piano keys. Of course he would first have to buy a piano. And where to find a teacher? Perhaps the people on the Music floor would know. Liszt would never be within his grasp, but some Mozart perhaps? His mind drifted to Austria and the Rheinland and all the music festivals advertised in his monthly BBC Music magazine. And cruises where experts gave lectures.

"Lesley, what do you think of cruises?" he asked.

She looked puzzled.

"Cruises. Holidays. On the crest of the wave, as it were."

He'd thought about them on and off since the day of the Jumble Sale, picturing himself in a deck chair, waiting for Italy to materialize out of the mist.

"Your mother might hate it. It's an awful lot of money to spend if you don't like the people you meet. And she doesn't eat much either. People who go on cruises always say the food is the best part. And then there's those dreadful bugs that go round the whole ship."

She had neatly summed up what he thought himself. These were exactly the reasons his mother would have given for saying no.

"On the other hand, it might be restful. I can understand why some people like them. You see different places, you have lots of people looking after you, even a doctor if you're sick, and you can do as much or as little as you want. And if you like food, there's plenty of choice, I suppose."

He felt a little sad without quite knowing why. Perhaps he'd hoped for more enthusiasm. More commitment, one way or the other.

"On that note, shall we have some supper?" he said, "Coffee or tea? Or something cold?"

"Tea, please. Just milk. No sugar."

"I broke a sugar bowl last week," he confided, "one of the good ones. I haven't mentioned it to Mother yet."

"Why not?"

"Isn't it obvious?"

Lesley let out a laugh. Or was it a giggle?

"This is serious," he told her, wishing he hadn't broached the subject.

"Not that serious, Duncan."

"No, really. She's had the set for years. I think it may have been a wedding present."

"Duncan, you're an idiot. You could probably find a replacement in ten minutes on Ebay."

"You told me you didn't have a computer," he said.

"I don't, but I hear the staff talking about the internet and Ebay all the time. What make of china is it?"

"I don't know. Blue and white, with handles. And in my defence, to be strictly truthful, it was Mrs Flaherty who broke it."

"Oh dear. Poor Mary."

"Yes. On top of everything else." He pictured again the dreadful son with his black coat dragging on the ground and his pointed shoes.

"I haven't been much help, I'm sorry to say. Going to the police seems a bit extreme, but it might come to that, I suppose, if Johnny doesn't go away."

"I thought his name was Ryan."

"No, that's the son. Her husband is Johnny."

Brendel was approaching the quiet passage with its wonderful descending notes.

"Why are we discussing the Flaherty family?" he said at last.

She looked up. "Because we're concerned. I hate gossip as much as you do. But how long has Mary Flaherty been part of our lives? I don't believe this counts as gossip, Duncan. The only person I've spoken to is Mr Smith and I didn't say who I meant. I'm glad she spoke to you," she went on. "I think she confided in me by accident, really. I was no use to her. It was just days after the funeral."

Brendel's magic was drawing him away. He tried to concentrate.

"And the boy, Ryan . . ."

"Oh, she hasn't told him or the daughters. I think she's afraid he would want to take the father on. He's very moody. I don't know. We see some people every day, and we don't see them at all. Not as real people. I wonder if it's because we just don't want to."

Purely by chance these last words sounded as the final crescendo gave way to silence. For a moment it seemed to him that the entire audience was waiting for him to reply.

After a while Lesley asked, "Do you want to look for a sugar bowl? All we need is the maker's name and the pattern."

"How do we find that?"

"Oh, Duncan. Go and look," she told him.

He paused with one hand on the half-opened door.

"On the bottom of a plate," she said. "Or a cup. Or a saucer. "

"That's what I thought."

He liked to see her smile. She was so sensible. And sympathetic, although he wasn't sure he liked the thought of her being involved with Mrs Flaherty and her problems. Whatever those were, exactly. It wasn't a matter of not caring. Anyway, women were better at that kind of thing. Take piano lessons, she said, as if it were the most natural thing in the world for a man his age to be queuing up beside five year olds. It would never happen, but it was kind of her to think it could. She'd called him an idiot. He didn't mind being called an idiot, not when it was said that way. And he'd made her smile. It was a long time since he'd seen her smile.

His mother was standing in the kitchen.

"We're wondering whether you and Lesley might like to join us for supper," she said.

How long had she been away from the sitting room? Had she stood in the hall outside his study, trying to listen in?

"I'll mention it," he lied.

She went back towards the lounge.

He made a mug of tea, and poured mineral water into a glass for himself. He studied the underside of a dessert plate. Of course Mother wouldn't have tried to eavesdrop, he rebuked himself. And yet, this taking orders from Lesley, being told by her to do something and being able to, made him feel . . . How did he feel? Reflected in the Gaggia's polished surface, his face looked squat and untrustworthy. It was the face of a man who could tell lies.

It was a small conspiracy. He did not feel in the least guilty. He felt cheerful. It was the only word he could come up with. Yes, cheerful.

"There is absolutely no reason why you cannot have a perfectly healthy tank of these stunningly coloured fish". Derek Jordan, Practical Fishkeeping.

Sadly, there was, and it was Ruby.

Walter watched his TV programme without seeing. Deception was not really his forte. He would have fared badly as a spy, or a member of the resistance in enemy-occupied territory. It was one thing to eat Dairy Milk en route to work, quite another to do what he was about to do.

He could hear Ruby moving about in the kitchen, making their suppertime cup of tea. Later she would go upstairs and run her bath. Twenty minutes with *My Weekly* in the hot water would follow. Walter Junior had got into the habit of sending expensive oil each Christmas. This year it was something to do with oranges, Mandarin Muse or some such name. The smell was not unpleasant: it drifted through the house each evening, and the association of the gift and the giver gave Ruby some comfort. He looked towards the kitchen. She'd driven him to it, really. Driven him into Lesley's arms, you might say.

He had given her every chance on that earlier night. He'd begun, as usual, by complimenting her cooking.

"Lovely soup, Ruby, is there something different in it?"

"It's organic celery," she said. "I told you the organic tastes better."

Harmless, these little compliments each night. His own father had done it all his married life. "A small price to pay, son." The thought that he might now be prevented from getting his heart's desire in spite of all such payments over the years was almost unbearable.

Would it have been different if they'd met and married earlier, or if Ruby had been younger than him instead of the other way round? More children might have helped. From time to time Ruby had asked him to speak to Walter Junior, to tell him that a personal visit was in order, instead of phone calls and the odd card from some exotic holiday, but he'd said no. They couldn't force him, Walter said wisely. The boy had to live his own life. At work he would now and then mention how Ruby seemed to have forgotten how much the boy's erratic comings and goings had disrupted their life, how his appeals for money had been such a drain on the budget, how he'd refused to even consider working in the family firm, and how often he, Walter Senior, had had to ferry the boy and his pals home when they couldn't get a taxi. Every one of the fathers agreed with him. They loved their sons, dearly, but life was a lot easier without them on the premises.

"Ruby, I think it's time we cleared out the back bedroom," he'd begun, "We'll get a nice new wallpaper. New curtains."

"Why?"

"We're not using it. I don't know how long that paper . . ."

"It's Walter's room."

"He's got three rooms of his own in Croydon. And when," (just in the nick of time he changed "if" to "when") "when he comes back for a visit, we've got the fold down settee in the front room."

Now, watching her put the cups and the plate of biscuits on the low table in front of him he reproached himself. Any other man would have grasped the nettle, produced a large box of Kleenex, and instructed his wife to phone the Salvation Army or whoever else uplifted unwanted furniture.

Once he was sure Ruby was in the bath, he called upstairs to say he was going for fuel. "Will you be all right, love? I'll lock the door when I go out."

He switched on the back porch light. As if in reply, Lesley's back door opened. Walter waved. Lesley nodded.

He looked back from the foot of the garden, but the Venetian blinds were down and closed at the bathroom window, small lines of light escaping at the bottom and sides.

Lesley's back gate was unlocked as promised. He put on his work gloves, manoeuvered the first tank from the back of the van onto the trolley and following the strong beam of

Lesley's torch, walked up the path. It had whin chips, not slabs like theirs. His shoes seemed to crunch more loudly with each step.

She had helpfully moved her back-room furniture closer to the fireplace wall and laid a strip of sheeting all the way to her front room. Painter's sheeting it was, judging by the dried-in stains. Not that anything had been painted recently, from what he could see. It wasn't dirty, just old. In his opinion, and he'd seen a lot of houses, there was 'lovely old' and there was 'ugly old.' This house was a mixture of both. And there was far too much in it. He'd grown up in a cluttered house and been glad to get out of it.

Ruby liked a good clear out each spring. Sometimes he rescued a few things when her back was turned, but on the whole he felt she was right. He looked round him at the anaglypta. A bit of pressure on those whorls and he could have picked it off with his thumb nail.

Another trip to the van, and the second tank was placed safely in its new home, beside its fellow on the sheeted carpet. Nice cornice though – he looked at the ceiling – quality plasterwork. If Ruby saw that, she'd want something similar.

"Just as well I didn't get the filters and fluorescents," he said. "I hadn't decided on the best ones." He peered through the plastic wrap once more. Nothing had been damaged.

"I can't return them, you see. It's the nature of buying fish tanks in the sales. "

"I've been thinking about your difficulty," Lesley said. "Would it help if you told your son all about this, and he told Mrs Robertson he was well and truly settled in London? You might have him suggest you go there for a visit. Wouldn't that help?"

Walter scratched the back of his neck. "It might."

It might not, he thought. Common sense was not always in plentiful supply where Ruby was concerned.

"You could stay nearby," Lesley suggested. "You wouldn't have to stay with him. That might be easier."

It touched him that she had thought all this through.

"She likes to get her own way, you see," he said. "No reason why not, as a rule."

"But if she knew how much you wanted this . . ." Lesley patted the rumpled plastic on the edge of the nearest tank.

"People think it's easy, breeding guppies, but it's not. You need to get the water quality just right. It's like, you have to keep them happy, but not too happy. I mean, if you overfeed them, they get constipation, just like us . . ."

She was looking at her watch. He remembered that he was on borrowed time.

He crunched down the dark path with a heart less troubled. It was a pity they'd not become better acquainted with Lesley years ago. She was quite different from the mother. There was more to her than met the eye, so to speak. Her encouragement, her suggestion about speaking to Walter Junior, her acceptance of his dream as something normal, all served to make him feel that what he wanted so desperately was possible.

It was a clear night. To the left of his roof, Orion's belt twinkled in the blackness. The only other constellation he knew was the Plough. He turned and there it reassuringly was, just where it ought to be.

This is the day the Lord has made. Let us rejoice and be glad in it.

It was hard to find much to rejoice about. In the moment before full wakefulness, his right arm had reached towards where his wife's warm, naked back was not. After breakfast he drove a silent Harriet to the station in the next village, his expressed hopes that the Geography exam would go well being met with a grimace.

His next task was to take Morning Assembly at the Primary school. For some reason it went well. He was forced to conclude that Miss Calvert, though lacking in subtlety, had a kind heart. He'd felt himself in danger of being quenched in the early weeks and months, but he had worked hard, prayed much, and, judging by the fact that chocolate biscuits were offered for the first time with his customary cup of tea, she seemed to be warming to him at last.

"Was that all right this morning?" he asked.

She nodded. "I was happy to hear you include the Royal Family in your prayer."

"I was happy to include them," he said, keeping his face solemn.

"Thank you."

Was that the key to acceptability? He'd assumed it was some deep-seated flaw in him she objected to. How strange people were. With all her enthusiasm for foreign travel, he'd never have guessed she was such a fervent Royalist.

"Will you be replacing the gerbils? I heard there were many tears yesterday."

"I suppose we must. Mrs Gibson diverted the children by suggesting they chose new names, which was rather unfortunate."

He nodded sympathetically. "Well, that tea was most welcome." He got to his feet.

"There was something I wanted to mention," she said, as they walked to the front door. "I'm hoping it's not going to turn into a problem. Some of the children have been chattering about a man hanging about, offering sweeties. You haven't heard anything?"

"No. Nothing at all. "

"We get these rumours every so often. When parents call us, we pay much more attention, of course. The children would believe you if you showed them a tinfoil hat and told them Martians had landed in the playground." She pushed a button to release the outer door. "We're not sending notes home yet. But naturally we're keeping our eyes open."

"I'll let you know if I hear anything," he said, zipping his jacket higher against the cold. "I tend not to ask questions when this kind of thing happens, in case it fuels the fire, but I'll call you if anything comes up."

The High School stood across the playground, behind a

tall wire fence. Just in time he stopped himself from saying how hard it must be for Lesley, being on her own. But of course she and Miss Calvert were very different women.

"Have you spoken to Miss Crosthwaite recently? Is she back at work yet, do you know?"

"I'm sure she's fine," Miss Calvert said. "She's her mother's daughter."

"I never met her mother."

Mrs Crosthwaite had withdrawn her lines from the church years before, as had Lesley, but if Miss Calvert didn't know, it wasn't his business to tell her. When Lesley had asked him to conduct the funeral, he'd felt obliged to say yes.

"She was a fine hard-working woman. She married late and Mr Crosthwaite was much older, so she had all the work of bringing up Lesley when he died. She chaired the Friendship Club committee for twenty eight years. "

"Yes," he said, remembering that he himself had mentioned the fact at the funeral. He waited for some reference to fruit scones, for which the woman had been famed, but enough had apparently been said.

Carrot cake

He had arranged to meet Lesley in The Sunflower. He assumed she would feel comfortable there. The Dirty Duck public house was not her style. If Jean had been at home, he would have suggested she do the counselling. She was far better at it than he was.

He arrived first. He was wearing his clerical collar so that all and sundry would know this was the minister meeting a member of the congregation. One of the lecturers at Divinity College had wanted to make all the male students swear never to be alone with a woman not their wife in a room with the door shut. Some laughed, a few booed, but most had taken it to heart.

The front of the place offered a mixture of gifts and cards. He studied the nick-knacks on sale. There was some jewellery Jean might like. He was doing his best, but his misery at her absence was getting worse as he scored off the days.

The tearoom had originally been a house. The old fireplace remained, with a proper coal fire burning. The Van Gogh reproduction hung above. There was something mildly disconcerting about a vase of sunflowers above a coal fire. Each table had a small white vase with three fake miniature sunflower heads stuck in it. The plastic covers were white with a pattern of bunches of pale green grapes. He recalled a sunny vineyard they'd visited near Sirmione, their last holiday before Kerr arrived. Picking some grapes when the guide wasn't looking, he'd been momentarily shocked to find them warm. All he'd known were grapes cold from a supermarket shelf, or at room temperature in a bowl on the sideboard. It had been a small but profound epiphany, as his tongue gently rolled the warm illicit fruit.

Lesley was on time and apologized for being late. She had come from work. She was doing two and a half days. One of the other women wanted a job share and she hoped this might become permanent.

The waitress, still in her teens, with a shiny multi-coloured brace on her upper teeth, suggested carrot cake with their coffee. The carrot cake was always popular. Lesley agreed to share one. When the girl brought it to them she said, "Will there be anything else, Father?"

"And I thought I was universally known," he said, when she was out of earshot. "Isn't it strange how even in a place this size we live in separate worlds with different information in our heads?" He touched the small beads of clear acrylic on the sunflower leaves and petals to confirm that they were artificial. "Years ago when my wife was still teaching, she told me she'd had to explain to some of her pupils that Sir Winston Churchill was not a member of the royal family. And these were teenagers, not little ones." He put half of the cake onto the spare plate and pushed it over to her.

"They don't read anymore," she said.

"That's true. Although I think it's more than that. I think it's getting harder for all of us to concentrate. We don't retain anything. Everything whizzes past, without making a dent. If my sermon lasts more than twenty minutes, I'm in deep trouble."

In his first month the Session Clerk had taken him aside for a quiet word. Could he perhaps shorten the sermon? "You see, Minister, quite a lot of the older folks are incontinent," he'd whispered. He had responded, cunningly he thought, by missing out a hymn and changing the offering from the middle of the service to the end as folks were leaving.

"Speaking of trouble," he went on, "the last time we met we were talking about your friend." He was still not sure if the friend existed, or if the trouble was Lesley's own. "I spoke to one of the policemen in the congregation. The first thing she must do is have the telephone company interrupt her calls. This is the number she should ring," he detached a leaf of paper from his Filofax. "Then she has to see a solicitor."

He explained as simply as he could about Non-Harassment Orders, and interdicts. And how there was a criminal route and a civil route, but getting a solicitor was by far the best thing when there hadn't been actual violence. He had been wrong about the police, he told her.

"She needs to go to them. They might go and visit the husband, and that might be enough to stop him. The word 'harassment' seems to take in almost anything that makes someone frightened."

"Even if he hasn't broken the law?"

"So it seems. You said he abused her in the past. What has he been doing all these years he's been away?"

"I don't know." She folded the page in half and put it in her handbag.

"Lesley, the one other thing I wanted to say was, I'm not sure you ought to get too involved in this."

"Why not?"

The short answer? She was female, single and vulnerable. He hated short answers. Too often they led you into conversations where you felt you were moving from one stepping stone to another, except that the stones were floating in the air. He was learning, or trying to learn, not to guess where the heart of a problem lay when the person involved wasn't ready to confide. In his previous life he'd pounced on problems shaking them by the neck till they gave up, but people were very different from pipelines. It was far from easy. "Be still and know that I am God." was his least favourite Bible verse.

"I know that you want to help this friend of yours," he began, "but by listening to her you've probably helped already, more than you realise."

She didn't look convinced. He took a little step backwards. Keep it light, he told himself. Once upon a time the clerical collar had meant something, had signalled the wearer's trustworthiness. Not any more. He'd been told that lawyers were the only professionals trusted, ministers and doctors were out. But that had been at least ten years ago. Who was trusted now?

"I've heard it said that being bereaved is like walking on a leg that's been broken. You might feel it's mended, but too much pressure too soon, and you're back to square one. Sometimes we need to be kind to ourselves," he added. "Fair enough?"

She nodded.

When they parted outside the tearoom, he was left with the feeling that he might have helped the mystery friend, but not her. She'd listened, but she hadn't thanked him. Which was fine. He didn't need thanks. Were the friend's problems a useful distraction? Whatever she was feeling about her own situation, he wasn't going to get a glimpse of it here. She hinted at so much before the funeral: old hurts, resentments, opportunities not taken. He had hoped to talk about the need to forgive and be forgiven. About love, and the impossibility of getting it from the dead. He was worried that this sad, loveless woman would now waste the rest of her life trying to gain her mother's approval.

Kids

Monday afternoons were not peak times in the Sports Centre. Dr Gordon glanced at the two middle aged women and the elderly man reading a newspaper. None of them was a patient. Radio One was playing in the background, but not too loudly, the smell of toasted sandwiches hung in the air, but not too strongly, and the immense TV, perpetually tuned to Sky Sports, was easy to ignore if you sat a distance away with your back to it.

He and the Reverend Smith had met here by chance some weeks earlier, and now it had become a habit. They arrived separately, allowing themselves enough time before the schools closed and the kids arrived. After a while Smith would come down from the gym and salute him through the glass wall that separated the pool from the café area. They had the timing down to a fine art. Smith waited the requisite number of minutes then ordered two double espressos, which arrived on the table just as he came through from the pool changing room.

"So how was the water today?"

"Chilly. Had to keep moving."

For the first fifteen minutes, before some senior citizens arrived, Gordon had been able to pretend it was his personal pool. An infinity pool was at the top of his fantasy "must have" list. There was something wonderful about standing in a completely motionless sheet of water then crouching down to begin, something almost sacred, with the hands coming together as if to pray, then pushing out, caressing the water with the first breaststroke.

"I suppose I should try the pool, but I'm not much of a swimmer," Smith said. "No, I'm trying to give up sugar," he added, pushing the bowl of sachets back across the table.

"You're far less likely to damage yourself with the water supporting you."

"I know. But swimming makes me feel sleepy, whereas the running and cycling wake me up a bit. And I like to see how many calories I'm burning. I get so many cups of tea and home-made cakes when I do my visits, and it's kind of encouraging to see if I'm using up any."

"What happened to resisting temptation?"

"Sorry. I can't hear you."

"You don't have much to worry about yet," he said. "You look pretty good for your age."

"Have you any idea how much those three little words hurt?"

"How many pills do you take a day? "

"None."

"Exactly. I have patients your age who can't see their toes when they stand up or climb a flight of stairs without getting breathless. Stop complaining."

"I gained more than a stone the first year I was married.

Jean put me on a diet. I'll be in trouble if I'm any fatter than I was when she left."

Men did gain weight after marriage. Many a research paper had confirmed it. He himself had gone up a trouser size, only to find the pounds dropping off when things went sour. At present he was living on microwave meals and toast, distrusting the gas cooker in the flat. He envied Smith his Jean. He was looking forward to meeting the woman, if only to see whether she was worth all this devotion.

"When does she get back?" he asked.

"Another three weeks. The fact that she says how hot it is in every e-mail doesn't help. They're on the beach, and I'm in the graveyard in the rain. Enough of me and my moans. How's your week been?"

"Awash with winter vomiting, as we say in the trade. The thing is, nobody believes you when you say stop eating, drink lots of fluids and wait for it to go away. All they want is antibiotics. The best one was Thursday. A chap who waited till he recovered, and then came to see me."

"Why?"

"I haven't a clue. I wouldn't mind but I always have a queue of people waiting, some of whom are, in fact, rather ill."

"We must be a bit late today," Smith looked at his watch as the first of the adults with children arrived. "Here come your favourite little people."

He wished Smith wouldn't keep saying things like this. He forced a smile.

"How many times do I have to defend myself? I don't dislike children. I just don't like sharing a swimming pool with them. They're dangerous. See, that one's actually been labelled."

The child trying to wriggle out of his father's grasp was wearing a white woollen hat with a black skull and cross-bones on it.

Smith said, "It's interesting how it's the Dad's job to take them swimming these days. I suppose they're on shifts, or unemployed. Maybe it's a good thing. At least there's a male role model."

If they stayed long enough, Gordon thought. The world was insane. An awful lot of kids had a series of men in their lives, none of whom would be considered suitable if they applied to adopt. Children were fragile. The lines of an old poem came into his head, 'She was beautifully delicately made, so small, so unafraid . . .'

". . . I'm a bit jealous. The minister used to be the most important man in the village. We're only called in when it's too late . . ."

It was a wartime poem about a child being killed, Gordon remembered. The poet had compared the child to the bomb that killed her. It was a horrible poem. How could anyone who hurt a child stay sane? He could never hurt a child.

"I'm sorry. I'm moaning again," Smith was saying. "Monday's my worst day. I'm a different person once I get Monday out of the way. But I do envy you. Sometimes you save lives. That boy in the primary school who collapsed. . . . Miss Calvert was telling me you ran from the surgery to the school."

A peanut allergy, a severe first reaction. One of the new intake had accepted a home made biscuit from a small friend. He'd been standing by the Surgery reception desk, bag in hand, when the call came. A few days later, the parents left him a bottle of wine. "It's our own," they told the receptionist. Dutifully she passed the gift and information on. He'd been impressed, imagining they had a patch in some Mediterranean country. He'd seen such schemes advertised as a gift for those who had everything. On stripping off the paper, he found it to be a Rhône.

It was a nice tale, but before he had the chance to tell it, the Reverend redirected the conversation. "Kerr was constantly at our doctor's when he was small. His first hospital visit took place when he was less than a year old, after he swallowed one of those large nappy pins."

"Open or shut?"

"Shut, thank God." His hat, balanced on top of his anorak on the back of the chair, fell to the floor. He bent to retrieve it. "Nobody warns you. You look at this little thing in your arms, and you wonder who's in charge, who's going to protect it. Then you realize it's you, and a wave of pure terror sweeps over you. You think I'm exaggerating?"

"No, I'm sure you're right."

Sometimes it was the child who felt the terror. He would never have any of his own. He'd hated his time in the neonatal unit. There was only so much one could do. Or rather, so little. He wanted to say these things, but hesitated. The trouble with Smith was, he was too bloody direct. Too ready to make things personal. You had to stay alert. You never knew where a conversation would lead or what you would find yourself saying. Now he was playing with the hat, a greyish knitted object like a tea cosy.

"We can't keep them behind railings the whole time. I was reading an article somewhere the other day," he frowned, plucking some fluff from the wool. "Some scientist, I think he was Danish, he was suggesting that with serious child abusers, there could be faulty wiring in the brain, that their urges didn't just come from trauma in their own childhood. Is that possible?"

What an easy solution that would be. And next we cure the common cold . . .

"Then we wouldn't hold them morally responsible."

"I know. But everything in me says we should." Smith glanced at his watch again. He lifted his jacket and put on the tea cosy, adjusting it to cover his ears.

"Thanks again for the coffee. My turn next time."

The carborundum stone

All of Ruby's knives were sharp. Several times a week she sharpened them on a grey carborundum stone which had belonged to her grandmother and then to her mother. There was no need therefore to chop the leeks, potatoes and carrots with such vigour, but she banged on nevertheless, hardly seeing them. While they sweated, she poured two pints of boiling water into the measuring jug and dissolved two organic herbal stock cubes – this to be added to the soup pot when the sweating was complete. The process was orderly, the ingredients were fresh and free from MSG. One thing only prevented her from feeling satisfied with life's rich feast.

Walter had lied.

When he came to bed she had pretended to be asleep, and for much of the night she had pondered. At breakfast she gave him a fresh chance to confess, feeling that she had perhaps been unfair. She was not ordinarily one who rushed to judgement, not like some.

"Was there a queue at the garage last night, Walter? You were gone a while," she'd begun, pouring tea for them both.

"Was I?" he said, with an air of unconcern. He was reading his newspaper as if nothing was amiss. "Not much on the telly tonight," he said. "Unless you like snooker. It gets worse and worse. I don't know."

Clearing the cereal bowls, she gave him yet another opportunity. "I didn't even hear the car. I suppose I must have fallen over quickly."

"Mm," he said, turning a page.

Ruby stared hard at the back of his head, willing him to confess and save himself, for had she not seen him with her own two eyes, tramping down Lesley's path? The window was open an inch to allow steam to escape. Had she not heard his familiar whistled rendition of "Scotland the Brave", heard too the squeak of that woman's gate, and seen the silent opening of their own before she let the white metal slat of the Venetian blind fall back into place? She'd barely had time to dry herself and get into her nightie before he came into the house.

She was meant to be in the shop at twelve, but as the morning progressed she felt more and more upset. Should she phone June and say she was ill? Certainly she was very tired. Her mid-morning tea, normally so welcome, tasted strange. Her head felt light, and there was a constant sensation in her bowels as if she needed to go to the bathroom, despite the fact that the needful had already been done.

She phoned June, changed back into her nightie and dressing gown and sat down on the front room settee with a crossword.

Just after one a knock at the kitchen door startled her.

Surely June hadn't come to see how ill she really was? She buttoned up her dressing gown, and unlocked the door.

"Hello," the young woman said, holding out a box. "I need a signature. Would you be able to take it for . . ." she looked down at her clipboard, ". . . Crawfurd?"

"There's no one here by that name," Ruby told her. "Not in this street."

"It's care of number four, Crosthwaite."

The woman pronounced it "crosstait" and it took Ruby a moment or two to realise what was meant.

"But this is number six."

"I know," the woman said. "It's for your neighbour." She spaced the words out as if Ruby was deaf. "Will you take it for her? It needs to be signed for."

"Oh, all right," Ruby said reluctantly, taking the fancy machine and stylus to sign. What a coarse rude woman. Her hair looked as if it had been chewed by a dog. She was surprised that the Post Office employed such a person.

She relocked the door and studied the box. Bold red letters on white tape said "Fragile" on two sides. It was addressed to a Mr Duncan Crawfurd. There was no clue as to what lay inside. She gave it a gentle shake, close to her ear, then placed it on top of the biscuit tin.

As soon as he came in, Walter noticed it.

"What's this?" he asked, "Something from the boy?" It was the way he always referred to Walter Junior.

"It's for her next door," she said. "She was lucky to

get me. I've not felt well all day. I didn't manage to the Shop."

"I could have come back earlier. You should have phoned me, Ruby." He was still holding the box. "I'll take this round after dinner."

She let it pass, but she was ahead of him. She had changed back into her clothes mid-afternoon, and had finished preparing the evening meal. She had eaten her own and there was a plate in the fridge covered with cling film, ready to be microwaved for him.

"Aren't you having any, dear?" he said, when only one bowl of soup was placed on the table.

"I had mine earlier," she said. "I thought it might make me feel better."

"No croutons tonight, dear?" he said.

He liked his croutons. Cubes of wholemeal bread were bathed in Extra Virgin olive oil, then toasted in the oven. Sometimes Italian seasoning was added, or cracked black pepper. Toast Melba, which he also enjoyed, needed more care; the slices were thin after being split, and when the raw sides were put under the grill, they tended to burn if unwatched. But there were no tasty extras tonight, peppered or otherwise. Nor would there be until he stopped keeping secrets from her.

She waited until he was halfway through the soup.

"I'll think I might take that parcel round next door, Walter. Your main course is in the fridge. I'll just pop it in the microwave when I come back."

She went to Lesley's front door, rather than the back one that faced their own.

Lesley came promptly.

"I took this in for you, Lesley," Ruby said. "Although I wondered if it might be a mistake, because of the name."

She couldn't help noticing Lesley's necklace, plastic beads like big chunks of sweetcorn, yellow and pale brown, and some darker ones, as if they'd been cooked too long.

"This is getting to be a habit," she began. "I meant, like your boots. Not that we mind, of course."

"Thank you," was all Lesley said. She was holding the parcel up to the light, reading the address label, and her face cleared. "Oh, that's fine. I know what it is."

But she didn't tell. Nor did she invite Ruby in, not even when Ruby said she hoped she wasn't interrupting Lesley's tea, and the answer was no. She tried another approach.

"You're back at the school, then, Lesley. Is that going all right?"

"Well, it's tiring, but I quite enjoy being back, seeing all the children. Anyway, thank you so much for taking this in for me." She was moving to shut the door.

"I didn't recognise the name, you see. I said to Walter, I hope Lesley's not taking in lodgers, now that her dear mother's gone."

Lesley stared at her.

Ruby said hurriedly, "I almost didn't take the parcel, you see. Is Mr Crawfurd new to the village?"

"But you've met him, Mrs Robertson. I'm sure Mrs Crawfurd often sends him with things to your shop."

She nodded and smiled as if of course she had. But had she? What did he look like? Why was Lesley getting parcels for him? But Lesley was saying goodnight, and thank you again, and better not keep you standing in this bitter, cold wind, and abruptly, quite rudely in fact, the door was being shut in her face.

"So what's the news?" he said.

"This and that. She's back at work. Said she missed the children."

"It's a shame she never had any."

Ruby made no comment. She lifted Walter's empty bowl and went to microwave his main course. The roast potatoes looked a bit leathery, as she'd half expected – roast potatoes never reheated well – but Walter ate without complaining. Nor did he push the green beans to one side. The minute she observed this, Ruby felt sure in her heart that something was amiss.

"Well, I think I can solve your mystery," he said. "I remembered after you went out. We put in a new boiler for a chap called Crawfurd about three years ago. He said they knew our next door neighbours. He lives in that great big house across the river, the one with the turret. Sandy hair and a big droopy moustache, like one of those wee terrier dogs. I see him at the bus stop some mornings."

When supper was over, the mugs dried and put away and all the worktops disinfected, Ruby sat for a little while in the front room, fighting vainly against the hardening of her heart. She looked over the top of her magazine at her husband of thirty years. His curls had receded neatly, like his late father's, leaving his head looking very clean. His eyebrows had become bushy, but she encouraged him to trim them each month with the help of her needlework scissors. Not that she sewed these days. Fine stitching made her finger joints ache. Walter's hands, reddened by honest toil, lay one on top of the other on his cardigan front.

She had always respected Walter. He was the breadwinner, and his firm had an excellent reputation because of his own high standards and his insistence that the men follow suit. He kept his tools out of the house, and took off his shoes as soon as he came in. He knew how to fix almost everything so that she rarely needed to have workmen in her house, and he always showered before bed, where he was affectionate but undemanding. Until now this had always been enough. There had never been a shadow between them until now.

Old friends

Wisdom, Roderick McKinnon reckoned, had been simpler in the old days. Before medical progress rendered it redundant, he had devised a foolproof method of predicting the sex of the next baby. He would write down "Boy" or "Girl" in his personal diary, on the day of the first visit, while assuring the mother verbally of the opposite. By this means he had quickly acquired a reputation for astonishing insight and cleverness. Some of his patients possibly still believed it. He himself felt less and less certain. He hoped he was still learning. It was just that the amount one had to learn seemed to grow greater with every passing year. The very concept of wisdom had become more obscure to him. He had seen great courage, and more determination to fight the odds than he himself would have possessed given the same circumstances, but he had also watched seemingly "intelligent" men and women ignore his warnings and bring themselves to a premature death. He had an idea in his head now as he walked towards the Crawfurd house, where the cold February sun hung motionless in the bare branches of their ancient beech trees, but he wasn't sure if it was a wise idea or a foolish one.

"Just passing, Edith. Thought I'd check up on you, since you never come to see us at the surgery."

Old friends

She led the way to the front sitting room. As always the room overwhelmed him with its beauty. He and Marjory came from working class backgrounds. They'd inherited nothing but their genes. *My shoulders and your mother's brains, and thank the Lord it was yon way round,* had been his father's pronouncement. Even now, accepted without question as an equal by Edith Crawfurd, in a room like this he felt very aware of his roots.

"Sherry?" she asked.

"A small one."

He sat in the rocking chair, a modern heirloom. Hand carved with its trademark Mouse, it had, he recalled, taken three years to come after the order was placed, arriving perfectly in time for her seventieth birthday. But who would inherit after Duncan died, apart from the taxman?

"Well then, any problems, or just the same old friends?" he began. It was impossible not to rock. He placed his glass on the shelf beside him.

"Fit as a fiddle," she said.

"Let's have a wee look at your blood pressure."

She unbuttoned her sleeve and let him tighten the grey cuff around her upper arm. The pressure was a little high, but he felt there was no need to up the dose. Duncan's grandmother, deaf but otherwise hale, had lived to well over a hundred. Edith's arms and legs were losing bone mass – few woman her age could defy osteoporosis – but she was still straight, still elegant. Was that important in these times? To her it would be, he thought. Her hair had a natural

221

wave, with whiter strands around the face. Marjory had told him, not disapprovingly, that she paid an expensive hairdresser from the city to come to the house.

"So how are the legs? Still getting down to the shops and back again?"

She had broken an ankle some years earlier, which had taken its time to heal.

She made a little face. "Not so often. We go into town sometimes but Duncan does a weekly order on his computer. I'm fine on the flat, though."

"I wanted to talk to you about Duncan," he said. He took a small sip of the sherry.

"Yes?" she said.

The moment of truth. He felt as he had felt in his youth, waiting for the whistle, when his broad shoulders had made him an obvious but unenthusiastic prop forward.

"I'm feeling a little concerned," he began.

"About Duncan? My Duncan?"

"Yes. And I hoped you might help me, keep me right, as it were."

She had poured sherry for herself, although she hadn't touched it. Nor did she now. She picked what might have been a hair from her skirt, then placed her hands in her lap.

"Tell me," she said, looking beyond him at the now shadowed garden.

Hurt

The box wasn't very big. It looked old but nice. Dark red, the shape of a heart. It took her a while to get it open, because the gold hook and the button it was caught on were so small. If it was sweets inside, they'd be really wee ones. The last time, he'd left chocolate coins wrapped in gold paper. Just two, but they were big. She'd eaten one on the way back to the van, and one in the dark after she was in bed.

But this time it wasn't sweets. It was a ring with a stone on it. It was the smallest ring she'd ever seen. She didn't know you could get rings that small. She thought maybe it was a pearl, because her Nan wore pearl earrings. It was too big for all her fingers, but stayed on her thumb without falling off. It was like a crown for a fairy queen.

Chocolate was better. If she wore this, they'd take it off her. If she hid it, they'd find it. They'd ask where she got it, and she had promised him not to tell anyone they were friends, not ever.

She put it back behind the stone. Then she changed her mind and, leaving the box, put the ring back on her thumb. It was so small, there must be somewhere in the van to hide it.

The twins found it before supper. She saw them whisper-ing. They whispered together, then Josie got her by the ankles, and Martine pushed her over and sat on her tummy, holding one wrist down on the floor between the bunks, pulling at the arm which ended in the hand whose thumb was locked in her mouth, pressing hard against her teeth. Then Martine started bouncing on her, really hard, thump-ing the breath out of her body.

It hurt so bad she opened her mouth and screamed as loud as she could.

The door of the van opened. The twins instantly jumped off her and onto the beds. She rolled over on to her front, the thumb with the ring again wedged against her top teeth.

"She's got a gold ring! She let a dirty man touch her bum an' she's got a gold ring!"

Dad yelled at them to be quiet, grabbed her by the arms, and got her to stand.

"Shut up! An' take that bloody thumb out yer mouth!"

The thumb was red, and white where she'd bitten down on it, but there was no ring. It had slipped silently past her tonsils and down into the dark.

Amber

At three am Lesley gave up trying to get back to sleep. She put on her dressing gown and went downstairs to make some hot milk. Last night's scrambled egg pan sat in the sink. It was an easy, filling supper, but there was something so disgusting about a pan with water and the remains of cooked egg in it that she had left it unwashed. Now that she could. Now that there was no-one standing behind her.

The Robertsons' outside light flashed on, then off seconds later. A cat on patrol along the bottom of the hedge? Mrs Robertson was getting sillier and stranger by the day. *I hope Lesley's not taking in lodgers.*

The glass disc began rattling in the milk pot. She lifted it off the heat before it could boil over. Had she been unkind, not inviting the woman in? She poured the milk into a mug, stirring in a squeeze of honey. *You're doing so well, Lesley. You're being very brave.* Being back at work had nothing to do with being brave. With her financial situation more secure than she'd expected, she could stop working, but who would there be to talk to? Her days would be as lonely as the nights.

Duncan looked so much younger without his moustache. When they finally found a website with what they needed, he'd let out a sound that was almost a boyish whoop of glee, before pressing a finger to his lips. It cheered her to see him enjoying their conspiracy. That's what he called it.

She'd meant to phone earlier to let him know that she'd left the minister's useful information on Mrs Flaherty's answer phone and that the replacement sugar bowl had arrived. She'd checked to be sure it hadn't been damaged in transit. The staples were embedded in the cardboard, and she had to use a nail file to lever them out. Inside, the bowl and lid were separately wrapped in tight layers of bubbled plastic.

She had to find scissors to cut the plastic wrapping, so much Sellotape had been used. The last piece of wrapping fell away and to her great relief all was well. It looked like new, although it had been advertised as "Used." Did any-one ever use their best china? The cabinet in the dining room contained a set of the same vintage, rarely used even when Mother was alive, *and* what was left of her grandmother's dinner set.

Mug in hand she went back upstairs. The string of beads she'd been wearing all day lay coiled on the bedside table beside her watch and reading glasses. She'd never been much of a one for beads, or jewellery of any kind. Wearing them to work had been rather out of character, but finding them in a drawer, she had liked the feel of them, and the colour.

"Lesley, are those amber?" someone in staff room said. "Can I have a look?"

She'd begun clearing out, Lesley explained, handing them over for inspection.

"They're gorgeous. You know, if they're amber they might be really old. I saw one like this on the Antiques Road show. It made more than £400."

"Lesley, anything else you're thinking of throwing out, could you bring it here first?" one of the other teachers said.

She wondered if she might ask Duncan to look on the web again. On the other hand, she'd be nervous about wearing them if they were really valuable.

Being the centre of attention was embarrassing but gratifying at the same time. She didn't usually wear beads, although she liked seeing jewellery on other women, earrings in colours that matched a blouse, or enamelled lapel brooches to brighten dark suits. Where then had it come from, this misbegotten, perverse idea that while it was fine for other women, wearing jewellery was in her case a sign of vanity, something to gain attention from men, or provoke envy from women? Even if it had been true once, it wasn't now. She was too old to make other women jealous, even if she wanted to, and the contents of an entire street of jewellers' shops would hardly be enough now to attract a man.

The sugar bowl had been a wedding present, according to Duncan. Not something she would ever have. This mug in her hands was stoneware, with the school crest on one side, and the dates of the centenary on the other. Not that she needed presents. If she needed anything, she could afford to buy it herself now. She might buy a new washing machine, the kind with the tumble dryer function. It would be lovely to get rid of the pulley. The women in the staff room would know which make was best.

Duncan was so funny. He thought he lived a very simple life, but really he was fussy about so many things. Proper coffee. Writing with a fountain pen, and blue-black ink. He refused to wear synthetic materials. Braces on his trousers rather than a belt. Proper shoes no matter what he was doing.

What had made him shave off the moustache? She'd always assumed he wore it as an act of homage to the Captain, whose portrait hung half way up the stairs. She remembered him as a silent figure in the background of parties, or rather of the beginnings of parties, as he never seemed to stay long.

If she ever had to choose wedding china, she'd have something without a pattern. No tangled roses or butterflies or hand-painted gold rims. It would be beautiful, of course, but plain. The way the amber necklace was plain. The way the full moon was plain. It would be used every single day of its life.

As she switched off the bedside light, it occurred to her that she was involved in three conspiracies, not one. She'd shared Mary Flaherty's troubles with the minister, helped Duncan find a sugar bowl and she was storing Mr Robertson's fish tanks. All conspiracies with men, and two of them married!

Don't let her spoil the rest of your life.

Easy for Dr Gordon to say. Young and handsome and kind to stupid middle-aged women who thought momentarily and quite mistakenly that he resembled their lost lovers. How easy life was for men like him. She felt for the necklace on the bedside table, and raised the cool, uneven lumps of amber to her lips.

"I would have been a good wife," she told them. "I would have let my husband have all the fish tanks he wanted."

The world too much

When Dr McKinnon left, Mrs Crawfurd returned to the kitchen. The pleasant, authoritative female voices on the radio which had previously been discussing pension plans were now debating the virtues of breastfeeding. She switched them off. She had been weighing flour for a batch of fairy cakes – most of them to go into the freezer, but a dozen to be iced for Duncan to share with the library staff. He was well regarded at work, she believed.

The daisy-patterned paper cases were as she had left them, crisp and frilly in their trays, and the cooling racks were waiting on the worktop. The maxims of Miss Scott the Cookery Mistress, immaculate in white, spoke to her still across the decades. *Good cooks think ahead and tidy as they go.*

Instead of putting her apron back on, she switched off the cooker, and made her way, one hand lightly touching the dado rail, through the corridor and up the back stairs to the small second floor room which had begun life as a maid's bedroom and was now her sanctum. Duncan had helped her with the colours. They had found a replica Owen Jones wallpaper in exactly the correct shade of muted pinkish red to suit the ancient Crawford tartan curtains and carpet.

North-west facing, the quality of light in the room was often poor, which was a soothing thing when the world became too much. It pleased her that there was no clock, no calendar, no rack of magazines, nothing by which to guess the date or time. A gold-framed blackwork representation of York Minster hung above the mantelpiece, silk on linen worked by herself when a girl. On the opposite wall was a back and white photograph of her late parents in front of the bungalow in Rangoon. Her father had one hand on the bonnet of the newly arrived Austin 12, the other arm round her mother, tall, slim and looking like a film star in her sunglasses.

She sat in the Indian rosewood armchair. Turning it slightly so that she could look out at the hills, she settled a mohair shawl over her knees. After a little while she drew it higher, until it was over her shoulders. She fussed at it, trying to tuck the sides in tight around her.

Once upon a time there had been nothing but fields beyond the mixed hedge of holly, hawthorn and beech, planted in her grandfather's time. As a child she had crouched to look through the gaps at the Clydesdales, with their pale brown foals sleeping in the sun. She had only one other memory of that era; being given a white enamelled pail with a royal blue rim (or was it a colander?) to fill with gooseberries – pale green, perfectly veined, enormous to a child's eyes. Hard and sour when raw, they were wonderful when grandma's cook made them into pies with the thinnest, crispiest pastry in the world.

Under siege

"I'm not asleep, dear."

Dr McKinnon ceased tiptoeing and approached the bed in a normal fashion.

"Your feet are freezing," his wife added moments later.

He removed them from her pleasantly warm calves, switched on the bedside light and opened "Fortress Malta: An island under siege." He had left the submariners trying to maintain good spirits the previous evening in Chapter Seven, and was not hopeful that things would improve. Chapter Eight was entitled, "Valour at Sea", which was worryingly unspecific.

"I'm sorry, I tried to be quiet," he apologised, as his wife turned onto her back.

"You were quiet, dear. I can't sleep. I've been thinking about Eunice Calvert and the Primary children and all these terrible rumours."

"I'm sure she'll appreciate that. I'll just phone and let her know."

"Don't be silly. It's after midnight," she told him.

He tried to get back to the brave submariners, but his mind was elsewhere. Had Edith Crawfurd been offended? Would she take up his suggestion? More to the point, would

Duncan? Had he acted with valour, or was he meddling where he had no business to? He had no faith in a Supreme Being, and no desire to begin acting like one at this stage of his life.

Squadron Leader Peter Townsend was just beginning to train a younger airman in the art of dog-fighting when a small voice said from beneath the quilt, "Darling, you don't suppose there could be any truth in what they . . ."

"No," he said firmly. He closed the book and laid it on the floor. "I must confess I've sometimes been tempted to start a rumour. Something harmless about myself. An ingrown toe nail, or something of that ilk. I'd tell three different people in complete confidence, and see how long it took to come back to me transformed into chronic gout or gangrene. Please don't get yourself agitated, Marjory. It won't help."

She turned to cuddle into him. "Why is the world so terrible? It wasn't like this when our girls were growing up."

She was quite wrong, the world had always been terrible but he was too tired to argue. He tried a different tack.

"You did a good job with them. You were always there for them."

"Well I didn't have to work. They were my work."

She seemed to settle, and after a while he switched off the light. But there was one more question. Later he would remember how it had come last, like the question patients would ask on the point of leaving, casually mentioning what was uppermost in his or her mind.

"Roderick. Mrs Flaherty's one of your patients, isn't she? The woman who cleans for Edith. "

"Yes."

"Someone said her husband's back in the district."

"And?"

"They thought he'd been in prison. Mrs Flaherty threw him out years ago, because he. . . ."

"Johnny Flaherty wasn't a paedophile, if that's what you're thinking. He was an alcoholic and a womaniser, and he battered his wife when he was drunk, but I am absolutely certain he never hurt his own children or anyone else's. Now please can we go to sleep?"

She was silent. After a moment an apologetic arm crept round his stomach. He patted it through the quilt. *Never let the sun go down on your wrath*, his father had told him, the day before the wedding. A very wise man, his father. Some clichés were worth holding on to.

Pals

"Daddy."

The Reverend Smith typed on but mentally readied himself. When Harriet used that word instead of Dad, it was usually a signal that something with the potential to ruffle feathers was to follow.

"Can I talk to you?"

"Yup." He misspelled "apocalypse", and pressed the plus sign instead of the delete.

"It's quite important."

"Mmn."

"Very important, in fact."

"Right."

On the third try it was correct. He peered at the rest of the paragraph.

"I went into town this morning, and I've just had my belly button pierced."

"No, you haven't, but you can if you want to."

"Really?"

"Of course not. What's the problem?" He pressed "save" and swung round to face her.

"Ryan wants me to do something, and I'm not sure if I want to do it."

So it was Ryan now, not Ryan Flaherty.

"Go on," he said. And silently, *God help us all* . . .

She'd taken a jar of coloured paper clips from the window ledge and was picking out the white ones. "Someone's been making funny phone calls to his house. Not obscene calls exactly, just not speaking . . ."

"Heavy breathing."

"Well, not even that, actually."

She sat on the rug beside the desk, so that her back was against his left leg. He had to stop himself from touching the fair head so close to his hand. Those days were gone. How he hated it that they were gone. In the bookcase against the wall, almost exactly level with Harriet's shoulder he saw "How to understand your teens." An excellent book. He recalled reading it. In fact he had underlined several useful passages. Sadly, the book on how to handle Harriet had not yet been written.

"He says his mother's all worked up about it, making herself ill, but she won't do anything."

The paper clips were being linked into a necklace. He had a sudden memory of summer daisies being made into chains in their first garden, Harriet sitting against her mother on the back doorstep, concentrating fiercely, tongue between her lips, carefully inserting the stems into one another after Jean had made slits with a pin, while he and Kerr practised putting strokes on the tiny strip of grass where an empty soup tin had cut out a circle of turf and been reversed into the hole to catch the ball.

"And what does Ryan want you to do?"

"Phone the number and find out who's calling them."

Thank you, God. Thank you. Thank you.

"And he can't do this himself because . . .?"

"I'm not sure. That's what worries me. But I don't want to say no, either."

Was this their fault, this unwavering determination in Harriet to adopt every lame duck in sight? One day a duck more lame than any who'd gone before would limp across her path, and some completely unworthy young man would take her from them.

Every milestone had hurt. Her first period, not that he was supposed to know; her first bra, ditto; the first phone call from a boy whose name he didn't recognise; the first party when he wasn't allowed to come inside but had to wait in the car.

"But she doesn't fall out with you," Jean told him. "I'm the one ruining her life. She still thinks you're her pal."

It was nice to know, but it wasn't enough to make him feel secure. Pals came and went.

He cleared his throat. "What do you want me to do? Would you like me to talk to him?"

"Maybe."

"Well, I suppose you could suggest it. If he says no, we'll go to plan B."

With a faint smile she raised her hand, "What's plan B?"

"I've no idea."

This was the question and answer always used in family

'discussions' when they took wrong turnings and got lost, or forgot to set the oven timer to cook Sunday lunch, or put diesel in the new car (an opportunity for grace). This time it sounded worn and tired, and not terribly amusing.

Harriet got to her feet. When had she got so tall? Something seemed to go 'ping' between his ribs, like a button flipping out of its hole.

"Are you going to unclip those for me?" he said.

"Of course not."

She draped the long loop over his head and left.

He turned back to First Corinthians. Some time later, in mid sentence, it struck him that he knew who the mystery caller was, knew who Lesley Crosthwaite's unnamed, unhappy friend was, knew more about Ryan Flaherty's troubles than the boy did himself.

Waifs and strays

"So how are Harriet's exams going?" Dr Gordon asked, watching the Reverend lower his trousers.

"I don't think they're causing any real trouble. She'll do well in the subjects that interest her and not so well in the ones that don't. With Harriet it's always been a case of whether she likes the teacher or not. That's it there," he indicated the small dark shape on his inner thigh.

"Skin tag," Gordon said, after a close look. "Fibroepithelial polyp, to give it its Sunday name. Completely harmless. It's gone dark because it's not getting any blood supply. It'll fall off pretty soon. You could put an Elastoplast over it when you get home, if you like, but I wouldn't bother."

"I was a bit worried."

"Absolutely nothing to worry about. But you were right to get it checked. We might as well do everything since you're here. If you roll up your sleeve . . . You know, I can't imagine Harriet being bad in class."

"She isn't bad. She does this passive aggressive thing, not doing more than the bare minimum required to pass. She's too proud to actually fail, unfortunately."

Gordon watched the dark red fluid enter the Vacu-tainer, then handed Smith a small pad of cotton wool, telling him to press down on it. He applied an adhesive strip. "Why 'unfortunately'? No, keep the arm up for a couple of minutes."

"She's never failed at anything in her short life. It's not good preparation for the big, bad world. I worry for her."

Was this said as a joke? He'd never trusted grand statements about learning from failure; they generally came from people who eventually found success. Failure seemed to him a little like salt in your soup, fine in very small doses. He'd had enough failure in his life to last him for the next few decades. Chiefly his marriage. Two years that had lasted.

"Ok, blood pressure next. Other arm. So what did you fail at?"

"Depends which day of the week we're talking about."

"No, I'm serious. Major failures. You can put that one down now."

Smith obediently rolled up his other shirt sleeve. "I'm not telling you about those. Those are gone. Even God's forgotten those."

Gordon said nothing. When God occasionally strayed into the conversation, it wasn't a problem. He'd discovered early on that the Reverend was too polite to continue in a religious mode when met with silence. He liked the man, admired his love of family, his genuine concern for his parishioners, even the occasional naivety he'd first interpreted as an ironic take on life.

"That's fine. Nothing to worry about," he jotted down the figures. "Maybe Harriet's tougher than you think. Or wiser."

"Wiser? It's a nice thought. Her intentions are always good, but not necessarily wise. I'm supposed to be helping one of her lame ducks tonight but I've a feeling the duck might not want my help."

"Surely that's your job, helping waifs and strays. "

"It's not so easy when the waif in question isn't in the least waif-like. Strange word, waif. One of those words that loses its meaning when you say it over and over."

"Most words are like that," Gordon suggested. "I take you to mean you can't help someone who doesn't admit he needs help. I had a patient in my last practice who kept coming for weeks before I found out what was actually wrong with her, and when I did, she stopped coming. Now then, no headaches, chest pain, dizzy spells?"

"No. What was wrong with her?"

"She was a kleptomaniac, though she'd presented with back pain. Because she only stole from department stores, and nothing she stole was valuable, she didn't think of herself as a criminal. But at the same time, she was crippled with guilt."

"And that caused the back pain."

"No, it was postural. We solved that with a new office chair. But I wanted her to get counselling. It was such a shame, because kleptomania is one of the few control disorders that people can recover from."

"What's the current thinking on paedophiles?"

The question startled Gordon. Where had it come from?

"We're not talking about Harriet's lame duck, are we?"

241

"God forbid. Is that me done?" Smith reached for his jacket. "No, I was thinking of these rumours going round the village."

"I've been warned that most of them begin in our Surgery," he said lightly. "You think this one's true?"

"Who knows? But what you were saying about control disorders . . . Can paedophiles recover? Supposing they want to?"

Surely they'd been over this before. "Recover? Huge question." He went to the sink to wash his hands. "I don't think so myself, but that's more of an instinctive reaction on my part. Why does it happen? I honestly don't know, and I don't know anyone who does. It's not the same as alcoholism, for example. Alcoholics are never cured, but they recover in the sense that they stay well, provided they don't touch alcohol. But that's incredibly simple in comparison. There are so many different forms of paedophilia. I can lend you some books if . . ."

The minister shook his head. "No, don't. I've a stack of books a foot high beside the bed already."

"Let me give you a question," Gordon said, irked that his offer had been so flatly dismissed. "The Bible says that man was made in the image of God, right? So whose . . ."

"Whose image is a paedophile made in?" The minister made a face. "I had an awful feeling you were going to ask that. I'd have to lend you a whole library of books on that one."

Black

Ryan stood at the manse gate. He crunched through what was left of an extra strong mint and put another in his mouth. He'd resisted the urge to put on a shirt and tie for this. Now he wished he had. "You're so bloody depressing," his sisters said. "Why d'you wear black all the time? Black's for funerals." He'd never been to a funeral. On the way in he'd tried not to notice the old graveyard with its shaggy yews and leaning slabs. He didn't ever want to be dead.

He wore black because you didn't have to make choices in the morning. Black didn't bother him one way or another. And he didn't feel depressed the whole time. Sometimes there were good things no-one else noticed. Like the smell on the leaves of old Crawfurd's pot plants or the green lines inside the snowdrops growing at head height beside a wall he walked past near the Art School. They were early, he guessed, because they faced south, and the stone wall sheltered them. He was ready to bet that no-one else he knew had ever looked inside a snowdrop. A small thing like that was sometimes enough to keep him from giving up. Did anyone else wonder why flowers were scented and coloured? He knew the slick answers, different coloured molecules make different colours, different colours attract insects or birds, different fragrances do the same thing at night. He remembered that much from Biology in first year. But this was like saying snowdrops have to be white because they're white. Why shouldn't they all be shades of grey? Why did they have to be beautiful? Why did his brain tell him they were beautiful?

Harriet was a beautiful thing. Her name was wrong, though. It was a hawk's name, ugly, nothing soft or smooth about it. Not that any name really fitted her. He'd gone through the alphabet more than once trying to find one that was right. It would be enough just to watch her every day, see her doing ordinary things, like lifting roast potatoes from a dish onto his plate the way she had that time he'd eaten with them. When one landed in Kerr's lap, her laugh had got right inside him.

He should have known Harriet would talk to her father. She'd no reason not to. For her, talking to a parent made sense. She was one of those lucky people whose whole life made sense. She could even laugh when things went wrong. It was like she'd had happiness or whatever it was pouring over her since she was a baby. He could picture it, like a shower of gold, like glittering special effects in a TV ad.

The outside light came on.

"Why the fuck am I doing this?" he said aloud, pressing the doorbell.

She was wearing a sweater he hadn't seen before, a pale

pink v-neck that showed her collar bones and the smooth hollows above them. She led him to the sitting room. Her father was reading a newspaper, which he folded and laid on the coffee table. He was wearing a dark green fleece over a tee shirt, and jeans, not the priest's outfit.

They shook hands. Harriet said something Ryan didn't catch, and went out of the room.

"So how's the new term treating you?" The man gestured to a chair.

"It's OK."

"Kerr went back a couple of days ago. We haven't heard from him, so I suspect he's probably not out of bed yet. Did you ever hear anything about your mobile phone, by the way? Did you get a replacement?"

Ryan shook his head. In fact he'd bought one from another student without questioning the ridiculously cheap price.

"Harriet's going to come back in a minute. I wanted a word with you on your own first."

He didn't like the look on the man's face. "I haven't touched her, if that's what you want to know."

Why did it sound like a lie? He shouldn't have sat down. He'd be at least three inches taller than the man if they'd both been standing.

"That wasn't what I wanted to talk to you about, Ryan, but thanks anyway."

The sarcastic smile was too much. "This is a fucking mistake," he said, getting to his feet.

"Ryan, wait. I think I know who's making these calls to your house."

He turned slowly, his hand still on the door.

"That's why I asked Harriet to give us ten minutes. I wanted to discuss it with you first. By a series of small coincidences . . ."

"Who've you been talking to? Father Breslin?"

"No. Nobody else knows about this."

"Yeah right. You can't fart in this fucking place without someone knowing. You think you. . . ."

"That's probably true. But I'm pretty sure no one's talking about you. I hear things because of who I am, but what I know stays here," he tapped his forehead. "It was all in small, disconnected parts. No-one else could put them together. Harriet doesn't know."

"Doesn't know what?"

"I may be wrong, Ryan, but I believe these calls are coming from your father."

It was exactly what he'd thought himself.

"If you want to be certain, I'll call the number for you. My feeling is that it would be better to keep Harriet out of the loop, at least until we know for certain. What d'you think?"

What did he think? He didn't know. He'd never even seen his father. There wasn't a single photo of him in the house.

"If it is him, what will you do?" the man said finally, "Would you want to meet him?

Overcome by virtue, Harriet had gone to the kitchen and

switched on the radio. She had grown up in an old house with walls made of grey Aberdeen granite. This manse was less than ten years old. Simply by standing in the corridor beside the closed sitting room door, she could have heard every word, but there were times, and this was one of them, when her father stopped being Dad and became someone else. She took out a can of Coca Cola, and rifled in a drawer for one of the pink swirly straws which were kept for the youngest of the Scottish cousins. Needing more comfort, she went back to the fridge and took out the remains of a chocolate cake. The sponge had gone a bit dry, but the icing was still good; thick and dark, with just the right amount of apricot jelly under it. She broke off a piece, decided it was too small, but managed with a struggle to close the door on what remained.

Was being good a virtue if it was just a habit? She was probably the only one in her class unable to drop litter, the only one who had to carry an empty crisp packet in her blazer pocket until she came to a bin. She couldn't lie about undone homework, or make believable excuses for not going to things. Because, basically, she was a coward. She'd been afraid to do what Ryan asked without consulting the Fount of Wisdom, and now he'd taken over. She stuck out her tongue at one of the fridge magnets. "Do you want to speak to the man in charge or the woman who knows what's happening?"

Just give me a few minutes with him.

Why? What for?

Was he warning Ryan off? Telling him to keep his distance?

She had her back to the corridor, and her legs under the table. When the door opened behind her, she turned round too slowly. Ryan was at the outside door and gone into the night before she could stop him. She ran to her father.

"What did you say to him? What have you done?"

Before he had a chance to speak, she flew back to the kitchen, grabbed the first coat her fingers found on the pantry door and rushed down the steps.

Ryan had only reached the far side of the car park. She ran after him, not calling, in case he too would begin to run. When she caught hold of his arm, he went rigid.

"Don't," he said, so quietly she could hardly hear. He spoke to the ground, didn't look at her.

"What's wrong? What did he say? Did he tell you to stop seeing me?"

Slowly he pulled his arm free. "This isn't about you, Harriet."

"Don't make it sound like that. I meant him . . . I wanted him to help you."

"Yeah, right. After I jump off the bridge he can do the fucking funeral."

He pulled a small bottle from an inner pocket, took a swallow, flung it towards the graveyard and started walking away, still facing her. "Would you miss me, Harriet? Would you cry? My Mum would, but that doesn't count. She cries all the time. Just promise you won't wear black."

"I'll wear black if I want to." she called back. She tried to match her steps to his, not wanting to get closer, not wanting to lose him.

"You won't look good in black."

"Maybe I won't come. Maybe I'll have something better to do."

They were yelling now, as the space between them grew. A large yellow Labrador with a man at the other end of the lead came out from one of the bungalows further ahead. The man glanced at Ryan, then tugged the dog over to the other pavement.

Harriet hesitated. The raincoat she'd thrown on was unlined. Her shoes were more like slippers with thin soles and the cold of the pavement was already seeping up her body. She turned back.

"You have to come! Harriet!"

Frightened, she stopped. In the same moment, there was the sound of a car horn. On the other side of the road, a car was pulling to a halt.

She went over.

"Get in the back," her Dad said through the lowered window, "And stay put."

She watched him cross to where Ryan was standing. There was a brief conversation before they both came back to the car. Ryan got into the front passenger seat.

In silence they drove down the first side road, turning towards the centre of the village and along Main Street. Her father pulled into the car park beside The Dirty Duck.

"Fifteen minutes," he said to Ryan, "Then we'll take you home."

"Why are we going into the . . ."

"*I'm* going in, Harriet. I have to confirm the booking for the Pie and Pint night. You and your friend are waiting for me."

She hated it when his voice took on that flat, sarcastic, superior edge. Undoing the seat belt, she slid over so that she could see Ryan's face. He was quietly, rhythmically thumping the window. The thumping stopped.

"So do you want to know or not?"

She didn't care, didn't want to talk, didn't want to listen. She didn't care what happened to him next or ever.

"Yes," she said.

"He said it's my dad. Makin' the phone calls. He wants to come back. He left when I was younger than Chrissie."

"Why?"

"I don't know. Maybe he didnae like the look of me."

It wasn't what she meant. Later she was to give thanks that she hadn't tried to explain, or worse, made some kind of flip remark.

He went on, "It's like everybody's going one way, and I'm being pushed in the other direction. Every fucking day. I'm a joke. It's no' as if I don't know."

Was he talking to her, or to himself?

"It looks good, but it's no' real. It's pure shite. All of it. I just want . . . I don't fucking care what they want from me."

"I have this weird dream sometimes," she said. "I'm in some kind of Army, and people are ordering me to do things I don't want to. It's not our Army, it's some foreign place, and they're evil, and I know I'm not supposed to be there, but I can't get away from them."

He didn't say anything. What could he say? He probably wasn't listening anyway.

When her Dad came back, there was no more conversation at all, apart from Ryan's brief directions to his home. He left the car without a word.

Caruso

Lesley lifted her mother's fur coat out of the wardrobe and laid it out on the bed. The colour was richer than she remembered from childhood. It was the shade a woman's hair might be if you began with dark brown and added something like a maroon rinse, but there was a gloss on it no woman's hair could ever have. She trailed the back of her hand down the sleeve. The outer hair felt cool and slippery but next to the skin the softer hair was unexpectedly warm. The lining matched the colour of the fur. Her mother's initials were embroidered across one corner in copperplate, two inches high, as if to say, let there be no doubt whose coat this is. Had furriers done this on all coats in the days when furs were common, where two might hang together side by side, and be so alike that the owners needed to initial their property? Perhaps they still did in countries where fur was worn. A few years back one of the staff had returned from a Christmas honeymoon in Athens. "I couldn't believe it," she told them. "I counted seven women in furs before we even got to the hotel. They all wear fur over there."

This wasn't Athens. She didn't think she would ever wear it. Mother hadn't worn it for years. She put it back on the rail. It could wait. Many things could wait.

She glanced at the black bin-bag, into which she had

earlier emptied two drawers of underwear. She'd done it quickly. No-one wanted anyone else's smalls. But the cardigans and blouses were different. You couldn't bin them without thinking. She had divided them into three piles: worn/bin, worn/still decent, and unworn. The worn/decent pile could go to Mrs Robertson's Hospice Shop, and Mrs Flaherty could have her choice of the unworn. It was difficult to imagine when Mrs Flaherty might wear a fur coat. Ought she to offer it anyway? One of the daughters might take it and shorten it into a jacket.

She had decided not to feel guilty about Mrs Flaherty. She'd put a note through the door with the information from the Reverend Smith about diverting calls, repeated his advice to contact the police, and assured the poor soul that she was not to come back until she felt strong enough. What more could she do?

The mantel clock downstairs chimed the half hour. One chest of drawers and half a wardrobe cleared. The smallest of beginnings, and she felt drained. Now she needed to bathe and change. What time had they decided on? Seven or seven thirty?

Mrs Crawfurd picked up the phone. Duncan? Duncan was at the computer. Was it something she, Mrs Crawfurd, could help with?

"We're having tea tonight," Lesley said, "but I can't remember what time . . ."

"It's seven, Lesley dear. When I suggested he should take you out, I said to make it seven. The service is always better, and it's so much quieter. I do hope it's all right. It's under new management, but Eunice Calvert went with her staff at Christmas. She said the food was very acceptable."

Lesley turned on the hot tap, and regarded the floor of the bath through the steam for some time before actually seeing it and realising she'd forgotten to put in the plug. A shallowish bath would still have been possible, but instead she turned off the tap, went to her room and lay down on top of the bed, pulling the top quilt over her.

A cream silk blouse and a pleated black skirt hung on two hangers on the door knob on the inside of the door. The curtains were open, and the blouse buttons, mother of pearl, caught and reflected the light from outside. On the dressing table lay two packets of tights, "one to wear, one for spare", the cellophane wrappers still sealed. On the floor beneath next to a pair of black patent court shoes, size 4, C fitting, sat a matching handbag containing a purse, a small comb, a white handkerchief with embroidered gentians in one corner (Made in Switzerland), and a tube of Taylor of London's Lily of The Valley hand cream.

She cried a little, though without passion. For a time she watched the unmoving shadow stripes on the Paisley patterned wall paper, before turning on her side, away from the window and the street lights.

Duncan had tried on three different ties, and was not convinced about the one he was now wearing, a cream and pale green stripe. It looked almost colourless in the restaurant's dim light. He sat perched at the very edge of the bench seat, next to the passageway, in case Lesley, being short, might not see him when she arrived.

Paper-wrapped breadsticks filled a grey stoneware jar in the centre of the table. Product of Firenze, according to the labelling. It was quite disconcerting to be less than a mile from home in a room that tried to convince you that you were in Italy. A continuous mural on the longest wall represented a summer lakeside scene, viewed through windows. In one alcove, real water trickled from a stone spout into a stone basin, draped above and below with ivy and other greenery, which might have been real, and black grapes which he assumed were not. The smells coming from the direction of the kitchen were exactly those he remembered from the long ago school trip, olive oil and garlic frying, coffee beans freshly ground.

"Would you like to order, sir?" It was the thin young waitress who'd earlier led him to the table and lit its candle.

Duncan explained that he was a little early. He would wait for his friend.

Would he like something to drink, then? Perhaps the house red? One glass while he waited?

She made little marks on her small square pad, and turned to the couple in the next booth. The man could have been any age. He could only see the top of the woman's hair, puffed up like white candy floss. The waitress was pretty, but terribly thin. Sideways on, she seemed to have no flesh under the short, black skirt and blouse; her legs were like straight poles, the same circumference from thigh to ankle.

"So how's life treating you, Diana," the man was saying.

The girl leaned towards them, out of his line of vision.

"You're absolutely right," the woman's voice, "And I can tell you what I'd . . ."

"Margaret," the man said sharply. 'Mahgrit' was how he said it. Duncan transcribed the next sentence on the table cover with his index finger. *We're here tae enjoy wurselvs.*

Music came on, very loudly at first, then reduced after a few seconds to something more reasonable. Il Trovatore. Duncan listened carefully to the voice. Caruso? Could it really be Caruso? Astonishing. He willed Lesley to come quickly and share his delight.

The glass of house red arrived.

"Is that Caruso?" he said.

The girl looked blankly at him, managing a diffident smile as she withdrew.

For years he had walked past this restaurant, never dreaming that such pleasures lay within. He would have to compliment the owner. Unable to stop himself, he un-wrapped one of the breadsticks and bit off a small portion.

Over the next three quarters of an hour, with two whole breadsticks nibbled to extinction and the glass of bright wine drunk, sip by increasingly anxious sip, his sense of delight gradually evaporated. He dialled Lesley's number. After several tries he gave up. The staff were beginning to glance at him, and the restaurant was filling with cheerful couples. Finally he went to the bar.

"I'm terribly sorry, I think something must have happened to my friend."

"We can't keep the table, sir," the man said. "Unless you'd like to order . . ."

Duncan put more than the cost of the wine down, and fumbling his coat and hat off the crowded rack for himself, made for the door.

In less than fifteen minutes he was at Lesley's house.

There was a light on in the hall. The storm door wasn't locked. He pressed the doorbell. Nothing. He tried the inner door. It opened.

With a sense of mounting anxiety, he stepped into the dimly lit hall.

"Lesley?" he called hesitantly. "It's me."

He tiptoed through the ground floor, glancing fearfully into each darkened room. He'd never thought of himself as particularly imaginative, but now one image only presented itself to his brain. Lesley struck down by a burglar, lying in a pool of blood. The kitchen light was on. Nothing seemed out of place. A few dishes in the draining rack. The pulley overhead was draped with drying clothes, including several feminine garments. Hurriedly he tried the back door. It was locked. Should he call the police? If not the police, then who?

Lesley's window faced straight into her neighbours' kitchen across a thick privet hedge. There was a woman at the sink. Would she think he was the burglar? Hesitantly he raised one hand in greeting. There was no answering wave from behind the net curtain,

He moved back to the hall. "Lesley? Are you here? Are you all right?"

He had one foot on the bottom stair when she appeared at the top, smaller somehow than she ought to be, a pale yellow quilt gathered round her.

"Duncan?"

"Are you all right?" he repeated. He began to climb.

"No! Stop."

He stopped.

"How did you get in?"

"The door . . ." he said falteringly.

One small hand emerged from the quilt, reaching for the newel, as if to steady herself. She was barefoot. Had she been in bed?

"Are you unwell? I phoned several times. . . ."

She began to speak, then sighed.

"Should I call a doctor?"

When she still didn't answer he said desperately, "Should I make some tea? Or a Lemsip?"

"Fill the kettle, Duncan," she said. "I'll be down in a moment."

Averting his eyes from the pulley, Duncan prised the lid from the kettle and filled it from the tap. Like most of the things in the kitchen, it had seen better days. The gas cooker in particular worried him. He might suggest she had it tested. Thank goodness nothing was seriously wrong. A chill, a sore throat. A migraine perhaps. Mrs Fleming occasionally suffered from migraines when she hadn't had enough sleep. Over the last year he had come to understand that there was a world of difference between his occasional bad headaches and a migraine. Poor Lesley. She never complained. He imagined she'd lost track of the time. And how thoughtless of him, phoning so many times if she'd been trying to sleep. But now he could make amends. He lit the gas, put the kettle on the ring and prepared to listen for the first sign of a whistle.

It was just beginning to shrill loudly when she appeared. The quilt had been abandoned in favour of a grey cardigan. She had brushed her hair, and her face was less pale. Probably she had splashed some cold water on it. It was a trick he often used himself to wake after a nap in the chair.

"Let me do that," he said, as she opened the cupboard.

"It's all right. You sit down. Here's your mother's sugar bowl, in case I forget." She put a box on the table.

He watched her come and go from fridge to drawer to cupboard. How pale and small her feet were. Didn't she mind the cold linoleum?

"There's some biscuits in the tartan tin. Behind you."

Obediently he stretched for it, and took off the lid. Inside were what his mother called "bought" biscuits; custard creams and ginger nuts and dusty-looking chocolate chip cookies.

Lesley put a mug of tea in front of him, and one for herself on the other side of the table.

"Milk?" she said.

He poured a little from the jug, then a little more. Too much. It slopped over onto the brown oilcloth.

"I'm sorry, I wasn't watching properly . . ."

Lesley pulled some sheets of kitchen paper from a roll and put them down over the puddle of liquid.

Why didn't she say something? What was he doing wrong? He wasn't really a tea drinker and he'd put in so much milk it was lukewarm. He took a large swallow, as if it might improve with familiarity.

"I don't think I've ever been in your kitchen," he said desperately.

"What do you think of it?"

He tried to think of something positive and polite. The yellow vitrolite wall-tiles reminded him of old hospital corridors. The Belfast sink had a brown streak below the cold tap, though he didn't doubt it was clean.

"I hate every inch of it," Lesley said. She took a sip of tea. "I hate this house, I hate this village, and I think I might possibly . . ."

She broke off. She straightened, as if there were hooks in her skin, as if invisible cords were pulling her head and shoulders towards the ceiling.

He'd never seen her like this. Slowly, slowly, he put down the mug, as if sudden movement might panic her, make her fly into the glass like the collared doves when he went out to refill the seeds. He hated that sound, hated to see the imprint of their fawn-coloured bodies on the patio window . . .

"I ought to go. I'm so sorry I woke you. I just wanted to make sure you were all right. When you . . ."

"I'm not all right, Duncan. And I don't think I'm ever going to be all right, whether you're sorry or not." She drew the cardigan tight, folding her arms. "I mustn't blame you, I suppose, since you haven't a clue, have you?" She unlocked the kitchen door and pulled it open. A cold draught swept in.

"What have I done?" he said.

She shook her head.

"Go home, Duncan."

He was at the front gate when he remembered the sugar bowl. It would have to stay where it was, he decided.

Guilty

June was already in the Hospice Shop when Ruby arrived. She was applying mascara, using the mirror on the wall behind the cash desk.

"The kettle's just boiled," she said, "but Letty isn't back yet with the milk. I told her not to rush, the pavements are that slippery this morning."

Ruby looked at the high heels on June's suede boots, and thought her own thoughts. June was in charge. Which was why they were always behind in the opening and sorting of bags. June would rather chat with customers than get down to work.

"Shall I get started on the bags?"

"Oh, thank you pet," June said.

Pet. Not for the first time Ruby wanted to scream. It was infuriating to be "pet'd" by someone younger.

She gave the back room a brisk spray of Woodland Breeze then emptied the first plastic bag onto the table. Shirts and trousers. Men's tan leather shoes, a good make, nicely polished. They'd soon sell. Men didn't seem to mind wearing other people's shoes.

She hoped Walter wouldn't have to wait long at the Surgery. He'd left the house before her. She'd told him to phone and let her know how it had gone before he went to work but whether he'd heard and whether he would remember was not certain. He was becoming very absent minded, just like his father. She frowned at a tie with a distinct mark over the stripes. Neglected gravy stain? Too late now. Into the Discard bin it went. She heard the door open and the sound of Letty's voice, cheerful as ever.

She herself could hardly remember what it felt like to be cheerful. She generally slept like a baby, but in recent days she'd found herself lying awake next to Walter's snoring body. Once, when the sound reached a crescendo, she had actually kicked him. It had achieved nothing; he was asleep again before she was.

And now he was looking for sympathy, complaining of stomach pains. For years she had devoted herself to this man, making nutritious, economical meals, catering to his every whim. The idea that there could be something wrong with his stomach was a piece of nonsense.

"It's wind," she told him. "You eat too fast. I've been saying it for years."

It wasn't wind of course. She knew fine what it was. A guilty conscience. She'd waited and waited for him to tell her why he'd been in Lesley's garden in the dark. This pain was his guilt breaking out. She tugged in vain at the imitation gold clasp on a white handbag. Sometimes money was left in handbags, or nice little handkerchiefs that could be washed and sold separately. Less nice were unwrapped mints that had melted into the linings.

"That's the tea made, Ruby," June called.

". . . Mrs Birnie was buying bread for Sammy's sandwiches, and she said it was a disgrace." Letty had evidently returned from her errand with much to tell. "and the police no' takin' a blind bit o' notice."

"You shouldn't listen to Mrs Birnie," June said, bringing the biscuit tin from under the counter. "That woman picks up gossip like a cat picks up fleas." She took up her mug, then put it down as her mobile phone rang. "Back in a moment," she said.

Ruby had frequently found out interesting things about the village from Letty, but it was important to ask at the time, because the girl forgot quickly. She offered Letty a chocolate digestive.

"Start at the beginning Letty dear, and go slowly," she said. "What else did Mrs Birnie say?"

Kettle Chips

As the train drew in to her station, Harriet pulled on a light waterproof over her blazer and took off her uniform scarf and tie. From here on, it was safer not to look like someone from a private school. It had been a long, exhausting week of exams, and she felt completely miserable, not helped by her period starting that morning. One more miserable thing to do and she would be free to lie on the sofa with a large bag of salt and balsamic vinegar Kettle Chips and watch junk TV.

A bus took her to Hartsend. She didn't know the name of Ryan's street, but she remembered where it was: beside a street lamp, with low hedges in front and all the curtains the same, upstairs and down in brown and white stripes. There was no name on the door. She rang the bell, and when nothing happened, knocked on the glass panel. Moments later the door opened a few inches. She saw a chain stretched across.

"We're no' wantin' anything."

"It's just a letter," Harriet said. "For Ryan Flaherty. Is this his house? "

The chain was loosened, the door opened, and the woman stared at her. Harriet hadn't really looked at her that day in the shop. Her hair was held back from her from her forehead by a pink plastic band with teeth, the kind that little girls wore. A dark green jumper stretched over her front. Either she wasn't wearing a bra, or it was too loose to give her any shape.

"It's . . . it's just a personal letter," Harriet said.

Ryan's mother, if it was she, took it without speaking, and closed the door. Was he at home or not? Harriet walked quickly away in case the door should reopen and a familiar voice call her back.

When she reached her own house, the kitchen light was on. She took out her key, but the door was unlocked. Which it shouldn't have been.

"Dad?"

"I'm in the sitting room."

He was on the sofa, shoes off, and a mug balanced on his stomach, watching football.

"I thought you were going to be late home," she told him.

"Oh, they cancelled it, thank goodness. Not enough to make a quorum. Combination of illness and road closures. I'm so glad. I'm absolutely knackered." He turned the sound back up.

"Why didn't you come to the station, then?" she asked. She had to say it twice, dropping her bag for emphasis.

"I'm sorry, sweetheart, I'm really not that long in."

Long enough to make yourself coffee though.

"What's for tea?" she said.

On the screen, a man in a white shirt jumped high in the

air, his foot striking a red-shirted man in the groin. Her father groaned loudly with the rest of the stadium.

"My exam was very hard, since you ask. And my period started and my stomach's very sore."

"Fine," he said.

"Dad!" she yelled.

He started, spilling his drink over his shirt.

"Harriet, what are you . . ." he got to his feet, wiping at himself with short, exasperated bursts of words and half words.

"I've just told Ryan Flaherty I don't want to see him ever again."

He seemed to struggle for a moment, then he said, "Why?"

"Because that's what you told me to do."

"When did I say that?" He seemed genuinely puzzled.

She gripped the top of the sofa. "On the way home the other night. You said you didn't want me to see him."

"I think I said you ought to. . . ."

She hated it when he began to slow down his words as if she was stupid, as if she was five years old . . .

"No, you said, 'I want you to keep away from him.'"

And now he was using the hand gestures as well, "I said you should keep away from him if he'd been drinking, Harriet. I didn't mean . . ."

"Yes, you did. And I've just seen his mother and his house and the hedge is all weeds and holes and it's awful. No wonder he's miserable. Anyone would be miserable in that house. I wish we'd never left Aberdeen. I wish we'd never come to this horrible place. I can't even travel on the bus home without getting spat on, or chewing gum in my hair. And I'm tired of making the tea every night, when I'm not even hungry!"

She slammed the door behind her. Half way up the stairs she conceded that her last statement was not completely true. She went furiously through the kitchen cupboards, grabbing the Kettle Chips, a family pack of Kit Kats, and a can of Coca Cola. As an afterthought, she twisted two sensible bananas off the bunch in the fruit bowl and stuck them in her blazer pockets.

Rumours and confusions

Rumours are spreading through Hartsend. Passed like a virus from one human host to the next and minutely altering, they are turning back on themselves and turning again, until they become quite different from their original selves.

In the Primary School the staff complain that the children are becoming increasingly excitable. The place is already something of a fortress, has been since Dunblane, with cameras, tall locked gates, and staff patrolling the play areas at lunch time, but Miss Calvert has now had to send out reassuring letters. She is certain that the rumour about High School pupils selling drugs disguised as Love-Hearts through the Primary railings is completely without foundation. Vigilance, she assures all parents is high. The security devices are in working order. All the same, she suggests that children if not accompanied by an adult should walk to and from school in groups if possible.

The bank, the chemist's, the fish-shop, and the baker's are all abuzz, and in the heart of the village, Dr MacKinnon, after a quick word with the other doctors, has asked the

Practice Manager to mail a firm reminder to the admin staff about confidentiality. Mindful however of the old maxim – a secret is something you tell one person at a time – his hopes are not high.

High on the hill, Mrs Crawfurd has chosen to ignore the whispers on the wind. Besides, she is preoccupied with her own thoughts. Too much time has passed to inquire about the mystery blonde. To ask now would be ridiculous. As far as she knows, the woman has not called again, but she cannot be sure. She is beginning to doubt her own judgement. When Dr MacKinnon had said, "Duncan is looking rather morose these days. We have to cheer him up. If he took an old friend like Lesley Crosthwaite out for dinner, I think that would do him a power of good.", she had acquiesced, but Duncan had come back that evening in a very angry mood, and she is afraid to ask why in case it makes things worse. In fact, Duncan is becoming rather annoying. She feels herself becoming tense when they are in the same room and he doesn't speak.

Life is beginning to confuse her on many different levels. A neatly ironed handkerchief, was lying with the post behind the door one morning, and the postman denies all knowledge of it. Mrs Flaherty is still unwell and has stopped coming to clean, which is not good. More curiously, the Spode 'Camilla' sugar bowl has disappeared. Did she herself put it somewhere? A few days ago she found her pension book in the fridge without the least memory of how it got there, and just recently, when she looked at her old school photographs, she could not immediately recall the other Prefects' names.

Down in the Dirty Duck, where memories tend to linger, and where the regulars energetically maintain a weary, cynical consensus about wives, politicians, footballers and life's other disappointments, there is a new swelling sense of outrage. Many of the pub's patrons are underdogs, done for by their genetic inheritance, unfairly treated by fate or baffled despite their own best efforts. They, out of all Hartsend, are the ones most instinctively sympathetic, most vocal, most outraged by the intelligence that someone is preying on the children of the village, for who is treated more unfairly, who is more regularly baffled in this life than a child?

No difference

The child was found, before anyone knew she was lost, by local man Albert Falconer, aged 43, who had just come off night shift, and whose habit it was to exercise his two Alsatian dogs on the edge of the golf course before going to bed so that they wouldn't wake him mid morning. The brief exposure to silence also helped him to relax, washing the din of the factory out of his head. Albert was a single man of quiet habits, one of a family of eight children, who enjoyed spending time with his siblings and their offspring, though as he liked to say, the dogs were less bother, they went to bed when they were told and didn't ask so many questions.

As always, he carried a large torch by which to see his way, a walking stick, for no real reason except that he liked a stick in his hand, and plastic bags to scoop up the dog dirt, because he wanted no trouble with the green-keepers. In truth, he felt a sense of ownership and responsibility when he walked through the grass. He had lived in the village all his life; he and his two older brothers had played in these fields before they'd become a golf course. There was a thin layer of frost on the ground, but Albert remembered proper winters, when the small loch in its middle had frozen. His elderly father spoke of even colder winters, when the waters had frozen long and hard enough for a bonfire to be lit, and bonspiels held.

The younger dog had run ahead and didn't come when called. Its barking grew more energetic. Albert shouted again, thinking it had found a rabbit or an injured bird. When he came close, he told it to be quiet. It switched to growling. The old dog went forward a few paces, then stopped, looking back to his master, back to the young dog, echoing its low growls.

In the light of the torch Albert saw something half in, half out of the shallow stream. A bundle of clothes, he thought. Another lazy git, too idle to take their rubbish to the dump. He went over to pull the daft dog away. A second look, and his heart failed him. He knelt down, heedless of the wet soaking his corduroys. His vision blurred. Only when the young dog began whimpering did he realise how tightly he was twisting its collar. Albert had never married, never had children, but it made no difference, not with this before him. No difference at all. Not with this.

Late night

"Hello, Father," the barman said. He was holding the phone to his ear.

The Reverend had given up trying to get the man to call him John, or Mr Smith.

"The room's all ready. And the food's to hand, though I doubt you'll have many in tonight." The man spoke hurriedly, as if his mind was elsewhere.

This was the fourth meeting of the Men's Pie and Pint Night, held in one of the upstairs function rooms. He had persuaded Dr Gordon to talk about Overcoming Stress but some of the regulars had sent their apologies, the weather was so foul. He'd wondered about cancelling the evening. The news about the dead child had depressed the whole village, including himself. It seemed almost wrong to talk about anything else.

It looked as if the weather had kept even the usual clientele away. The immense TV had been switched off, and the background music, normally loud and pulsating, had been muted, so that the rain could be heard battering hard on the stained glass panels of the upper windows. Two women sat at the far end of the bar, and an older man was working the slot machine. All three looked up and immediately lost interest.

"I'm on the phone to the polis," the barman said. "They're all on a mission, Father, off to deal with the bastard that killed that wee girl from. . . ." He broke off to speak into the phone.

Moments later, the street door opened. Dr Gordon, one elbow against the inner door, gave his umbrella a vigorous shake before coming fully into the room.

"That's some night out there," he began.

Smith held up a hand to quiet him, as the barman hung up the phone.

"What's wrong?" Gordon asked.

"I was just telling the Father here, somebody said he knew who'd done it, they'd known him from the old days, known him for a fucking bastard, excuse my French. So they're off to Whiteford to sort him out."

The Reverend forced himself to unhunch his shoulders and relax his grip on the wheel. He didn't enjoy driving at night, and bad weather made him nervous, gusting wind and darkness and the windscreen wipers at full speed making not much of a difference. Gordon's Lexus was heavier, far better equipped for this kind of weather, but the good doctor had come to the pub by taxi, anticipating more than one pint with his pie.

"Maybe this is a mistake," he said, not taking his eyes off the road. There was a car in front of them, but not near enough to illuminate the winding country road and it was impossible to put the lights on full beam with cars coming towards them round the bends.

Gordon said, "Did we have a choice? I should warn you, though, I'm not the heroic type. My usual role in a fight is to stand well out of the way with my eyes shut. Ouch," he exclaimed as they encountered a flooded patch, cascading a sheet of water over the field beside them.

The minister didn't consider himself the heroic type either. His own last involvement in a brawl had been twenty odd years earlier in a pub in Malaga. He could recall little of it, having been drunk at the time, but he'd a lasting reminder in the form of back pain that recurred when he least needed it.

"Hopefully the police will be there before us," he said.

"Don't count on it. I had a patient a couple of weeks ago. Manic depressive and off his meds. He told me on the phone he was going to slit his wrists, and mine if I tried to stop him. His social worker was elsewhere and occupied, no surprise there, but the police said they'd be within the half hour. So I sat outside in the car."

"And?"

"They weren't, so I went in."

"That sounds heroic to me."

"It's all role play. I'm very convincing. I should have been on the stage. Anyway, I'd seen a lot of him at the start of the week, and we both knew he didn't mean it." He made a sound between a cough and a laugh.

They stopped at a crossroads. Two miles to their destination, according to the sign.

"You said you knew this man?" Gordon asked.

"I know the family. Not very well." Saying more would take him into deeper waters. He didn't want to go into explanations that involved Harriet. She had begun speaking to him again, but not with any enthusiasm. Most of the time he didn't know whether she was listening to anything on her iPod, or whether the earphones were merely a declaration of mutiny.

Long night

"Mr Smith?"

"Yes."

"The Doctor's asking for you. Can you come with me please."

"I've lost my hat," he told the Police Sergeant's back, immediately realising how pathetic and pointless this sounded. He could explain death and hell with logic and conviction, but all he could talk about here was the fact that someone had knocked his woolly hat off.

They'd shouted, trying to get through the crowd. Dr Gordon ploughed into them but he himself faltered after a glancing blow left him hatless, unnerved by the looping wail of sirens, the cries and calls of neighbours, the barking of stray dogs. Before he knew it, Gordon was out of sight and he was alone on the edge of the disordered mass of bodies.

Now he followed the Sergeant up a badly-lit stairwell, which smelled of damp and burnt fat and pee. Even here there was a lot of noise echoing around. He felt, rather than saw, those they had to squeeze past, all wet like himself, some with heads down, some in black raincoats and police caps, one bulky man in a soaked tee-shirt who was doing most of the shouting, and at the top, a woman in uniform, her face impassive, her one glance memorising everything about him.

The room seemed full of people. All the lights were on. He called Gordon's name and the man's head rose from behind a toppled armchair, followed by the rest of him. He'd taken off his overcoat and pushed up his shirt sleeves. "Your man's going to be all right. Probably. I don't know if he'll hear you. He's coming and going a bit."

Had Gordon himself been hurt? His curls were dishevelled, and he was holding himself awkwardly.

"That's the ambulance now," someone said above the other voices, and for a moment there was silence while everyone listened.

Gordon insisted on staying with the injured man, deferring to the paramedics in all else. His earlier cheerfulness had gone and his face seemed ghost-like to Smith in the criss-cross of headlights and yellow streetlights. The wind had dropped but the rain was still falling.

"No, I'm fine. There's no need," he told the Reverend. "You go home and get on your knees." As the ambulance door closed, he gave a half lift of his hand and a brief nod.

Smith tried later to think what exactly he'd done after that, and couldn't, although he did recall a plain clothes officer taking some details, and asking him questions. Then the Sergeant came over. Actually he was a member of the Church, he said, introducing himself, grown up through the Sunday School and the BB, though he didn't get along much, what with overtime and shift work and that. They'd made several arrests, he said, though many of the culprits had disappeared into the night as soon as they'd heard the squad cars. They would probably all be well-known characters. It could have been much worse. They'd used fists and boots, not knives. They might have tried to burn Flaherty out, endangering the lives of all the building's occupants. They'd been drinking but were not as drunk as they might have been later in the evening. The doctor's intervention had given the man a chance.

"How did you know what was happening?" the Sergeant asked.

"We were in the pub. Pie and Pint night."

He watched the Sergeant consider whether or not to delve deeper.

"Aye well, it's going to be a long night for some," the man commented at last. "Drive home carefully, sir."

All the slow, cautious way home, Smith listened to loud music on the radio, afraid he might fall asleep at the wheel. When he reached the manse and checked his watch he was astonished to see that it was closer to four than three am. Every part of him was exhausted. He took his sodden shoes off in the kitchen, went upstairs, stripped, and fell into bed without his usual scrupulous brushing and flossing of teeth. He tried to pray, as was his habit, but couldn't manage

more than a few words. God and the dental hygienist would
have to forgive him.

When he woke, he was surprised that he'd slept so well
despite all the night's events, only to find, glancing at his
phone, that it was just after five. He switched on the light.
They had promised to use email and not to phone one
another. It wasn't expensive to phone, but hearing her voice
made the separation unbearable. He had never been good
on the phone, not when it mattered. Skype wasn't much
better. He always felt afterwards that no-one had said what
they meant to say. Now he stared at the other half of the
bed, flat and forsaken, and dialled the sunny side of the
world. It rang a few times, then his father-in-law's voice,
formal, but having lost none of its Scots accent, told him no-
one could come to the phone, but please leave a message.

Santa Claus

The room felt very chilly. Duncan pulled the quilt closer, hoping he might get back to sleep , but it was no use. Once more consciousness brought with it thoughts of Lesley.

And a feeling of guilt. He'd been very upset that night, hurt by her lack of explanation. He'd pondered deeply on what he might not 'have a clue' about, and come up with nothing. But for Mrs Fleming, he might never have found an answer.

She'd been in need of painkillers. Apparently the box in the First Aid kit was empty. Negligence on the part of the Miss Guthrie the First Aid officer. He offered ibuprofen, which she accepted gratefully. Then, with a small fluttery gesture of one hand towards her middle, she mouthed the words 'time of the month.'

He was embarrassed, but later realized that she had done him a service. She had solved the mystery. Everything now made perfect sense. He supposed in a way it was something of a compliment, since it suggested Mrs Fleming didn't see him as an old fuddy-duddy. Lesley, being the person she was, would never dream of mentioning such things. Not to him, certainly.

At once his anger had evaporated. Her name now conjured up for him only vulnerability. He felt terrible. His heart ached with sympathy. Lukewarm tea, custard cream biscuits too long in the tin, a kitchen tiled in ancient, pale yellow Vitrolite – he saw now with miserable clarity how everything fitted together to make a sort of metaphor of her life. No wonder she disliked it so much. It reminded one of old hospital corridors, and boiler rooms in school basements. And yet, if she hated it, why didn't she change it? Surely there was something childish in this refusal to change things?

The temperature, as forecast, had fallen overnight. In the dim garden below the cracks in the tarred paths were frost-rimmed, the lawns altered to rough expanses of greenish white. Time to take the first suet balls from the freezer. Breadcrumbs. Beef suet from the local butcher. Oats and raisins. Chunky peanut butter. Sunflower seeds got from the Pet Shop, and polenta from the Co-operative.

He was proud of his suet balls. He gave some to a select few of his colleagues in the library each year as an early Christmas present, with a note on the gift tag, "Not For Human Consumption," because as someone had jokingly said, they had more nutrition in them than supermarket sausages.

The sparrows would find them first. He'd changed his mind recently about sparrows on learning that they were in decline and it cheered him to feel that they'd found a haven in his garden. The starlings would squabble over them. *Not* the favourites of his flock. Their sheen reminded him of petrol on water. Greedy, vicious in their intentions and unintelligent, they were the avian equivalent of bikers in black leather. (He wasn't sure whether this idea was his own, or whether he'd found it somewhere, but when he'd used it in conversations, it had been appreciated, which was quite satisfying). In contrast, finches and tits seemed to him to justify their existence merely by their bright defiant colours.

Washed and dressed, he made himself an espresso, set bread in the toaster, then decided to make porridge. While it rotated slowly in the microwave, he opened the blinds. He had neglected the feeders. The male robin was looking directly at him from the hydrangea. It might as well have been carrying a protest placard.

"I know they're empty, but I'm having my breakfast first," Duncan said. "Would that be all right?" It was as much of a bully as the starlings, but it was a loner, that was the difference. He would order mealworms if he could ensure that only the robin got to them, but they were very expensive and a gang of starlings could devour an entire tray in minutes. He'd put some out once when he had workmen installing a new boiler. The chap in charge had watched it happening and compared them to piranhas.

In an ideal world, he mused, birds could be trained to fetch seed for themselves. The shed door was never locked. Apart from the bird seed mix, nothing of value was stored there, their present gardener preferring to bring his own tools, but it was a useful repository for items that might yet be used; hairy balls of brown twine, ceramic bowls once faithfully filled each autumn with hyacinth bulbs, screws and nails in jam jars attached by their lids to the undersides of shelves, hessian potato sacks, rolls of netting for the long-abandoned strawberry bed, mousetraps (not the humane kind), wooden-handled hoes and forks not used since Mr MacKenzie's day. A tired but somehow reassuring smell of dust hung in its air.

The door wouldn't open more than a few inches. Assuming it was to do with either the previous rain or the present hard frost, Duncan put his weight on it. When he heard sounds from inside, his first thought was that it might be a hedgehog or a cat. But what animal would close the door behind itself?

He scraped the frost-encrusted side window and peered in. There was a body on the floor, face down, wrapped in sacking. Male, judging by the size of the shoes. He breathed on the glass again, making a wad from his handkerchief this time rather than using his leather glove.

All Ryan wanted was to be left alone, but Crawfurd wouldn't let him be. He'd been forced to sit up, then get up, his arms and legs totally numb, as if they were sub-stitutes, his own taken away, and prosthetic parts attached to him in the night. Crawfurd half dragged, half carried him into the house. Now he was in an armchair, with a scratchy rug round his shoulders, another round his legs and feet, in front of an electric fire, his teeth vibrating against one another, and his throat feeling like it had been scoured with one of his mother's sink cleaners. A cup took shape in the space just beneath his nose. Crawfurd told him to drink. He did as he was told. It was coffee, but there was alcohol in it.

"How do you feel? Any better?"

Fuck this guy who kept waking him. He looked like a teacher, the kind who needed to be liked, the one nobody took seriously, not even the rest of the teachers.

"You haven't done any harm, except to yourself, so I suppose I should just turf you out onto the street . . ."

Ryan bent down, trying to find his trainers and socks, then decided against it. His head felt like it was going to break in two.

"I don't think you quite realise how stupid you've been. D'you know what the temperature is out there? Once your jacket's finished drying, I'll drive you home."

"Fuck you."

The old guy seemed to explode. "Don't you dare use that language in this house!"

"Stop it. You're doin' my head in."

The shouting stopped. When he next opened his eyes, Crawfurd was sitting across from him on the other side of the fireplace, with an expression on his face Ryan couldn't interpret. It could have been hatred or disgust. Or maybe the opposite. This was, after all, the man his mother spoke about as if he was next in line to Santa Claus for sainthood.

"Your mother must be worried to death about you."

"She's no' worrying about me. She's got a hell of a lot more to worry about than me."

"What d'you mean?"

Ryan shook his head, and wished he hadn't.

"We knew she was ill, obviously. Is it . . . something serious?"

Was the guy being stupid on purpose?

"I don't want to intrude of course, but if it's . . . something that a specialist might . . ."

Ryan looked at the room, seeing it properly for the first time. Rows of books, gilt-framed mirror above a marble fireplace, paintings, heavy dark green curtains with tasselled tie-backs, the B&O music centre and the stacked CD's, the brass-studded tan leather of the chairs they were sitting in – it was a different planet. Nothing ugly, nothing cheap, nothing that would have looked at home in their living room less than a mile away. Three times a week his mum had come into this world and back to theirs. How had she stayed sane?

"I'm sorry. I didn't mean to upset you," Crawfurd said.

"You're no' upsetting me. It's having a fucking paedophile for a father that's upsetting me."

The word was out before he could stop it. He waited for Crawfurd to shout at him again. Nothing.

Next moment, the door opened.

"Duncan? I thought I heard voices."

Crawfurd stood up.

"Raised voices, Duncan. What is happening? Who is this person?"

Influencing the situation

The Manse door was opened, by the daughter, the pretty blond girl. She was yawning, only belatedly remembering to cover her mouth.

"Good morning. Is your father at home?" Lesley asked.

"I'm sorry, I think he's still asleep. There was an emergency last night. He didn't get back till this morning . . ."

Clearly this was why the phone had been ringing out. Lesley stood her ground. Saying she would go and see, the girl showed her into a small book-lined room. Old weighty volumes stood neatly along the bottom shelves. Others more modern lay at odd angles or on top of one another. Facing the door was a small desk with a computer and a telephone. A poster of a black motorbike, with the word Honda in bold red letters, took up most of the other wall, but the oddest thing was a penguin, at least three feet high, hanging on a hook next to the window. It was made of black and white fur fabric, with spiky black hairs on the top of its head, a garish orange beak and over-large shiny eyes.

The daughter came back into the room. She had straitened her hair a little, and put a long jumper over her rather skimpy pyjama top.

"I'm really sorry," she said again. "If it's not desperately urgent, could you leave a message, and he'll phone you in a little while?"

The penguin seemed to Lesley to be staring at her, trying to read her mind. She turned her back on the glittery eyes.

"Please tell him my friend's husband was attacked last night. He's now in Intensive Care in the District General."

The girl wasn't looking at her, more interested in the garden outside, where nothing at all was happening.

"I'll certainly pass that on. Thank you for . . ."

"The point is, she can't stay in that house."

The girl retreated into the hall. Lesley followed her.

"I don't make a habit of interfering in other people's lives," she said as the girl opened the front door to let her out. But her response was nothing more than a faint smile.

Clearly the Reverend Smith didn't want to be disturbed. And indeed, why should he do anything? Mrs Flaherty was not one of his flock. But with each homeward step Lesley felt more and more annoyed. Johnny Flaherty, perpetrator of unspeakable crimes, lay safe in a hospital bed being looked after, while Mary sat behind closed curtains, too scared to show her face. The police didn't have the manpower to watch the house constantly, no surprise there, and she refused to go to either daughter. "Come to me then." The words had formed in Lesley's mind, but she hadn't said them. There were all sorts of reasons why this was impossible.

Once back at the house, she took out two shopping bags and placed various basic foodstuffs in them. As she walked past the end of the Crawfurd's street, she told herself that she did not need help. A grown man who couldn't ask a friend out for dinner without his mother's permission, correction, on his mother's instruction, was hardly likely to help in this kind of situation. If there were troublemakers outside the house, it was very likely that she would know them from school. She would know exactly who they were.

Her feet, however, seemed to contradict her. Against her will she found herself turning, making her way up to the Crawfurd mansion. No-one answered the doorbell. She went around the side, avoiding the overgrown pyracantha and its sharp thorns, glancing into Duncan's study. He looked straight back at her through the glass, then signalled towards the kitchen door.

"Good morning," she said. "I just wanted to tell you that I've . . ."

"I'm so glad to see you, Lesley. Please come in. I could do with your help. I've got Mary Flaherty's son in my study," he said.

"What? Why?"

"I found him in the shed, half-frozen. Come in, please."

She followed him into the kitchen.

"He's sleeping at the minute. But he says he won't go home, and I don't know what to do."

"What does your mother advise?"

"I sent her back to bed with a cup of tea. She hasn't come down again," he glanced at his watch.

How could someone so intelligent be so dense? How

could a grown man be such a child? He wanted shaking or slapping, or something.

"I feel completely at a loss."

He was. She saw it and rebuked herself. This at least was admirable. She could see he wanted to do good. There was something of the hero inside him, in spite of everything.

"And by the way," he went on, "forgive me for the other night. It was complete thoughtlessness on my part. It won't happen again."

She swallowed what she'd been about to say. There was a helpful stool just beside her and she sat down. When she looked up, Duncan was sitting on the opposite side of the table, watching her.

"I was just on my way to their house," she said at last. "Mary left a message on my phone. She said Johnny was in the hospital."

"Johnny?"

"Her husband. And there were people outside, throwing stones at her windows."

It was his turn to ask why.

It took time to explain but she did the best she could, leaving out completely her fruitless visit to the manse.

"Good Lord," he said, when her tale came to an end. He raised his hand to his upper lip, in search perhaps of the lost moustache. "I'll phone the police," he said.

"I think she already has. I couldn't sit at home any longer. At least I can see she has enough food."

"No, I'll go," he said. "You should stay here. Go and sit

with the boy. I will make some calls first though. I know one or two people whose word might influence the situation. If he wakes up, talk to him. I've a feeling he doesn't like me very much."

He showed her into the study. The boy was asleep in the reclining armchair, his feet on a stool, a cushion beneath his shaven head and a brown and white mohair rug wrapped over him. She understood why the boy had run away, but why had he taken refuge in the Crawfurd's garden shed? And what was she meant to say to the lady of the house if she appeared before Duncan came back? Before she could ask, Duncan caught her hand, gave her a quick peck on the cheek and was gone. Actually, it was more than just a quick peck. Lesley had received enough quick pecks to know the difference.

Glory

Thanks to calls from the local undertaker, a visit to a bereaved family, and a Presbytery committee meeting, it was late in the afternoon before the Reverend had time to think again about the Flahertys. He worked his way up to a senior member of the local police, only to be told that the Chief Inspector would call him back. While he waited it occurred to him that he might get the latest news from Dr Gordon, but a voice at the Surgery told him that Dr Gordon was taking the day off. He tried the man's mobile. No reply. He texted Harriet to say where he was going, and went out.

He could hear music playing in the flat, and knocked hard on the door when his first tentative push at the bell brought no response. Then, bending to the letterbox, he shouted, "Gordon, it's me. Open the door."

"I'm not here."

He knocked harder.

Gordon looked terrible. He was wearing a navy dressing-gown minus its belt and brown pyjama bottoms. His hair had not been combed: it rose at each side of his head, as if straining to meet in the middle.

"Are you all right?"

"Absolutely tip top."

"Tell the truth."

Gordon gestured towards his ribs: on his left side there was a large discoloured area of skin. "Two cracked ribs. Not a problem. I have a smallish private store of painkillers. Very naughty of me but that's the way it is."

"I was worried about you."

Gordon didn't react. He was still hanging on to the door. Smith sensed it was about to be closed in his face.

"Any chance of some coffee? The traffic from the city was terrible." This was probably true, though he hadn't been in it.

The flat had so obviously been inhabited by a series of temporary tenants that Smith felt instantly sorry for his friend. The armchairs, high backed with dark wooden arms, took him right back to his grandparents' house in Elgin. Married during the Second World War, they had lived in a house full of Utility furniture and being canny Free Church folk had never replaced it with anything more beautiful.

Gordon had gone to the bathroom and was taking his time, so he made himself coffee. He glanced round the kitchen: stained vinyl walls, net curtains, a lethal looking gas cooker. He had never invited the man round for a meal. Once Jean came home, he would.

"I made myself a cup," he said, when Gordon came back. He had put on black jogging bottoms, and there was a white sweatshirt in his hand.

"Shall I make you one?" he went on.

"No, no. Help me on with this."

They did the sleeves first. At one point Gordon let out some small grunts, undermining his claim to be pain-free. It was like putting clothes on a child. He'd learned how to stretch the neck of T-shirts when he dressed Kerr. Gordon hadn't showered, he thought, just sprayed on deodorant. It put him in mind of how Kerr used to rub soap on the back of each hand before meals, and splash a little water on the palms. You had to admire the cleverness, but he could never understand what the point was. It was so much effort, and fooled nobody.

He sipped his coffee. They watched the steady red glow of the electric fire.

"I think I really came to apologize. For not following you in," he said at last. "I feel very bad about it."

"Forget it. This way I get all the glory. I'm hoping for a brass plaque above the bar at the Dirty Duck."

"I'm not sure the regulars would approve."

"You're right. I spoiled their fun. Next time make me count to ten. Or twenty, whatever it takes."

The man seemed determined to avoid being serious.

"You are going to have to cope with a lot of gossip. Some will love thee, some will hate thee, that kind of stuff."

More silence.

"How is he?" he asked.

"Flaherty? I've no idea."

It sounded as if Gordon didn't care. Fair enough. He'd possibly prevented a murder, which was a good thing, but Flaherty's future, his innocence or guilt, was none of his concern. If only he himself could be so . . . dispassionate? Was that the word he wanted?

"Well, if it's any consolation, I've just ruined Harriet's life. Again."

He went on, though knew Gordon wasn't listening.

"Not deliberately. She thinks I told her not to see this particular boy." He shied away from naming Ryan. "Not that she was particularly serious about him, until I banned him from the premises. According to her. You know, there must be some technical term for what happens to words when they leave your mouth meaning one thing, and enter a teenager's head meaning something totally different."

"What would you do to someone who hurt her?"

"Hurt her?"

Gordon nodded.

Smith thought of the Flaherty boy, (the smell of strong mints failing to mask the drink on his breath), who didn't need to lift a single finger to draw Harriet after him into the night. He'd thought he'd handled it pretty well, wise as a serpent, gentle as a dove. Harriet had somehow turned it into a battle. And let him win. What was the name for a battle that cost you more when you won? It would come to him. He'd prayed and prayed for her, far more than he'd ever prayed for Kerr. Sometimes he wondered if praying made things worse.

"Well, if someone hurt her, they would be held accountable," he said slowly, "but as a Christian, I would have to forgive."

"No, you wouldn't."

Gordon's certainty cut like a whip.

"We've talked about this before." He tried to stop thinking of Harriet, and focus on what he was trying to say. "I'm not saying it's easy, but there is a logic to it. If Christ commands it, it must be possible. I have to forgive if I want to be forgiven. You have to take into account the . . ."

"And that makes sense to you? You have to forgive, but God doesn't? He separates the sheep from the goats and the poor goats don't even know they're goats. They're in the same field, eating the same grass. What choice did they have? They didn't ask to be goats."

"That's a parable. You can't read it in that . . ."

"No. Speaking as one of the bloody goats, I think I have the right to read it anyway I like."

Smith couldn't think quickly or clearly enough to refute him. Later he thought it was just as well. Any reply would have been wrong. Later still, he wondered if he should ever have gone. If it was his own sense of failure that had taken him, not concern for his friend.

"Maybe I should let you go back to bed," he said, getting to his feet. He tried to sound amicable and generous and untroubled.

"Maybe you should."

After all this time.

Marjory McKinnon adjusted the velvet cushion behind her head. The head rest in this car was too hard for her.

"I hate to mention it, dear," she began, "but people have been asking me why after all this time there's no word about a funeral for poor Dr Gordon."

"You'll know when I know," he lied. Of necessity he'd been lying to more and more people with each passing day. All would soon become public knowledge. Then he corrected himself. There had been no suicide note, no last minute phone call, no diary revelations. "All", therefore, would never be known.

"Warm enough?" he asked, keeping his eyes on the busy motorway.

"Yes, thank you, dear."

And really, he reflected, there was a great deal that the public would never know, that even Marjory would never know unless he decided to tell her. The Factor had gone to Gordon's flat in response to a complaint about damp, lodged at least a month earlier. Finding the body, he'd phoned for an ambulance and the police. The police summoned the police casualty surgeon, a GP from a city practice, who attended the scene and confirmed life extinct. A syringe and ampoules were bagged, to be sent in due course to the forensic laboratory. The casualty surgeon came to McKinnon at home because they were old friends, having stood round the same dissecting table as students, and because she trusted McKinnon would have done exactly the same if their positions had been reversed.

She told him all the sad, unsavoury details – how one of the officers had touched the sleeping computer, and come back through to the living room saying, 'Don't bloody move anything. We need the CID."

McKinnon's mind had made the terrible leap almost at once, but he'd taken his time before replying.

"I'm thinking of another recent death," he told her. Meaning the death of the child. Meaning that Gordon might have been involved somehow.

His colleague understood perfectly. "Such thoughts would certainly occur," she said, "though one would hope to be proved wrong. I gather they're calling it "Accidental Drowning" at the moment. Who knows? We'll all have to wait for the pathologist."

Should he have known? The government had spent a very large amount of money training him to observe and recognise symptoms and years of practice had taught him more. The young man's looks and charm had blinded them all. Hindsight, that old retrospectoscope, was such a wonderful thing. With the benefit of hindsight, there were certainly some indicators. Shortish spells in different jobs, a failed marriage, few close friends . . .

"He saved that man's life. I think it'll be a big funeral, even though he wasn't here long," Marjory said.

McKinnon thought not. Not when the facts came out. The Fiscal was still waiting for a Pathology report on the death of the travellers' child. Depending on that, Gordon's funeral might be weeks or even months away.

It would be conducted by someone from the Humanist Association, he'd been told. None of the local ministers would have to participate. Who would be there, besides himself and the practice manager? He thought it unlikely that the ex-wife would make an appearance. The executor was some kind of cousin.

"I thought we might stop at that garden centre," he said, glancing at the dashboard clock. "I told Lillian she needn't make lunch."

Soup and bacon sandwiches at the Garden Centre was a far better deal than one of his daughter's lunches, which featured low fat ingredients; something called humus, which looked like farmyard slurry, bits of leaves and raw carrot and crispbread. No wonder she didn't have a husband yet. No sensible man could live on rabbit food.

He would need to let Marjory wander; she had a passion for looking at nicknacks they didn't need, but he would read one of the newspapers provided for husbands over a second cup of coffee. They would then drive on to Lillian's house, where they would, as usual, have a pleasant enough time.

After all this time.

He would wash her car, give it a polish, then doze on the couch while mother and daughter walked to the local retail park where they would spend many happy hours buying a pair of pillowslips or something of that ilk.

When he'd come home that day with the news of Gordon's death, he'd found Marjory in the kitchen. The pulley was down and half-covered with sheets, with her barely visible behind it at the ironing board. She was folding one of his shirts. The iron, vertical on the end of the board, was giving out little snorts of steam. She'd refused to believe him. "Are you sure?" she'd said, several times.

Johnny Flaherty, minus his spleen, was still in the High Dependency Unit. There was no evidence whatsoever that he had been involved with the dead child or indeed any child anywhere. The ringleaders of the mob were being rounded up. Inquiries were proceeding. Meantime, Hartsend abhorring a vacuum, opinion was beginning to harden against the child's parents.

He'd spared Marjory all but the barest details. Her only comment that evening, as she helped herself to more peas, was, "He had such lovely hair." He'd looked up from his roast lamb and mint sauce, aghast. Granted she had only met the man on a few social occasions, but a death was a death. It seemed to him the most fatuous statement he had ever heard.

He'd lain awake long after she fell asleep. This was the woman he loved. He expected more from her. Ridiculous tears formed in his eyes. For her, for himself, or for Gordon?

Perhaps. For the whole human race? No. Not any more. The planet was far too big for him now, it had long since slipped beyond his grasp. He wasn't alone in this, most of his contemporaries felt much the same. They had believed at the beginning, knowing their cleverness, eager to get into medical school. Once in, they'd quickly become cynical. He'd read someone's comment in a recent BMJ, warning of the danger of being like crabs or oysters in a pot, gradually losing strength as the heat, paperwork and targets, and political meddling increased. In like manner, he had given up on the wider world, given up on the nation, given up rationally if not emotionally on the NHS. Protecting the people of his village was something he would fight to the death for. But here in his own small corner, in his own bed, he wanted help. He wanted some deeper, more profound verdict on all that had happened, something more than the fact that the man had lovely hair.

Home

"I stink of garlic," Harriet said. "I've been making meat-loaf." She sniffed her fingers.

"No more cooking after tonight. No more cooking after tonight." She made it into a song as she went to the sink, rocking her hips. Without the slightest idea of the effect she was having on him. She had a very pert little bum. Tight denims might have been invented just for her.

"I can't wait to see what she's brought for us."

"You are so greedy," he told her.

"I am not. Everybody likes getting things. Anyway, Mum took Christmas presents for all of them, so they'll be sending stuff for us."

She was too fond of stuff, though. He'd have his work cut out trying to make her less materialistic. He thought of old Crawfurd, sitting up there on the hill with all his beautiful stuff, like the Crawhall original on the landing that was probably worth thousands. "They're only things, Ryan," he'd said. "They don't bring any comfort when the cold wind blows."

"Anyway, I made this for you. For your Mum coming home," he said, taking a roll of paper out of its cardboard tube. He let it unroll across the floor.

"Wow! It's brilliant. Thank you so much. I love all the gold bits." She fingered the letters. "Is that bubble wrap?"

"They never throw anything out. They have a whole room stuffed with things they're never going to use. He told me to help myself."

When he'd explained to Crawfurd that he wanted to make a 'welcome home' banner, and who it was for, Crawfurd had said, "A nice girl, Harriet." With a thoughtful expression, as if he was thinking, "Too nice for you." Or maybe he was thinking, treat her properly, which was ok, because that was exactly what he intended to do.

He didn't completely get Crawfurd. He'd been treated decently from the moment he'd been brought in from the shed, more than decently, but in a kind of hesitant way, as if Crawfurd wasn't sure he was allowed. It was like how Chrissie looked round to see who was watching when there were plain biscuits and caramel wafers on the plate.

"It's so-o-o good. Should we hang it inside or outside?" Harriet asked. She knelt to roll it up.

"I would say inside, but it's up to you. OK, then. Phone me later?"

"But you just got here," she stood up. "And I want you to meet Mum."

That's going to happen, he thought, but not right now. He'd seen photographs. She was an older, plumper version of Harriet, with darker hair. There was no way of knowing how she'd jump. Weeks of absence, a long flight. Better not to make his entry this week. He thought he'd be pretty much ok with Mum but only if he kind of tiptoed into her life. And more like a dancer than a burglar.

He had his excuse ready. "I'm moving back home soon. I haven't packed my stuff yet." Not that there was much to pack. And not that he wanted to go, but he could feel his mother's silence getting louder every time he saw her.

"There's loads of meatloaf."

It was tempting. The Crawfurds lived on microwave stuff, It was ok, but it came in microscopic quantities. Hand on the door, he turned. "Phone me soon, ok?" He tried standing on his toes. Not so easy. He laughed at himself.

Harriet flung a towel at him. He laughed again, threw it straight back and closed the door behind him.

Well, that was something, she thought. Usually it was hard work just trying to make him smile. Even though good things were happening, the bad things were still pulling him down. He'd passed his first assessment, despite all the time missed. The graffiti on the pavement outside his house had been cleaned off, and his mother had moved back from his sister's. Someone from the Community Council had even come round to see what else they could do for her. But none of the big things were being talked about.

"Kid gloves," her Dad said, meaning, don't ask questions, let him talk about what he wants to, when he wants to. She was trying, but it was hard. She hadn't realised how much her life depended on being direct with people, and expecting them to be direct back. Being gentle with people wasn't in fact her strongest point.

The potatoes were on the work top, waiting to be peeled. She put Ryan's three back in the vegetable box, and looked at the clock. It had occurred to her that it would be a noble and generous thing to let them have time to themselves. She'd invented an excuse to conceal her generosity. "I hate waiting, Dad. It drives me crazy."

"You'll be waiting here. Longer."

"I can tidy up a bit. I might go to bed and read. You should get some flowers," she told him, "but not the ones at the petrol station. Get them at that Sainsbury's on the way."

Thank goodness she had given up the Hospice shop. No early rising tomorrow. She wondered if Mum would sleep all day, or if she had slept on the plane. It occurred to her that their bedroom might be a better place to hang the banner, but when she went upstairs she couldn't go in. She hardly ever went into their room. Hardly ever needed to, but it was more a feeling of respect that stopped her. It was their space. She would have died rather than open any of the drawers. If they had secrets, she didn't want to know, not ever.

She went into the downstairs study to find something to read. There was a lot of nostalgia in here. The penguin puppet who'd once starred in a holiday club, an aerial photograph of their old house in Peterculter, school photographs of Kerr and herself, and the beloved motorbike poster. Dad had given up the bike when she was small. Kerr remembered it, said it should have been kept for him.

She'd heard it used as a sermon illustration more than once. Giving up something you loved for something you loved better, Dad said. Mum had a different interpretation. He wasn't very good, she said. He fell off quite a lot, especially in the rain at traffic lights, so it was really self preservation.

He'd be less grumpy and smile more with Mum home. Exercise had helped him work off his grumpiness, but he'd stopped going to the gym now. He hadn't said why, but it was clear as the nose on your face. He was so angry at being taken in by that man. It made her skin creep. Only once he'd talked to her about it. She'd been in bed, with the light off and the radio still on. He'd opened her door.

"Time you were asleep, love," he'd said.

"I can't. I'm really really tired, but I'm not sleepy."

"It might be easier without Radio One."

She couldn't see his face. "Are you alright, Daddy?"

"Not really."

"Can I help?"

"You do help, Harriet. You help me all the time."

"Are you thinking about . . . That man." She couldn't bring herself to say, "Dr Gordon" or "your friend". It was unbearable to think that her father could have been friends with such a person.

"At least you never brought him home," she said.

He stood in the doorway for a long while.

"Try to sleep, darling," was all he said, as he closed the door.

A *little* strange

It had been well below zero during the night; the pot-holes in Lesley's back lane were frozen over. He drove very cautiously, trying to avoid the worst ones. She had evidently been watching from the house, and was at the back gate waiting for him. Well-wrapped up, he was glad to see.

"D'you have a wheelbarrow?" he asked, unlocking the car boot.

"It's very rusty. I can carry one bag."

To prove it she wrapped her arms round one of the seed-filled plastic sacks, shouldered the gate open and made her way to the old boiler house. Duncan followed with the other sack, the box of suet balls and the bird feeders.

Now that the heavy mist had cleared, pale sunshine had melted the frost on those parts of the ground not shaded by the house. The garden looked sadly neglected. A *hamamelis molis* was doing its best but the snowdrops and pink hellebore were practically hidden by weeds, creeping ivy, and withered beech leaves.

They opened one sack and filled the two bird feeders.

"You want to have these where you can see the birds, but they can't see you," he advised. He suggested a lilac bush near the dining room window. Together they tied them on, at a height where Lesley would be able to refill them without standing on a stool.

She suggested coffee. He accepted. The yellow kitchen tiles seemed uglier than ever in the morning light. He shivered, recalling what she had said about hating them.

"Go through and sit beside the fire," she told him. "And by the way, that's yours," She pointed to a small square parcel on the table. "Don't forget to take it this time."

He remembered this room from the day of the funeral. Apart from the rearrangement of chairs, not much had changed. The previous year's calendar still hung next to the fireplace at the December Page. The Rialto Bridge Under Snow. A *vaporetto*, interior lights on, passengers muffled behind steamed-up windows was emerging from beneath it. Dark water reflected pale gold light from shop fronts. In the foreground the intricate tracery of a metal gate opening onto the canal was powdered with white.

He cleared his throat carefully before calling to her in the kitchen.

"Lesley, could I perhaps have tea?"

"Of course. I thought you were a coffee drinker."

"Well, I am sometimes," he said, turning to look at the feeders. It would take a little time for the first birds to come, but the message would soon spread.

She brought through the tray. "I hope you don't mind sitting in here. The front room is temporarily occupied."

"Occupied?"

"Fish tanks," she said.

"Fish tanks." Had he missed something? Mother's cryptic reference to a gentleman visitor had never fully faded from his mind. He had settled on a cousin eventually, a distant and not very welcome caller, too insignificant for Lesley to mention at the time and of no importance whatsoever now.

"It's a long story. Walter next door bought new tanks to breed fish, but Ruby won't let him, so the tanks are here till he works out what to do with them."

Why would anyone want to breed fish? His sympathies were entirely with the wife.

"What kind of fish is he wanting to breed, flesh-eating piranhas?"

"Guppies."

He was none the wiser. "Well, it's very generous of you to store them. I hope he appreciates that."

"I'm not going to be generous indefinitely."

He was glad to hear it. "Why doesn't he build a shed? He's got the same amount of ground as you have. Plenty of room to put a big shed back to back with his garage. He could sit down there with his fish, put in a little TV set, some curtains and a kettle, and be out of her way completely."

"Oh dear," Lesley said. Her lips curved in a proper smile.

"What's the matter?"

"Nothing." She stirred her tea. "Sometimes I think I'm a very bad person. I have very bad thoughts."

This he could not believe, but he kept silent. He had kept

silent quite a lot recently in moments of female distress. He felt he was beginning to understand women.

"Talking of sheds," she began, "I meant to tell you, I asked Ryan Flaherty why he took refuge in yours that night. How is he, by the way?"

"He seems fine. He passed that essay I helped him with. I rather enjoyed it. He knows what he wants to say, but he's not terribly logical. I suspect he may be dyslexic. What did he say?"

"About the shed? He used to come to your house after school when Mrs Flaherty was cleaning. When he was in Primary school. Your gardener gave him Buttered Brazils and let him sit and play in the shed."

"Mr Mackenzie. Odd I never noticed him."

"Well, you would be at work. Your mother must have known."

He supposed so. Perhaps she had assumed that as long as the boy remained outside the house he was not a nuisance.

"How is she?"

"Mother? Fine. Well, a bit fragile. She said the strangest thing to me this morning. You know we put him in the back bedroom, downstairs. Now that he's gone home, she told me she'd felt safer with him there, because he would hear anyone prowling around in the garden, or trying to break in. Marjorie McKinnon comes round quite often but I'm wondering whether I might ask Mrs Flaherty to come in more, that is, on more days to make up the same hours, just to keep an eye on her. What do you think?"

"I think that would be good. Mary needs to be busy. Did he ever talk about his father?"

"Not to me. Dr McKinnon spent a while with him, but I don't know what was said."

Dr McKinnon had come to talk to Ryan several times. He must have known for a long time what the rest of the village was now coming to terms with. It seemed the little girl had run away that night, and that her death had been accidental, The new doctor's suicide was generally talked of as a "good thing." Duncan preferred not to listen. He had only met the man once after all and could barely remember his face. Lesley's response troubled him. She had been incredulous at first, and she was still quite strange about the whole business. She would go to Dr Gordon's funeral, she said, when there was one.

"You can't possibly," he'd told her, but had left it at that. She would see sense and change her mind when the time came.

She was looking at his cup. He'd taken a couple of sips, and no more.

"I know why you asked for tea," she said abruptly. "We've never had anything but instant. You could have said, Duncan. I'll buy some proper beans and a percolator. But you'll have to tell me what to get."

"You don't want a percolator. Coarse ground coffee and a cafetière would be the best idea. Or an Italian stove-top pot. They're rather smart. A machine would take up too much room on your worktop. And it's not "we" any more, Lesley," he added. "It's you."

"Pardon?"

"The house is yours, Lesley."

She picked up the tray and went to the kitchen. After a minute or two he followed. She was standing at the sink.

Was he in trouble? He had no right to tell her how to live her life, what to think, how to mourn. She would go to Gordon's funeral. And, he realised, if he cared for her, he would have to go too.

"Am I in trouble?" he asked.

"No."

He put a respectful, brotherly arm across her shoulder. She turned, leaning her head on his chest. He could feel his heart thumping as his arms closed round her.

On Saturday morning he was on the back doorstep at ten o'clock exactly, having promised to take her on a shopping-for-a-cafetière expedition. She was already in her coat.

"Lesley, do you trust me?"

"Why?"

"I would like to do something . . . rather . . . odd."

"Odd?"

She looked closely at the jute shopping bag he was carrying but there was no way she could tell what was in it. He'd laid the day's Herald on the top.

"A little . . . strange. But in a good way. If you'll let me."

"When?"

"Now."

"Here?"

313

"Yes."

"Something good but strange?"

"Yes."

"All right. Should I take my coat off? Do I have to . . ."

"No. Just stand well back. No, further than that. In the doorway."

"Why?"

He didn't answer. He had some difficulty getting the overalls over his shoes, but managed at last. He took off his glasses, tucked them into their hard case, and laid it on the work top. He brought out the safety goggles and put them on. They felt rather tighter than they had in the shop, but now was not the time to bother with petty adjustments. The hammer handle was slippery: he must hold it firmly. He had brought a cloth, the plan being to tape it over the tiles, but now it seemed unnecessary, almost cowardly. He chose a spot near the outside door, far enough away from the window and the electric switch, steadied his stance, counted to three, and swung.